THE NANNY SHARE

BOOKS BY EMILY SHINER

The Wife in the Photo

The Hotel

Meet the Parents

DETECTIVE FREYA SINCLAIR SERIES

Three Drowned Girls

One Liar Left

EMILY SHINER

THE
NANNY
SHARE

bookouture

Published by Bookouture in 2025

An imprint of Storyfire Ltd.
Carmelite House
50 Victoria Embankment
London EC4Y 0DZ

www.bookouture.com

The authorised representative in the EEA is Hachette Ireland
8 Castlecourt Centre
Dublin 15 D15 XTP3
Ireland
(email: info@hbgi.ie)

Copyright © Emily Shiner, 2025

Emily Shiner has asserted her right to be identified as the author of this work.

All rights reserved. No part of this publication may be reproduced, stored in any retrieval system, or transmitted, in any form or by any means, electronic, mechanical, photocopying, recording or otherwise, without the prior written permission of the publishers.

ISBN: 978-1-83618-348-8
eBook ISBN: 978-1-83618-346-4

This book is a work of fiction. Names, characters, businesses, organizations, places and events other than those clearly in the public domain, are either the product of the author's imagination or are used fictitiously. Any resemblance to actual persons, living or dead, events or locales is entirely coincidental.

For my mom.
For all of your support over the years, and for wearing me down until I finally caved and wrote a book. I guess you were right all along.

PROLOGUE

Nealie's screaming yanks me out of my daydream.

I stumble to my feet, knocking over my iced coffee in the process. I'm barefoot and feel the splash of ice cubes and cold brew on my toes, but don't look down.

My eyes are locked on the girl I'm nannying.

I'd only closed my eyes for a moment, but I should've known better than to look away from her even for a second. Nealie and Emma, the two girls I nanny for, move faster than you would think possible. Nealie especially. She's always halfway up a tree by the time I close the front door behind us.

Or under a fence before I can stop her.

"Nealie!" Her name bursts from me, and I rush to her. She's upside down on the swing, her ankle caught in the chain. I grab her around the waist and pull her to me so I can unhook her. "Hold as still as possible, okay? I'll get you out in just a second."

She's not screaming any more, but she is crying, sucking in huge gasps of air as tears fall. "It huuuuurts!"

"I know, darling," I tell her, hoisting her a bit higher so I can free her leg. Finally, the chain comes loose, and I lower her to the ground, sitting with her so I can pull her into my lap. "Let me see if you're bleeding, but I don't think you are."

"It hurts," she gasps, and I kiss the top of her head while I run my hands up and down her leg.

No cuts. She'll bruise, I'm sure of it, but right now she's fine. Relief washes over me when I realize she's not hurt nearly as badly as she could be.

"Wiggle your foot for me," I tell her.

She does, her sniffles slowing as she watches her pink sneaker move back and forth. The sparkles catch the sunlight and make her sneakers seem to light up.

"Nice job. Now, can you bend your knee?"

She nods and does just that, the tip of her tongue sticking out from the corner of her mouth.

"You're a champ. Now I need you to stand up and jump for me. Show me that you can do that." I pause, thinking, then clamber to my feet, pulling her up with me. "I bet I can jump higher than you can."

"No way!" She grins at me and starts jumping, her long ponytail swishing from side to side as she does.

"Yes way!" I jump too, then reach out and grab her hands. Squeezing them, I pull her into me for a hug. She's hot and sweaty from playing outside, but at least she isn't seriously injured. That's what matters.

"Can I have some ice cream?" She uses her little baby voice and looks up at me, blinking hard so a few remaining tears roll down her red cheeks.

"Of course! Let's go, kiddo." I swing her up and rest her on my hip before bending down to grab my empty plastic cup. Yes, she's perfectly able to walk on her own. Heck, as excited as she is to get some ice cream, she'd probably beat me to the house if I tried to race her.

Carrying her isn't about speeding up the afternoon and

getting inside as fast as possible though. It's about holding her. Loving her.

Without thinking, I snuggle her to me and kiss her on the cheek. "Sorry, kiddo."

"Because I got hurt?"

No. "Yep, but I'm glad you're all better now. You're so brave. So strong."

I *am* sorry she got hurt, but that's not what's bothering me right now.

A wave of guilt washes over me. Not about her almost falling off the swing, although I do feel bad that I wasn't paying attention, but guilt over what's going to happen.

By now, the phone call has been made. The threat passed on. And things are set into motion. Nealie deserves to have stability in her life; she deserves to have people around her who love her and would do anything for her.

That was me, for a while. But not any longer. We've put something into motion now; the ten-day countdown is on.

And there's no stopping it.

ONE

One Week Before

Dinner's almost ready when my phone buzzes in my hand. We're having spaghetti, our daughter's favorite, and I hear her singing as she comes down the stairs. I should go to her, should scoop her up, should hold her close.

But gnawing dread makes me check the message I just received.

I thumb on my phone, ignoring the way my hand shakes. The message pops right up, glaring. Angry.

What did you decide?

I want to scoff. Tuck my phone into my pocket. Ignore the text.

I want to pretend it doesn't mean anything, when I know full well it does.

The four words are an accusation. I've deleted the prior messages, the ones that would make this one make sense.

But as quickly as I delete them, they keep coming. At first, it was once a day. For a week, it felt like they were sent on a timer. I grew nervous around 9 a.m. waiting on them, but then one morning... that first message didn't come.

It was a relief, the break, like it was finally over, like I could breathe, like maybe it was all a bad dream and then—

It came that afternoon.

And then the next morning.

Over and over, text after text, building and coming faster and faster, flooding into my phone to the point where I'm now getting five, sometimes six a day, and it feels like I can't close the valve, can't get them to shut off and—

Tick, tock. You're running out of time.

I delete both messages, and then, even though I should leave my phone on in case someone needs me, I turn it all the way off and shove it into my pocket.

It's out of sight but not out of mind.

All through dinner, I imagine texts pinging into my inbox, waiting to assail me as soon as I turn my phone back on. I consider dropping it in the toilet, getting a new one and changing my number, doing everything I can to stop the messages from getting to me.

But that won't change a thing. It won't matter if I get a new number, or if I move, or even if I die, because this is the type of secret to follow you to your grave.

Hell, it's the type of secret to drive you to an early one.

TWO
ALISON

9:33 a.m.

God, I need coffee.

A Friday evening Pre-K school play and sing-along, with all of the little kids squealing and giggling as they'd stuffed their faces with cupcakes and candy after their performance, had worn me out. When I finally coaxed Nealie into bed, I swear the girl had enough energy to power a rocket to the moon.

The final time I'd checked on her last night was at... ten? No, eleven. It was eleven, and I'd heard her giggling in her room. What she was doing awake and not sound asleep, I'm not sure, but I'd wager the excitement from the party and seeing her friends had been making it hard for her to sleep. I'll get her some breakfast, and then she'll be happy to talk to me.

My phone buzzes, and I grab it to check the email. It's automated, from the bank, and one I should have expected since I've been getting them for months now.

We've noticed an unusually large balance in your personal

savings account. Our associates would love to talk to you about—

As quickly as possible, I delete it.

"Please tell me you made a double pot."

My husband's voice makes me jump. Ryan swoops into the kitchen in the way only a man who's never been told *no* can. He grabs the pot and pours a cup of coffee with a flourish before bending to give me a kiss.

I force myself to kiss him back, but all I can think about is the lipstick I saw on his collar when starting laundry yesterday. It was a different shade than the lipstick I've seen before.

I push that thought away, just like I pushed the email out of my mind.

But it pops right back up.

Is it a new woman? Or did she just go shopping? I shouldn't let it bother me, not when I have a plan to end all of this, but I can't help but be angry about it.

My hand shakes as I reach behind me and put my phone back on its stand.

"You must be tired if you're asking about a double pot." My voice sounds natural. Good. He'll never guess that I know about the affairs. We'll have to talk about it, of course, but not right now. Not when Nealie's going to get up soon, not when I don't think I have my mental ducks in a row.

He nods, scrubbing his hand down his face. "I'm exhausted. And I just got this email from the security company about them having *technical difficulties* last night. It's been happening more and more, have you noticed? And now they're saying the cameras might not be functioning correctly for a few days. What are we even paying for?" He groans. "Maybe it's time to look for a new company."

He doesn't say it, but I know what he's implying: that I

should be the one to do the research into a new security company, but my plate is full right now, so I ignore him.

Ryan yawns. "Who knew preschoolers could party so hard? Is Nealie up yet?"

"Not yet." I turn away from him back to the stove where I already have pancakes ready to come off the griddle. After putting them on a plate and sliding that into the oven to stay warm, I swipe butter over the griddle, pour more batter onto it, then flip the bacon. "I keep thinking the smell of bacon will get her out of bed, but she must be wiped out."

"I can man the pancakes if you want to get her up." Ryan takes the spatula from me without waiting for a response. He flips it between his fingers like it's a baton. "You know Nealie. She responds best to you in the morning."

"You're still her favorite," I point out, leaning against the counter as I take a sip of my coffee. "She's always been daddy's little girl."

"Just not when she's sleepy."

I watch as Ryan pokes at the pancakes. "But you're the one she turns to when she's upset about a bad grade at school. Or when she falls and scrapes her knee."

"She'll turn back to you. Girls do that." He sounds all-knowing, like he's raised a pack of girls before, even though Nealie is an only child and, at this rate, she's going to stay that way.

I don't fancy trying to have another kid at close to forty-five, and with Ryan five years older than me... let's just say the math ain't mathing, and our ages aren't the only reason we're not going to have another child after four years.

"Girls are tricky beasts," I say over my shoulder as I leave the kitchen. "Trust me, I was one."

Whatever Ryan says in response is quiet enough that I can't make out the words. Grabbing the banister, I hurry up the stairs to the second floor, pausing at the bathroom door long enough to see that she's not in there. It's silent in the hall, even with the tempting smell of bacon filling the air.

Scientists say your sense of smell is diminished while you're asleep; it's the sound of a fire roaring and crackling that wakes someone up when their house is burning down, not the thick scent of smoke. But those scientists have never met Nealie.

I swear, she has some supernatural way of knowing when I'm making bacon and will rush down to the kitchen. The fact that she's not down there right now, shimmying her stool closer to the stove so she can snatch pieces right from the frying pan, tells me a lot.

I rest my hand on the doorknob and pause, listening for the sound of her waking up. Her rolling over in bed. Talking to her stuffed animals. Maybe groaning at the birds chirping madly in the tree outside her window.

I turn the knob and push the door open slowly, well aware that the hinge squeaks if you throw the door open. Early morning light fights against the venetian blinds, and I cross the room to open them, allowing slats of bright sun to land on the floor and on Nealie's bed.

Her blankets are pulled up over her pillow. There's a lump in the middle of the bed that looks like her when she curls into a little ball to sleep.

"Nealie," I whisper. "Nealie, good morning."

Silence. Carefully, I put my hand where Nealie's head should be, but the light pressure from my touch compresses the blankets flat to the pillow. My heart hammers and bile rises in the back of my throat.

I rip the covers back.

Empty. The bed is empty.

I gasp, my head pounding, and turn in a slow circle even though I know there's nowhere in here for her to hide. It's a small room, with a bed, bookshelf, and desk. A few stuffed animals are shoved in the corner.

I drop to my knees and look under her bed. She's not there.

In seconds, I'm up and flinging open the door to her closet. An overhead light clicks on, illuminating clothes, shoes, an errant stack of library books, but nothing more.

I push the closet door closed and turn back to the room. Nealie's good about putting things away, but she always leaves her kitty backpack by her bed. It should be right—

Gone. It's gone.

I drop to her white rug. Her pink sparkly sneakers, the ones she wears all day, every day, are also gone.

Sweat breaks out on my brow, and I bend over, grabbing my knees and taking a huge breath to try to calm down. There's a pounding in my head, a squeezing like a vise, and I have to force myself to stand back up.

She has to be in the house. I missed her, I must have walked past her and not known she was there, because nothing else makes any sense.

"Ryan."

I think I'm screaming his name, but it comes out in a whisper. I try again.

"Ryan."

My foot catches on the edge of her rug as I stumble to the door. When I slam into the doorframe to catch myself, I clear my throat.

"Ryan!"

Nealie. We have to find her. I hear Ryan respond from the kitchen and slowly turn to look back over my shoulder.

She's gone.

"Alison. What's going on?"

It's Ryan, framed in the doorway, and I turn to him before slowly dropping to my knees. I don't pray, but I could start now.

"Nealie's gone."

"Gone? No." He frowns and shakes his head. "She has to be in the house somewhere, don't worry. We'll find her." He spins away from the door, hurrying down the hall, Nealie's name already echoing as he calls her.

I didn't tell him about her shoes. Her backpack. My legs are wobbly, and I force myself to stand, to pull my phone from my pocket.

I have to call 911.

It doesn't matter what Ryan thinks. Her shoes aren't here, and that tells me *she's* not here, and...

My eyes fall on her window. Ryan and I keep it closed and locked at night since the wrap-around deck on the second level reaches her room. It's always been my fear that anyone could get on the deck, could get to her window, could slide it open if it were unlocked...

But it's open right now.

And the screen is popped out and lying on the floor.

THREE
CARRIE

9:39 a.m.

Daniel calls my name, his voice tight, panicked.

I hear him. I know I should respond. But I'm caught in a fog, and I can't break free from it. Rolling over, I groan and press my face harder into my pillow. There's a spot of drool there, which always happens when I stay up late.

"Carrie." Daniel's in the bedroom doorway now, his tone insistent.

I was having the best possible dream. If I screw my eyes up tight and take a deep breath, maybe I can sink back into it.

If Daniel would just go away, I could do that. It's Saturday, and we don't have anything planned. He told me he'd get up and make breakfast, that he'd take care of Emma, that I could sleep in—

"Carrie, I need you to wake up." He grabs my shoulder and gives it a little shake before yanking the covers down. Cool air washes over me, and I wince, then plant my hands on the mattress and force myself to sit up.

"What is it?" I look up at him. For a moment, the room spins. I blink hard, and he snaps into focus.

My husband. Thinner now than he was when we got married, even though it usually goes the opposite way. His blond hair is pushed back from his face, and he's gripping his hands together, wringing them, like whatever's important enough for him to wake me up has him really worried.

"It's Emma."

Em-ma. Her name filters through the haze that always wraps around me when I sleep super hard. I really was having the most wonderful dream. I was back in high school, hanging out with—

It hits me what he said.

"Emma?" I swing my legs over the edge of the bed and plant my feet on the floor. Daniel moves to the side, already reaching for my arm to help me stand. "Is she sick? Did she eat too much sugar last night?" I swallow again and think about a glass of water. "I told her to lay off the cupcakes, that she'd be wired all night long, but you know Emma. When she sets her mind on something, she won't back down."

"She's gone." Daniel sounds like he's choking on the words.

"Gone?" I stop dead in my tracks and turn to look at him. He's so much taller than me, and I tilt my head back, back, before finally zeroing in on his face. "What do you mean *gone?*"

"I thought it was strange she was sleeping so late. It's already nine thirty," he says as I lift my wrist to check the time.

Not that I have a watch on. I haven't worn one in a year, but old habits die hard.

He continues while I struggle to focus on what he's saying. "I promised her I'd take her to the pinball arcade this morning, but she had to be up early."

I pull away from him. *This can't be happening.* Daniel's still talking, but I only catch snatches of it as I force myself up and stumble out into the hall. I have to brace my hand against the wall a few times before I reach Emma's room.

She didn't want the big one at the end of the hall, so I turned that into a craft area for the two of us. Right now, it looks like a glitter factory exploded in there. Her space is smaller, but it's closer to where Daniel and I sleep, just in case she ever needs me during the night.

The light is on, and I think for a second that Daniel was wrong, that Emma is right here, that she must have been in the bathroom or something and now is digging through her over-stuffed dresser for something to wear on their daddy-daughter day.

But when I walk through her door, I already know I'm wrong.

Her blinds are pulled closed. There's no music playing. Those are the first things Emma does in the morning—open her blinds to let in the light and turn on music so she can sing along.

"Emma?" My voice is thick.

My head spins.

"Where is she?" An idea hits me, and I whip around. "The bathroom! She has to be in there!"

"I checked." He moves in front of me and takes me by the shoulders. "I checked in there and downstairs. I looked in her tent downstairs to make sure she didn't take an iPad in there to watch cartoons. She's not in the house."

My knees give out, and I sink back to the mattress. "You're wrong," I say, even though I know he's not. Daniel might be a lot of things, but he's not wrong about this. He *wouldn't* be. He loves Emma more than anything, even though—

"I'm calling the police." His words stop my train of thought in its tracks. "Just sit there. I'll handle this."

I watch as he fumbles his phone from his pocket. Thumbs it on. Dials 911. I can't hear the dispatcher, but it's easy to follow the conversation just listening to Daniel.

He reports her missing.

No, he doesn't know where she might have gone.

I sit silently as he gives them our address and her description. Without realizing what I'm doing, I grab her pillow and squeeze it to my chest. It smells like Emma's strawberry shampoo, and my heart aches.

Daniel turns away, hunching his shoulders. Then he reaches up to cup the phone with his free hand.

"I need to tell you one thing," he says, and I stop squeezing the pillow.

Is he going to tell them about last night?

He wouldn't, right? The problems we're facing don't have anything to do with Emma going missing. This isn't my fault. Besides, she would have had to walk downstairs and through the living room to get out the front door.

And with Daniel sleeping on the sofa, he would have heard her.

This isn't on me.

"... was unlocked," he says. Then he pauses. "Thank you. I'll wait outside for the officer." He hangs up and turns back around, but doesn't meet my eyes.

"What was that?" I stand up, no longer feeling unsteady on my feet. I'm desperate to know what he just said to the dispatcher. "What was unlocked?"

"It doesn't matter."

"It sure does." I take a step towards him, then another, then rest my hand on his chest. When he doesn't respond, I tense my fingers, digging them into his chest. "What did you say to her?"

He closes his eyes. Looks up at the ceiling. "The back door. I... left the back door open last night. It was an accident. I'm sorry."

An *accident*?

He's *sorry*?

He may think he's sorry now, but if something happens to Emma, he really will be.

FOUR
KATE

9:44 a.m.

My phone wakes me up, ripping me out of probably the best sleep I've had in over a month.

My heart kicks into high gear, and I grab it from my bedside table. It vibrates in my hand like a living thing, its screen lit up, the sound so loud I feel my teeth grind together. Before answering, I squint at the screen, but I don't have my contacts in, so it's a bright blur. I clear my throat and swipe my thumb to answer.

"Detective Martin."

"Detective, this is dispatch. We just got a call about a missing girl and need you there."

I'm instantly awake. There are few things in the world that will get me up faster than hearing it's all about to hit the fan. Groaning, I sit up and swing my legs out from the bed. My slippers are right where I expect them to be, and I shove my feet into them.

"Text me everything," I tell her. "I'll be out the door in ten." Before she can respond, I hang up.

Ten minutes feels like you're taking all the time in the world when you're up against a hard case, but that's as fast as I can get ready from a dead sleep. Still, the thought of a missing girl drives me to hurry.

When the popular TV series *48 Hours* was at its peak, it taught viewers all over the world that police have two days to get their act together and find someone who's missing, or hunt down a killer, or perform TV-magic-DNA testing, but the reality is that the clock ticks much faster.

You don't want to give a kidnapper two days to get away.

Three years I've been at the Rockridge department after moving here to escape the big city life of Los Angeles. I came from a team of a dozen detectives, but now it's just me.

I have to hurry.

In just a few minutes, I finish up in the bathroom and pull on jeans and a navy short-sleeve shirt. POLICE is emblazoned in bright-yellow letters across the back. It's chilly this morning but will be hot by mid-afternoon.

It only takes a minute to run my fingers through my short hair, then I'm out the door, grabbing a granola bar on the way. Once I'm in my car, I turn on my laptop and pull up the case notes. Just like I'd asked, the dispatcher texted me, and I plug the address into my phone's GPS before I realize where I'm going.

Blackwood. It's probably the nicest gated community in town. Everyone who's anyone lives there, mostly doctors, lawyers, and trust-fund babies.

A kid missing in Blackwood should be easy to find. The last time I was in there, there weren't any thick brambles or errant bushes for them to hide in. The yards are all perfectly manicured. Anything out of place or wild is removed as soon as it's noticed. And that's not even mentioning the security cameras, the gated entrance, the nosy neighbors with nothing better to do than make sure kids stay off their lawn.

But if the kid was taken? I dealt with a few missing kid cases when I still lived in LA. Not all of them end up with the kid coming home in one piece, and the thought of that happening today is worrisome.

I scoff and shake my head as I reverse out of my drive. A kid taken in Blackwood? Where most homes have security cameras to protect their BMWs and Mercedes? When you have to enter through a security gate, and everyone's keeping an eye on anyone who might not belong?

"Not a chance," I mutter as I gas it.

Kids don't go missing in Blackwood. They wander off, fall asleep at a friend's house, hide from their parents.

But what if that's not what it was? What if every parent's nightmare came true in the safest neighborhood in town? My stomach twists. If a kid was taken in Blackwood, that only means one thing.

It was an inside job.

FIVE
JULIE

9:55 a.m.

My cramped walk-up apartment is a far cry from the houses I nanny in Blackwood, and I'm reminded of that fact when I stub my toe while walking into the kitchen.

"Holy heck," I say, dropping my book and bending down to grab my toe. It throbs under my touch, and I grit my teeth.

"Cute swear." Theo's voice behind me makes me straighten up. "Most adults aren't afraid of using the f-bomb." He wraps his arms around me and kisses my neck.

"Sure, but most adults aren't terrified of getting fired because they swore in front of their charges." I pull away from him and stare at him, take in his hair. It's thick, dark, and curly—the exact opposite of mine.

"They wouldn't fire you. Those kids love you."

"Eh." I shrug and pick my book back up before leading him into the kitchen. "The kids aren't the ones paying me, so I don't worry so much about them. It's the adults that concern me, and Alison told me on day one that if I swore in front of Nealie, she'd can me."

"Harsh."

I shrug again but don't respond. Instead, I busy myself with the kettle for tea. Anytime I bring up something about the families I nanny that Theo doesn't like, he points out how problematic they are, even though he's the one who found them me to nanny for them in the first place.

Sure, the moms can be demanding to work for sometimes, but the girls? Getting to nanny for two preschoolers is a lot of fun, and I love them both. Emma and Nealie know how to lighten my mood when I've had a bad morning. They're so innocent, so interested in the world around them. And their laughter?

It's cliché, sure, but it's like heaven to my ears. I'd stay here forever, be their nanny for as long as possible, but I know that's not how we do things. It's almost time for us to move on, no matter how happy I would be staying this time.

I thought... honestly, it's silly, but I thought this time could be different. That we'd stay. Make a home, make a family. That I could keep Nealie and Emma in my life, but I can't.

I push the thought of them aside and focus on Theo. I know what the problem is. We've been here too long, and he's getting antsy about finishing the job. But honestly, it's the parents' money—they get to do what they want with it.

They don't want me to swear around the kids? I won't.

They only want me feeding organic snacks? Fine. They're the ones buying them.

Are some of the rules a little crazy? I think so, but I'm not going to argue with the people paying me, even if what they're paying me is pittance compared to the payday we're working towards.

Still, this place is home. For now, at least. Until we move again. I keep thinking that each city we land in will be the one Theo decides we can stay in, but our plan has worked out perfectly so far, so why change things?

Maybe because I know he owns a house here. As soon as I found that out, I kept wondering if this was it, if we were finally going to settle down.

But not yet.

And sure, maybe I could use some of the money we've made on other jobs to get a nicer place, but it feels silly to do that when we're just going to pack up and move again soon enough. We just have to complete this job, get paid, and we're out of here.

"Earth to Julie. Hello, Julie." Theo utters some static noises that make me laugh. "I was asking what you want to do today. Any thoughts?"

"Oh, no. Hang out, I guess. Maybe watch some movies?" Every so often, I'm asked to nanny on the weekends, but this weekend I'm free. I don't love giving up my time off to hang out with the kids, but I don't mind the extra money, even though we don't really need it, and the girls are really sweet.

"Or hear me out." He spreads his hands in the air like a magician. "We could go out for a fancy dinner. Something with real cloth napkins and candles on the table."

"That's an idea." I click the kettle off and turn away from him to pour water over some loose-leaf tea I set out the night before. "But I don't know if I want to do something so off-the-cuff without planning it out."

"Sure, but I thought that would be the fun in it. We both like routine, but why not shake it up sometimes?"

"I don't know." Using my spoon, I poke at the tea leaves. They swirl in the hot water, smelling so good my mouth waters.

"It was just a thought." He leans forward and plants his hands on the counter. "But if you don't like the plan, we won't do it. No harm, no foul."

"Thanks." I throw him a grin. He returns it and opens the fridge.

"You know what I'm feeling? Those Chinese leftovers. How do you feel about lo mein and sesame chicken for breakfast?"

"They've never done me wrong, and I can't see them starting now."

Theo laughs and begins pulling takeout containers from the fridge. I take my tea strainer out of my cup and set it in the sink to deal with later while I wait for breakfast.

"Since we're staying in town," I say, "I want to walk to the farmers' market, then go to the library. Maybe spend the afternoon alternating between watching movies and reading. Thoughts?"

He stares at me. "You're joking, right? That's my perfect Saturday. Where do I sign up?"

A smile curls my lips.

"You can sign up after you heat up the Chinese. I'm famished."

"Love it. You name it, it'll happen." He moves past me and grabs two plates. It only takes a minute for him to dump out our leftovers and pop a plate in the microwave. My stomach grumbles as the scent of sesame chicken fills the kitchen.

"Okay," I say, turning to squeeze some honey into my tea, "but I don't want the day to only be about me. You can have a say in it too." What I don't say, even though I'm thinking it, is that we might as well enjoy Rockridge as much as possible now.

Who knows how much longer we'll be here?

"I might skip the library but watch movies with you later," he tells me. "I don't have to work today, but there are a few loose ends to tie up. I thought the perk of working for an online security company would be weekends off, but I have some coding to do. You know how it is. Rich people want their security issues addressed as soon as possible, and there have been some outages."

"They want everything as soon as possible. I remember when Alison and Ryan had their security system updated. I swear, the crew was there the same day Alison got the idea to enlarge it."

"Money talks." The microwave beeps, and Theo swaps out the plates. "Do you mind getting me some OJ?"

"Not at all." I grab it and a glass. Just as I'm about to pour him some, my phone rings. "It's Alison," I tell him.

"Don't pick it up." Theo waves a fork in my direction. "It's your day off."

"She probably needs me to watch Nealie," I say, but the puppy-dog eyes he gives me are too good, and I silence the call. "Happy?"

"So happy." He pulls the plate from the microwave and joins me at the counter.

I've just sat down and put my napkin on my lap when my phone beeps.

Twice.

Three times.

"Alison can parent Nealie herself for one day," Theo says, but I hold up a hand as I read the text.

"Oh no." My breath is caught in my throat. I'm suddenly very aware of my pulse, the feeling of my pajamas on my skin, how warm it is in the kitchen.

"What?" He stabs a bite of chicken but pauses to look at me. "Everything okay?"

No.

"I got texts from both Carrie and Alison. Emma wasn't in her room this morning. Carrie said she doesn't know where she is, that they're going to call the cops," I say, forcing my mouth to form the words. "But that's not all."

"What? What's going on?" His fork still hovers in the air, but his eyes are locked on mine. "Julie? Is everything okay?"

I swallow hard but can't respond. Instead, I turn the phone around so Theo can see the text from Alison for himself.

Nealie's missing.

SIX
ALISON

9:59 a.m.

"Don't tell me you were going to call the police."

I barely make it down the stairs before Ryan rushes me, his brows furrowed, his neck splotchy with rage. He moves faster than I do, stepping forward and yanking my phone from my hand. In one smooth move, he slips it into his pocket.

"Of course I'm calling the police! Are you kidding me right now?" I don't tell him I already texted the nanny, not when he looks so angry.

My heart hammers in my chest; my cheeks burn. I feel my hands curl into fists, and I force myself to relax them as I stare at my husband. He's sweating, beads of it forming on his forehead along his hairline. He wipes them away, the movement self-conscious, then shoves his hands into his pockets.

"Okay. Listen." He exhales hard, then grabs his hips, hinging forward to stretch before straightening back up. "We could have found her on our own. You didn't need to do that, not without giving me a chance to fix this."

"Fix this? Do you hear yourself?" My words are weapons, and he winces as I speak.

"Nealie wouldn't sneak out of the house without a good reason," he tells me. "You know that as well as I do. She's just a little kid! Unless something was really eating at her, she wouldn't leave the house in the middle of the night."

"And yet," I say, throwing my arms out to the side, "that's exactly what she did. I can't understand why you don't want to get anyone else involved. *The professionals*, Ryan. Why the hell would that be?" My voice breaks, and huge tears slide down my cheeks, but I don't move to wipe them away.

I don't know how to get him to see how crazy he's acting. There has to be some reason why he wouldn't want me to call the police.

I just don't know what it is.

"We can figure this out on our own—" he begins, but I cut him off.

"Are you in trouble with the law?" I blurt the words out without really thinking about them, but it makes sense. He did something, or knows something, and that explains why he doesn't want to call the police. But... no. He's a lawyer. I can't believe how buddy-buddy he sometimes is with the cops.

So why wouldn't he want to call them?

"What? Of course not." He's nervous and shakes his head. "Just... let me figure out what to do, okay?"

"That's it, isn't it?" I don't give him time to respond. My breathing is ragged. "You did something. Something illegal I don't know about. Did someone take our daughter?"

"Are you serious?" Frustration flashes across his face. "You're grasping at straws, Alison. I didn't do anything. It's just that I know how the police can be when they don't think you're telling the truth."

"But we would be telling the truth."

He sighs. "I know, but try to see it from my point of view. I work with the cops, and I know how they can jump to conclusions. If we can find Nealie and bring her home, then it'll be better in the long run if they're not involved. Trust me on this. They'll point fingers, they might talk about this being an abusive household. It's best not to involve the cops unless you absolutely have to."

I stare at him. "Do you hear yourself?" I ask again. "You can't possibly think the police would turn this on us, do you? She snuck out! We didn't do anything to make her think that was a good idea. And they know you! They won't doubt that we're innocent."

"It's always the parents." He stares at me like he can convince me of what he's thinking just by looking at me. "Think about it. The parents are always involved."

"Not this time."

"Alison." He sighs.

"I can handle this," I tell him. "Trust me. We didn't do anything wrong."

Or did we?

I push that thought away. The more I think about it, the less comfortable I am. The first thing the police are going to ask is if we can think of anyone who might want to hurt us by taking Nealie.

And I don't know if I can lie to them.

He blinks, and it feels like he puts on a mask before he looks me full-on again.

Is he lying to me?

I take a deep breath. "Think about how it will look: us dragging our feet and not alerting anyone to the fact our daughter is missing? If someone else finds her first and calls the cops, everyone will think we *did* have something to do with it. Or that we're just terrible parents."

"You should let me handle this."

I bark out a laugh. "Not a chance. We already looked

throughout the house and in the backyard, so where do you think—"

"The park."

"What?" I frown at him. "You're being ridiculous."

"Nealie loves the park."

"She also loves ice cream. But that doesn't mean she walked to the ice cream parlor downtown in the middle of the night." He looks ready to argue, so I keep talking. "Give me my phone, Ryan."

"No."

"Jackass." I move faster than him, lunging forward and grabbing for both of his pockets at once. Instinctively, he takes a step away from me, but he smacks into the door as I hit him with my shoulder.

"Alison, stop!"

But I don't. Not until I've shoved my hands in both his pockets. His phone is in his right pocket. It's bigger than mine, and I let it go before digging my nails into the back of his hand as he tries to stop me from dipping into his left pocket.

But I do, and when I pull my hand away, I'm clutching my phone.

"Lay off," I hiss, stepping back from him. "What is your problem? What could be more important than helping Nealie?" Another step away from him. His eyes are dark and locked on my face, and I feel sweat trickle down between my shoulders. "I'm taking this. Leave me alone."

He takes a step towards me, and I'm suddenly afraid. Turning, I race into the bathroom. At the last moment, I slip, my toe slamming into the doorframe. I yelp, but slide inside and turn around. Close the door. Lock it. Sink to the gray tile floor. My toe throbs, but that's the least of my worries. Breathing through my mouth, I try to listen for Ryan.

Is he coming after me?

I don't know what's going on with him, but I don't like the look on his face. I don't like the lies. My hands shake.

I dial 911.

Ryan's done something, but that doesn't mean Nealie has to suffer for it.

It was him. It has to be.

I refuse to admit to myself that I might have caused this.

SEVEN
CARRIE

10:01 a.m.

If Daniel is the reason my daughter is missing, I swear I'm going to kill him.

I haven't spoken to him since he told me he left the back door unlocked all night last night.

I groan and jam my fingers into my temples. I woke up with a splitting headache. I'll take a painkiller, but I already know it's not going to go away.

Not until Emma is home.

In the bathroom, I tip two Tylenol into my hand and swallow them dry. My hand shakes as I screw the lid back on the medicine bottle and drop it into the bathroom drawer. After turning on the faucet, I splash cold water on my face, then dry off with a towel. I knock the drawer back in place with my hip and heave a sigh before going downstairs to join Daniel in the wait for the police.

It's not just Tylenol I keep in that drawer, but right now I need to be as alert as possible, and I haven't used stronger pills in years. The thought of Emma going missing, that she's not in the house, that something bad might happen to her... it's terrifying.

Daniel's standing at the front window, the curtain pulled a little to the side, his phone in his hand. He's not talking on it and hasn't been—or I just haven't heard him. He turns it over and over, not looking down as he does, and I realize how scared he is.

He must be terrified, and I'm suddenly glad. He did this, after all. He left the door open, let my daughter sneak out.

But we'll get her back. We have to. I don't care what I have to do. I need my daughter.

"What are you looking for?" I join him at the window, reaching up and pressing my fingers against the cool glass.

He doesn't look at me when he responds. "Just waiting on the police."

"They should be here any minute," I tell him. As the words leave my mouth, a cruiser pulls into view. Then another. And another.

My heart starts beating faster.

I gasp and lean forward, pressing my nose against the window as if that's going to give me a better view.

"Carrie," Daniel says, and the next thing I know, his arm has snaked around my waist. "Carrie, we're going to get through this. I promise you. We'll find her."

I stand rigid. Melting into him, taking comfort from him, allowing him to love me... I should want that from him.

But I don't.

"Do you think we're being punished?" My voice is quiet, soft on purpose, because I'm honestly not sure if I want him to hear me or not.

"Punished?" His arm falls from around my waist. "Punished for what?"

I shrug. "You lost your job. I lost my best friend." My voice breaks when I think about who lives two houses down the street. So close and yet I never see them.

Daniel stiffens. We're not touching, but that doesn't matter. I sense the way his muscles tighten, how he moves away from me just a little bit, almost like I'm not going to be able to feel him step to the side.

"We're not being punished." His voice is flat. "We didn't do anything to deserve this, just like we didn't do anything for me to deserve losing my job. I didn't do anything wrong, Carrie."

A door slams outside as an officer gets out. She stretches, pressing her hands into the small of her back, then gives herself a little nod before walking towards our house.

There's so much to be said before she gets here, but there's no time. Daniel and I have avoided talking about what happened, and now that it's a subject we're willing to broach, we don't have the time.

He turns and walks away from me, rushing to get to the front door. Before he swings it open, he stops and turns back to me. "Aren't you coming?"

"Of course I am," I mumble, then force myself to hurry after him.

We'll step out onto the porch. Present a united front. It's what Daniel thinks we are, after all.

But that couldn't be further from the truth.

EIGHT

KATE

10:07 a.m.

Blackwood is gated, but all I have to do is slow down and flash my badge for the man in the gatehouse to let me in. Once inside, I take my time. I don't want to miss a thing.

It's the dream location for anyone rich enough to buy a house here. Kids don't have to worry about a creeper next door or darting into the road to grab a ball. Everyone drives slowly—the signs say 15 MPH—and everyone knows everyone.

Which is why this is even more confusing.

My GPS tells me to turn to the right and I do, slowly traveling away from the main road that cuts through the neighborhood. Two stop signs later and I'm pulling into a freshly paved driveway. I park directly behind a cruiser. Its number is 219, which means Sergeant Aletha Bradshaw is here.

She's focused. Determined. Exactly the person needed to run point on a missing girl, and relief floods my body when I think about how on top of everything she'll be. Sure, she made sergeant a bit young at only twenty-eight, but she's incredibly tenacious, and that's one of the reasons everyone in the department loves her.

Just like me, she moved here recently. Unlike me, however, she's never wanted to be a detective. When I approached her about the possibility of training with me to one day wear a detective's badge, she told me she doesn't want that pressure, that she prefers to be able to blend in, that she wasn't raised to stick out from a crowd.

Because of that, she sees everything. It's a talent—watching and listening, learning without overstepping. A lot of officers want to rush in and take control of the situation without seeing what's going on first, but not her. Aletha didn't have to be taught how to observe, she already knew how.

While I think about her; I stare up at the house towering over me. The Everett family lives in a two-story white home with a wrap-around porch, perfect landscaping, and an American flag flapping in the breeze. I take a moment to prepare myself, then get out of my car.

There's a woman on the front porch, her dark hair pulled back, her thin shoulders hunched forward. As I watch, she wraps her arms around herself and shakes her head.

Sergeant Bradshaw walks towards me. Her chin is high, her jaw tight, her thick black hair pulled back from her face. Her shift started at six this morning, but she must have had some coffee. You'd never know how early she had to get up to clock in at six. She looks well rested. Eager to handle this.

"Kate," she says, giving me a nod. "Thanks for heading out here so quickly."

"Of course." I glance back up at the house. The woman has been joined by a man who pulls her to his chest. "I saw the notes in CAD, but talk to me. What's happening?" CAD, or computer-aided dispatch, tracks calls and information from officers and dispatchers, making it easy for anyone who logs on to see what calls are active at any given time. If Aletha learned something and hasn't had time to enter the information, I need to know it.

"That's Carrie and Daniel Everett. He had plans to take Emma downtown this morning, but when he went to get her up, her bed was empty."

"Carrie wasn't going to join them?"

Aletha shrugs. "Daddy-daughter day, from the sound of it."

"Okay. Did you get a photo of her?"

"Already got it and I'm about to email it out." She holds her phone up for me to see.

"Good. Signs of foul play?"

"Back door was left unlocked, but apparently that's standard practice around here if you ask him." She rolls her eyes. "Carrie didn't seem happy about it, so I'd guess this has been an argument in the past. Daniel told me it's because the lock tends to stick but that's the best way for him to get to the backyard in the morning when he wants to do some yoga."

"Yoga every morning?"

She shrugs. "Just lost his job."

I stare at her. "You said Daniel Everett? I know that name... he was a lawyer, right? So he loses his job and now his kid turns up missing?"

Aletha pins me in place with a stare. "You're thinking something."

"Nothing's coincidental. You've searched the house and property?"

As if on cue, another cruiser pulls into the driveway. It slows and parks next to my car. Another continues past. We both watch the cruiser drive away.

"No way he missed the house," I say, and Aletha shakes her head.

"Not a chance."

"Being proactive and canvassing the area?" I don't mention the thought I had earlier, that anything that happened here probably originated in these gates. Aletha is smart. She'll have her own opinions about that.

"Something." She gives her head a shake. "I've searched the house and am going to have my officers put up a perimeter. You want to come talk to them?"

"You better believe it. And I want an officer talking to everyone on this street and getting security footage. And fingerprints from anyone who had a reason to be in this house. Handle it for me."

Before I can take a step, my phone rings. "Sorry, just..." I pull it from my pocket and frown. "Dispatch. Again. Think they're checking up on me, making sure I made it here?"

Aletha doesn't respond as I tap on my phone. She also doesn't linger to hear my conversation. I keep an eye on her as she walks over to talk to the officer who just pulled up.

"This is Martin."

"Detective, sorry to bother you when you're working the Everett case." The woman calling me sounds young. I used to know all of the dispatchers we had working for us, but that was before some huge turnover. Now I don't know them all by sight, but I recognize their voices.

"It's fine. I'm about to go talk to the parents. What do you need?"

She inhales hard. "We got another call from a mother in Blackwood and didn't know if you heard it go out over the radio."

I'm only half listening. On the porch, Carrie and Daniel have stopped embracing. They're now standing a few feet apart from each other. I can't make out what either of them is saying, but from the way he's waving his hands in the air, it's not good.

Aletha has noticed the change in the couple. Her strides are long as she walks up to the porch.

"This call was from a woman named Alison—she didn't give her last name." A pause.

Frustration bubbles up in me. I have no problem with young dispatchers, new dispatchers, ones who haven't been hardened by the horrors they're going to see day in and day out. What I do have a problem with is ones who can't spit it out.

"What's going on? I have a missing child to worry about and—"

"That's just it, Detective. There's not just one missing child. There are two."

NINE
JULIE

10:15 a.m.

There are so many police cars parked in Blackwood that when Theo slams on the brakes, he has to park three houses away from the Everetts'.

"Okay. I can do this." I take a deep breath and glance over at Theo. My heart's still beating in my throat, but I have to do this. I have to help try to find these girls. "Thanks for the ride."

He kills the engine, and surprise washes over me.

"What, you think I'm letting you deal with this on your own? No way am I dropping you off and leaving. Come on." He moves quickly, meeting me at the front of the car. For a moment, the two of us stand still, taking in the scene in front of us.

It's bedlam. Blackwood is quiet—that's its draw. That's why families want to live here. Sure, in the summer and on nice evenings during the school year, kids run around screaming and laughing, but that's part of the charm.

But there aren't ever cars parked halfway up on the sidewalk, and there certainly aren't ever this many police cars on the roads. Neighbors stand on their front porches watching, and right now there aren't any kids riding bikes up and down the sidewalks.

It's like we stepped into an alternate reality that *looks* like Blackwood but isn't.

"Hey, you okay?" Theo takes my hand and gives it a little squeeze.

Grateful, I look up at him. "Yeah, this is just terrifying. Why would they be missing? What happened in here?" I swallow hard and try to think.

"I don't know. Do you want to find Alison and Carrie? Or stay here?"

"I can't think." My words are slow, and my eyes are wide. It's almost as if I can drink in everything that's happening and make it all make sense. Before I can do that, though, Carrie rushes up to me.

"Julie! You're here!" Ignoring Theo, she throws her arms around me and pulls me into a hug. Her cheeks are red, her eyes puffy. Tears drip from her cheeks, and she wipes them against my shoulder. "Thank you for coming! I didn't know what to do, didn't know if I should call you, but Emma loves you, and I thought she might come out if she knew you were here."

"I'm glad you called." Her breath is warm on my neck, and I can only handle it for another moment before pulling back. "But, Carrie, you need to know something." I steel myself for what I'm about to say. "Nealie's missing too."

"Nealie's missing?" Carrie's eyes go wide, and she sucks in a breath. "What? What are you talking about?"

For a moment, I can't answer. My throat feels tight, like I've swallowed something I shouldn't. I stare at Carrie, then finally turn to look at Theo.

He clears his throat. "Carrie, we were at home, and Alison texted that Nealie was missing. But there are so many police cars here. Are they...?" His voice trails off when Carrie sobs again.

"Why would they both be gone? It doesn't make any sense." She wipes the tears off her cheeks with the backs of her hands before continuing. "I got up this morning and she wasn't in her room! You know how Daniel never locks the back door?"

I barely have time to nod before she's speaking again.

"She must have gone outside. That has to be where she is! I can't find her. But I had no idea Nealie was gone too." She closes her eyes, fat tears running down her cheeks. I appreciate the way she takes a deep breath to try to calm herself because when she speaks again, the edge of panic in her words has dulled.

"Alison didn't call me," she whispers. "I didn't know Nealie was missing too."

"We'll figure something out," I promise her. "The girls are friends! They love playing together. I bet they're off somewhere playing or hiding, what do you think? They probably missed hanging out with each other and thought they could sneak out together. We just have to find them, but that shouldn't be a problem."

I'm lying. To her, to myself, even to Theo. Without knowing where the girls are or that they're okay, what business do I have pretending like everything is going to be alright? Carrie's eating it up, though, desperation making her willing to believe anything I'm saying. I see the look Theo gives me, like he can't believe what I'm saying, and I choose to ignore it.

"You think they're together?" Carrie asks.

I shrug. "Maybe? I don't know." Tears burn my eyes, and I angrily wipe them away on the back of my hand. Freaking out and losing it right now isn't going to solve anything. If I want to be helpful, I have to keep it together as much as possible. "But it makes sense, doesn't it? As close as those two are."

Or as close as they were.

Emma and Nealie love each other. As different as the two girls are, I've never met ones more attached at the hip. Until recently.

Adults fight, but kids shouldn't suffer for their problems. What's going on between the two families should be put to the side so the girls can have each other. I zone out thinking about that while Theo and Carrie talk, their voices like static.

Guilt eats at me. It's easy to cast stones, isn't it? But if anyone knew what I'd done, what *we'd* done—

"Julie, I was just telling Carrie here that we're going to help look for the girls, okay? But you need your head in the game." Theo's voice is gentle. He puts his hand on my shoulder and helps pull me away from Carrie. Without me to cling to, she looks lost. Her hands hang at her sides, but she keeps opening and closing them like she's dropped something and isn't sure how she's ever going to be able to pick it back up.

"Right. That's a great idea, but I want to see Alison too. She has to be freaking out." I take a deep breath and try to calm down, then glance at Carrie, who's now chewing her cuticle. "We'll be back, okay? And you have my number. If we see anything at all, we'll give you a call."

She nods but doesn't look at me. Her gaze is far away, like she's lost. For a moment, I consider giving her a hug, but instead I reach for Theo's hand, and we walk away.

Every step I take away from Carrie fills me with guilt. She's distraught, and for good reason. Emma missing? And Nealie? I can't make it make sense. Not when both of the girls are so sweet. So innocent.

They have to be okay.

"You alright?" Theo asks. "This is hard."

"It's a nightmare." Each movement feels mechanical. We're close enough to Nealie's house now that I can see their yard, which is as lit up with police cars as Emma's was. "I just keep thinking that this is a sick joke. That they're suddenly going to pop out from behind a tree." My voice breaks.

"It might happen," Theo tells me. "You know this neighborhood: it's locked down to the extreme. And where would they go? They're, what? Four?"

"Four, yeah. Well, Nealie will be five in a few months." I take a shuddering breath as we pause at the end of the driveway. "They could be anywhere in here. You know how big this place is?"

"Right, but they couldn't have left it. That's all I'm saying. They're little kids, not wild and crazy teenagers."

"You sound confident." Doubt works its way into my voice.

"Are you questioning me? After everything we've been through? Because you don't need to do that. Everything's going to be fine."

"But what if it isn't?" My voice is soft. I can barely speak the words for fear that I might be right.

"Hey, listen." Theo stops and turns in front of me. He takes me by the shoulders and gives them a little squeeze. "Nothing like this has ever happened before, right?"

"Right." I whisper the word.

"There's no reason to think we're at all tied to this. What we do..." His voice trails off for a moment. "We don't hurt kids. We wouldn't. Hell, we never put them in danger. Never. Do you hear me?"

I nod but can't respond because Theo might think he's right, but he's wrong.

Blackwood is huge, he's not wrong about that. And man are there are a lot of crevices and hiding places they could sneak into. From culverts to garages, storage buildings to playhouses, the possibilities seem endless.

That's not what he's wrong about. He's wrong about the fact that the girls wouldn't have left the neighborhood and that we didn't have anything to do with them doing just that. That we might not have been the ones to put them in danger. Sure, if you're in a car, you have to come past the guardhouse, which means it's really unlikely anyone came through that way and took them.

But there are walking trails that lead out of Blackwood. They're not really well kept, and I don't think everyone that lives here knows about them, but they exist.

And the girls know about them—I know they do.

I'm the one who showed them how to sneak out.

TEN

I'm nervous as I thumb on my phone and open my texts. I never saved the unknown number that kept texting me, but I have it memorized.

My breathing is slow as I type out the words. I'm trying to listen for any sound in the house.

Nothing.

Did you do this?

I send it and wait. While I wait, I count.

I get to three hundred before I check my phone, but I would have noticed it ringing or vibrating.

No response.

Then, just as I'm about to send another text, the screen lights up.

I told you that you were running out of time.

ELEVEN
ALISON

10:17 a.m.

My interaction with Ryan terrifies me. It's been long enough now that the cops should be here, right? Moving as slowly and as quietly as possible, I walk to the bathroom door and press my ear up against it.

At first, I can't hear anything over the sound of my pounding heart. It thuds in my ears, and I force myself to take deep, even breaths.

Is Ryan right outside the door?

The anger on his face when I stole my phone and ran for the bathroom is seared into my mind. Even when he's lost cases at work, even when we got into a fight just a few weeks ago, when he slammed the door and tore off in his car, he didn't look this angry. And in the end, it all worked out for him, didn't it? I'd done the thing he'd wanted me to.

He got what he wanted. He forced my hand and, in doing so, made one thing clear to me. I have to look out for myself. For Nealie.

Luckily, I'd been planning ahead. I took what I wanted in

return to ensure I could always keep Nealie safe. But he doesn't know it yet.

I'm confident he doesn't because once he finds out what I've done, he's going to be mad enough to kill.

"No," I whisper and try to ignore that thought. Ryan is a good man. He is. He's kind and loving and goes out of his way to help people when they need it. What happened this morning wasn't usual.

But think about what he made you do.

He's good. He's perfect.

Except he's not, is he?

I push the thought away.

But if he's so good, then why did he get so angry that you called the police?

I can't think about that right now. My hands are pressed flat against the door, and I lean harder into it, searching for any sound.

Maybe I wouldn't be able to hear his breathing, but surely he'd clear his throat. Check his watch. Shuffle his feet.

But nothing. There's no sound, and it's only the hope that he's really gone and I'm alone that leads me to slowly unlock the door. The click is so loud in the silence that I wince and pause, sweat trickling down my back.

Still nothing.

"Ryan?" My voice is quiet. So quiet, in fact, that I don't think he could actually hear me if he wasn't standing right here. I stay still, listening for the sound of footsteps, for a creaking floorboard, for anything.

Silence.

"Ryan." I'm a little louder this time, and I take a step away from the bathroom. My ears strain for any little sound I might miss. My mouth is dry. When I swallow, it feels like there's cotton in my throat.

The house is still, like it's waiting. Holding its breath.

I'm feeling bolder now, and I hurry down the hall, my phone clutched in my hand, my head pounding. I'm not sure what I expect—is he going to leap out at me? Take my phone from me?

Again.

Will he be sitting at the kitchen counter scrolling through the news, looking bored, like nothing happened?

But he's not here. It's only when I'm halfway down the hall to the front door that I hear a floorboard squeak and I freeze, my heart kicking into high gear.

He's upstairs. There's one board in our bedroom that squeaks. Ryan keeps saying he's going to replace it, but his hours during the week are too long for him to find time to do that. And then on the weekends? Forget about it. He wants to watch sports, see friends, take Nealie to the splash pad.

So the board still squeaks, but that tells me where he is. My shoulders feel pinned to my ears, and I force myself to lower them.

I reach the front door. Turn the handle. Step outside. The day is warming up, the sun burning all of last night's rain off the grass. For a moment, everything feels normal, everything feels fine, then I think about Nealie, and I bend over, grabbing my stomach.

"Mrs. Brown?"

I jerk upright, my eyes wide. My hand finds the railing, and I grip it, trying to gain control of my breathing. The woman standing in front of me is tall and slender, her short hair messy, her eyes narrow as she takes me in.

"Hi. Yes. You are?"

"Detective Martin." Her grip is firm, her skin cool. She walked quickly up to the porch, so fluidly I feel like I didn't see her move. "You called about your daughter going missing?"

"Yes. Oh God." I choke out a sob. My eyes hurt from crying. I can't stop rubbing them, can't stop pressing my knuckles into my closed eyes like the pain will make me wake up from a nightmare. "I was making breakfast this morning and when I went to check on her, to get her up, she wasn't there. Nealie loves bacon. She wouldn't miss breakfast."

Tears burn my eyes. More sobs threaten to tear loose from my chest, and I clamp my mouth shut. Ryan had the porch railing replaced last year, so the wood is firm, the paint brand new, but I dig my nails in regardless.

"How old is Nealie?" She reaches into her pocket and produces a notebook. One flip of her wrist and it's open. Another swift movement and she's holding a pen. Either I can't focus on what's going on, or she's just that quick.

"She's four."

"Do you have a picture of her?" She waits while I nod and reach for my phone, then she continues. "And have you searched your house?"

"Yes to both." My hands tremble as I unlock my phone and pull up a photo from last night. "She's not normally this dressed up, but this is her."

The detective pulls out her phone and snaps a picture of my screen. "I'm going to have officers come search your house."

"We already looked."

"I'm aware, but this is our first step. We'll also spread out across the property, then expand our search as we need to. Do you have any idea where she might have gone?"

I think about Ryan telling me she could be at the park and shake my head, but then it hits me. "Oh, her window screen!" How could I be stupid enough to forget this? "Her window screen was out. And her window was open. We don't let her sleep with her window open just in case. There's a deck right outside her room, and I've always been worried."

Her dark eyes bore into me. "Where was the screen?" When I don't immediately answer, she continues. "Was it outside the house or inside her room?"

"Inside her room. On the floor." I pause. "I don't know how she got it open—we always keep it in place."

Because otherwise anyone could get into her room. The words hang silent, unsaid, between us.

"Who had access to her room? Anyone outside of the family?"

"Just Julie, her nanny." I pause, then speak faster. "She nannies for Nealie and Emma Everett."

The detective pauses. When she speaks, she gives equal weight to each word, and they hit me like bullets. "Mrs. Brown, Emma Everett is also missing."

Her words are like a punch to the stomach. I exhale hard, bending forward and wrapping my arms around myself.

This is all my fault.

The thought is instant, unwelcome. I fight to push it away. A wave of dizziness washes over me, and I close my eyes. Tears leak free, and I wipe them away before forcing myself to stand back up.

I can't claim responsibility for this. At least... not until I know what happened.

"What? Are you serious? You're wrong! They wouldn't both go missing like this! Who would do that?"

"That's what I'm going to find out." She reaches out and lightly touches my shoulder. "Trust me, my team and I are prepared to do whatever it takes to find the two of them, but you need to help me. I need you to think of anyone you might be worried about being around your daughter. Make a list. Are you married?"

I glance down at my hands, but they're free from rings. After I lost a diamond in some bread dough a few years into our marriage, I started taking off my rings before cooking. I guess in the craziness this morning I never put them back on.

"I am."

For now.

"I need to talk to your husband."

Behind her, two police cars pull into our driveway. My eyes flick to them, but I quickly look back at her. She's staring behind me at the house, her eyes narrowing, her mouth in a tight line.

Nealie?

The thought that it might be my daughter, that she might have been hiding all this time, tears through me. I gasp and turn around, excitement already bubbling up in me. Yes, I'll be angry at her for hiding, but it won't matter, not really, not when I know she's okay.

But it's not Nealie. It's Ryan.

He's halfway out the door, frozen in place like he saw a ghost. If I'd thought he looked angry before, now he looks positively pissed.

TWELVE
KATE

10:23 a.m.

What the hell is he doing here?

I swear, one look at Ryan and my brain short-circuits. I'm glad his wife is turned away from me, watching him as he walks out of their front door, because that means she can't see my face.

Years of learning how to school my expression when dealing with controlling men at work usually means I can keep my face neutral.

But this is a shock.

It feels like time stops as I try to catch my breath. Ryan's brows are knitted, his mouth in a straight line as he looks at Alison, then slowly turns to look at me.

I can't read minds, but I'd wager he's thinking the same thing I am.

"Mrs. Brown," I manage, clearing my throat to get her attention. "If you'll meet the officers on your driveway, they can talk to you about where they need to search and what else you might have noticed."

"Okay. Good. I'll do that." She hurries by me, leaving the

scent of an expensive perfume hanging in the air. I watch her out of the corner of my eye but don't turn as she races down the deck stairs.

Ryan closes the gap between us quickly. He's immaculately dressed for the day, just like he always is when he's in the courtroom. Even today, on the day his daughter has gone missing, he looks like he could stand in front of a jury and impress them all.

"Kate." His eyes flick to mine.

"It's Detective Martin." Best to let him know exactly how this is going to go from the start.

"Right. Detective Martin. So formal." He throws me a grin, but I notice how he looks over my shoulder. For the officers? For his wife? He's always been one for optics. That's part of his schtick in the courthouse, that he's perfectly in control, that nothing bothers him.

Shaking my head, I do everything in my power to put those thoughts behind me. I've wanted to scream at Ryan before when he starts parading around in the courtroom. He's a peacock when he gets up there in his custom suits and pocket squares, acting like he's on prime-time TV and not in a courtroom.

It's infuriating. And honestly, that's not the only infuriating thing about him, but I push all of those thoughts aside. How I feel about Ryan and what I think about him as a person and lawyer don't matter.

The only thing that matters is finding these two missing girls.

I can sort through my feelings later with a pint of ice cream and some *Gilmore Girls*. But only once I know the girls are home safe.

I flip my pad of paper back open. "Okay, Mr. Brown, your wife has already filled me in a little bit about what happened this morning, but I'm going to ask you to run through it for me as well."

He clears his throat and shuffles his feet. Is he getting ready to put on a performance? Or lie to me?

I look at him, trying to read the expression on his face. His neck is blotchy with stress, but not a hair on his head is out of place.

"Nealie doesn't miss breakfast," Ryan says. He was staring me down before, but now he's studiously avoiding making any eye contact. "She just doesn't. Alison went upstairs to get her, and she was gone." He lifts a hand and glances at it.

"How did you get those marks on your hand?" They look like they're from fingernails.

"It's been a stressful morning." Now he looks at me. "We're just trying to hold it all together."

He doesn't plan on telling me the truth, but that's fine. I saw his wife's face. She could have gripped his hand in panic while searching for Nealie. "Your wife said you searched the house and the property. How far away from the house did you look?"

"You're asking if we went to the neighbors?" When I nod, he continues. "No, I only looked in the yard around the house, and then Alison called you when we couldn't find her."

His face darkens for a moment before he catches himself.

"And her window screen?"

"Popped out." He shrugs.

"And you didn't think that was abnormal? Your wife expressed concern over it."

He's halfway through another shrug and stops to stare at me. "You think she went outside, don't you?" He scoffs. "No. She wouldn't. Not my daughter."

I don't immediately answer his question. "Mr. Brown, who had access to Nealie's room last night?"

"Just Alison and myself."

"And has Nealie ever popped the screen out of her window before?"

"No, Alison was worried about it a year or so ago, but it's

hard to do. You have to really lean into it." He stops abruptly, his eyes narrowing. "What are you saying to me? Do you think that Alison or I took out the screen so she could sneak out of the window? Do you know how ridiculous that sounds?"

I ignore him. He's upset, and I get that. His daughter is missing, which is the only thing that should matter. Finding Nealie. Finding Emma. Until I've brought both girls home safe and sound, I'll do whatever I have to, deal with anyone I have to.

Even Ryan.

Still, even though I know him, even though he's considered one of the upstanding citizens in town, there's more to this story than first meets the eye. There always is, in fact.

The parents are typically the first suspects. They're both claiming that their daughters wandered off, that they have no clue what could have happened or where they might be. That they're blameless.

Which is what anyone in their position would say, to be honest.

I already know how much of a smooth talker Ryan is. I don't know his wife or the other mother. And as for Daniel Everett? I've heard he's just as smooth as Ryan, although in a different way. A quiet way. Less prone to theatrics, more in touch with his emotions. But still smooth.

"I'm going to search your house after I get my fingerprint kit." As I speak, I tuck my notebook back in my pocket. "I'd like you to show me Nealie's room, then stay out of the way."

"I'll help you." He gestures towards the front door, but I don't move. Ryan is used to getting his way, I know he is. But he's not going to right now.

"No, you'll show me her room and then leave me alone until I fingerprint you and your wife. If that's a problem for you, I'll have an officer escort you outside while I look for any evidence." I pin him in place with my stare. "And I'll need access to the deck since her window opens up onto it. Are we understood?"

Ryan's jaw tightens. It's obvious he's not happy with what I'm telling him to do, but that's beside the point. I'm telling him, not asking. There is no professional courtesy when it comes to finding missing children.

"Nealie's room is the second on the left upstairs," he tells me. "Since you want to be alone so badly, I'll stay down here."

"Perfect." I spin away from him and hurry down the steps to my car to grab my kit. Just a moment later, I'm back on the porch, past Ryan, and in the house. Without slowing down, I hurry up the stairs and down the hall to Nealie's room. For a moment, I stand in the doorway and take it in.

The blankets and sheets have been thrown on the floor. The closet door stands open, but the space under the bed is empty. There are a few stuffed animals and a groaning bookshelf, but the rest of the room is unremarkable.

At least it's not crammed to the gills with crap. Looking for clues in a hoarder's house is my worst nightmare. This looks like everything was shipped directly from the Muuto website. I glance up to the ceiling, note there isn't a ceiling fan, then turn on the light.

There, leaning against the wall across from me, is the window screen. The window has been shut, and I snap on some rubber gloves to open it. Moving as quickly as possible, I dust for prints, carefully storing the print cards in my kit before turning back to the window. When I lean outside, I'm hit with a cool breeze.

The deck is right here. A preteen or teen wouldn't have any trouble slipping out of this window and escaping the house, but a little kid like Nealie? No way. Even if she worked up the courage to try, she'd fall, and her parents would hear her. I stick my leg out through the open window and carefully climb through it.

And that's when I step right onto it: the step stool someone left right below her window.

THIRTEEN
CARRIE

10:41 a.m.

There's only one person I want to talk to right now, and it's not my husband.

I watch Daniel out the corner of my eye as he paces up and down along the driveway. Julie and her boyfriend have scurried off down the street. Neighbors whisper from the sidewalk and yards. I see one busybody headed in my direction, and I turn, walking quickly around the side of the house.

I don't want to talk to her. Or the detective. Or more officers. I'm talked out, for the most part. Taking a deep breath, I look down at the phone in my hand.

Would it be stupid to make the call?

Instead of dialing, I shove my phone in my pocket and wipe my nose on my sleeve. Never in my life have I cried this hard.

Not when I lost the babies I was supposed to have before Emma came along. Not when I was begging the doctors for help. Not even when I had to take matters into my own hands.

Some people say that you can't mourn children you've never held in your arms, but they don't know how bad it hurts to know you'll never get to kiss your child's perfect nose, never get to snuggle them. And nobody tells you that losing one, two, *five* babies doesn't make the hurt of losing the sixth one any less.

And they also don't tell you that when you finally hold baby number seven, when you feel their fingers curl around yours, when their hot body is placed skin-to-skin against your chest, that you'd do anything in your power to protect them.

Emma. I'll do anything to protect her. To bring her home. To make sure she's safe. My mind races when I think about all the things that can happen to little girls who go missing. She could have fallen into a ditch and broken a leg. Or wandered so far away in the storm that she can't find her way back home.

She could be dead.

I don't like the thought I have, that I know *why* she's missing, even if I don't know where she is. But it's there, nestled down in the back of my mind, and I know full well that thought isn't going anywhere, at least not until I assure myself that there's no way anyone else knows the truth.

I pull the phone back out, but I don't thumb it on. I should make the call. Should reach out and see what's happening, but I don't think I can. I don't think I can hear their voice right now.

Where I'm standing, around the side of the house, it feels like nothing terrible is going on. Emma's sandbox is back here. Yes, she's gotten a little too old for it, but Daniel keeps saying that we might have another baby.

He has no idea I got an IUD. It's not that I don't want another child. It's that I don't want to go through the pain of losing so many more before we might have the chance of keeping another one.

And there's really no guarantee that we wouldn't lose more kids, is there? Emma is special, for a lot of reasons. We couldn't replicate her if we tried.

Holding my chin as high as I can, I walk back around the front of the house. From here, I can turn to the right and look into Ryan and Alison's front yard. That was part of the appeal of living here, of course. Who doesn't want to live two houses down from your best friends?

And Mr. Harriot between us knows the girls so well and hasn't ever cared about them cutting through his yard. He's never had grandchildren and has always treated Emma and Nealie like they're family.

But the worn footpath the girls made across his perfect grass is slowly filling in. The beaten-down brown blades are turning green again, perking up. The dirt path will be reclaimed by lawn, and there isn't anything I can do to stop it.

Not when Emma and Nealie no longer play together.

There's movement in front of the Browns' house, and I catch a glimpse of Alison. She's alone. My hand tightens on my phone as I think about making the call.

Not now. Maybe later, when things have calmed down. When there's no chance of anyone overhearing us.

FOURTEEN
KATE

10:59 a.m.

The young woman walking towards me knows something, I can tell. I watched her as she walked into the house, peeking around the front door like she wasn't sure if she was going to be allowed inside. She looked nervous then, and she still does.

She's chewing her lower lip, looking around furtively like she's afraid someone is going to notice her in the house and tell her she shouldn't be here. I watch as she clocks the badge on my hip and frowns.

Not everyone is happy to see the police. I get that, and it doesn't surprise me when I see people figure out what I am and turn and walk the other way. But for her to look so surprised—or worried, in fact—at the fact that there's a detective in the house of a missing girl? That's strange.

I make a mental note.

"Detective Martin," I tell her, reaching out and taking her hand before she can turn and run. "And you are?"

"Julie Staton." Her hand is sweaty, and I wipe mine on my jeans after we release. "I'm the nanny."

"Good. I need to talk to you." When I heard the girls shared a nanny, I'd been surprised. What kind of a case is this? "Were you supposed to work today? Is that why you're here?"

I wouldn't have thought it was at all possible for her eyes to get wider, but they do. She shakes her head, her cheeks already flushing pink.

"No, I'm off. I got texts from both of the moms letting me know what had happened. I knew I had to come right away, that my boyfriend and I would help look for them. Then we arrived and..." She waves her hand around her, encompassing the crime scene.

"Your boyfriend's name?" I have my notepad out and am writing as quickly as possible. Even though I generally don't forget the details of cases, I learned a long time ago that it's better to have things written down than question something I was told.

"Theo Roberts. He's sitting outside with Alison—oh, geez, Mrs. Brown. Sorry, I'm... shook up, I guess. This is awful, isn't it? What could have happened to the girls? Both of them going missing in one night?"

"That's what I'm here to find out." I pocket my notebook. I'll need to talk to the boyfriend and get a handle on who's around, who's saying they're helping but are just being nosy, and who is actually pulling their weight. I'm well aware that perps love to return to the scene of the crime. I'm also aware that this is a rich neighborhood, and those are generally full of busybodies ready to tell everyone else's business.

So why hasn't anyone come forward?

The young woman standing in front of me? The fact that she nannies for two families tells me a lot: mainly that she shouldn't have any problem driving in here without anyone raising an eyebrow. "Both girls going missing in one night is strange. Do you have any thoughts on that?"

"It's terrible! I don't know what to think. Nothing makes sense—"

I cut her off before she can really get going. "That's not what I mean. What I'm asking you is if there's any connection between the families other than the fact that they live down the street from each other." I pause for effect. "And that you nanny for both of the girls."

It takes a moment, but I see when what I'm saying sinks in. Julie takes a step back from me, her hand fluttering to her throat. Her cheeks, which were pink, deepen to crimson. She's flushed, she's nervous, and she's liable to make a mistake.

"You think I had something to do with it?" Her voice is a whisper, and as she speaks, her eyes flick around the room. "You can't... you can't be serious?"

"I never accused you," I tell her. "But surely you know more about the two families than I do. Why don't you fill me in?"

"Oh geez." She exhales hard, obviously trying to gain control of the situation. "The families, right." She takes another deep breath and runs her hand through her hair. "You know, besides what you mentioned, I can't think of a thing."

She's lying to me.

It's as obvious to me as if she had a neon sign blinking above her head. I don't know yet what she's hiding, only that she's hiding something.

"Not a thing?"

She closes her eyes and takes a deep breath. After a moment, she opens them to look at me. "They used to be really close, the families. But they had a falling-out." Her voice has gone flat.

"What was it about?"

She jerks one shoulder up then lets it drop. "The families used to all hang out, then two months or so ago, that stopped. Nealie and Emma were so sad."

I file that away and change tactics to try to keep her talking.

"Do you recognize this step stool?" I pull out my phone and show her a picture of the stool I found outside Nealie's window.

"Sure do. That's the stool from Nealie's mud kitchen."

"Mud kitchen?"

She nods. "It was actually my idea because Nealie loves playing outside so much. We got some pots and pans and set up a dry sink for her over in the backyard. That stool goes with it so she can wash her dishes after making mud pies."

"And it's normally kept..." I let my voice trail off in a question.

"By the mud kitchen in the backyard." Her smile is tight. "Is that it?"

"Not quite. Have you noticed anyone watching the girls? Anyone getting too close to them?"

She shakes her head.

"Have they mentioned anyone? Maybe someone at their preschool? Kids sometimes notice seeing the same person a few times before an adult does."

"Nobody." She wipes at her eyes.

"What places do you take the girls, Julie? I doubt you spend all day in their houses."

"The park, obviously. For ice cream. But only places we can walk—Alison can get funny about me driving Nealie around." Her voice trails off for a moment. "But, you know, mostly we're staying in the neighborhood because this place has everything. A playground, a gazebo, a little pond to feed the ducks."

I nod. She closes her eyes and sniffs hard. While she takes a moment to compose herself, I look around the foyer.

I've already been in here for an initial pass through the house. It's time for me to poke around some more, time to really dig into what makes this family tick. My eyes slide over the thick runner on the floor, the key hooks by the door. There's a table on the side wall with a vase of flowers. I take it all in and turn, soaking in all the details.

"That empty frame," I say, pointing to a gallery wall in the living room. "What was there?"

Julie turns and looks. She's still sniffling a little, but I see the way her jaw tightens as she realizes what I'm pointing at. "Let me think..." She pauses, then walks past me into the living room. I watch as she crouches next to the side table by the sofa, then returns with something in her hand. "This photo," she says, handing it to me. "Alison threw it out weeks ago, but it goes to show you how often they empty the trash."

I take it, turning it so it's right-side-up.

Ryan and Carrie.

"Alison threw this away?"

Julie frowns. "I'm pretty sure it was her, yeah. When she gets in her moods, anything goes."

"Moods?" I have to drag my eyes away from the photo. It's fairly recent—Ryan looks about the same as he did earlier. He and Carrie are clearly at some sort of fundraiser, both dressed to the nines, both grinning at the camera.

Julie glances around like she's afraid to let anyone overhear her. "Alison's great. She really is. But sometimes she gets really angry at Ryan. She'll take Nealie, even if I'm still on the clock, and leave for a few hours."

Interesting.

"Do you know where she goes?"

"She never tells me, and I'm not going to push to ask." A pause, like she's thinking. "She'd probably tell you though."

"This is good to know, thanks." I pull my notepad back out and click my pen. "I'm going to need your phone number so I can reach back out to you. And I'll need Theo's as well. I would hate it if I couldn't get in touch with him."

"What? Why do you think you might need to talk to me again? I just told you everything I know."

No, you didn't. I think she's holding back, and I intend to find out more about why these two families had a falling-out.

Ryan and Daniel worked together. Maybe a little rivalry at work?

"Phone number."

"Right." She rattles it off. "I'll do anything to help find the girls, but I don't know anything else. This is all so random. So terrible."

"You think it's random that they happen to have the same nanny? That they live right down the street from each other? That they worked together? They used to be close and now, according to you, aren't? I highly doubt that, Julie. But maybe you're right. Maybe there isn't any connection."

Her shoulders relax, and she draws a deep breath.

But I'm not finished.

"But you do know what that means, don't you?"

"What?" She barely breathes out the word.

"That I need to focus on you as the connection. And let me tell you, Julie, when two little girls go missing, you don't want to be the one thing tying them together. So if you know something you're not telling me, I suggest you come clean before I find whatever dirt you're trying to hide." I pause. "Where were you last night?"

"At home."

"All night?"

She nods, and I spin back to the stairs.

Yes, I've already been upstairs. I've already been through the entire house, but that was just my first time through. I want to see Nealie's bedroom again.

And then I need to head down the street and see how the investigation into Emma's disappearance is going. I'll have an officer dig into social media, see what there is on the two families. Instagram, Facebook, Nextdoor... it's grunt work I don't have time for, but I need to figure out why Emma and Nealie were targeted.

What's so special or important about the two of them?

There's no way these two girls went missing on the same night without a reason.

I'm going to find out what that reason was. No matter what it was, I'm going to tease it out. Solve this. Bring the girls home.

My cell buzzes with a text from Aletha, interrupting my train of thought.

Headed to the park to look for evidence there. I'll be back shortly.

Good. I don't like Aletha not running point here, but she has the right idea, and she won't be gone long.

Slowing down, I turn and look over my shoulder. Julie's standing at the front door talking to Ryan. She dips her chin; tucks some stray hair behind her ear. I watch as he leans forward like he's going to say something to her, then turns at the last second and makes eye contact with me.

Julie said that sometimes Alison gets really angry at her husband, and I can suddenly see a possible reason why.

Just how many women has Ryan been sleeping with?

FIFTEEN
ALISON

11:09 a.m.

Every fiber of my being screams at me to walk down the street and see how Carrie is doing, but I can't do that.

Not now. Not after everything.

I can't talk to her. I can't throw my arms around her and cry on her shoulder.

And it's all because I can't look her in the eyes. She doesn't know what I did, but that's only a small consolation because I know what I did, and I have to live with it.

The front door slams hard behind us, but I don't turn around to see who it is. An officer? Julie? That detective with the dark eyes who seems to see everything? It doesn't matter, does it? All that matters is that Nealie is gone.

Across the road, the Whitmires are on their porch, openly staring at the scene in front of them. They're old, and I know I shouldn't let them get to me, but I'm overcome with the horrid desire to run over there, to shake them by their shoulders, to scream in their faces until they tell me what they know or until they go inside.

But I don't do that, and in just a moment, an officer walks across the street to their house. I keep an eye on him as he talks to the two of them, but there's no big revelation, no Nealie popping out from behind a bush. After a moment, he points to the security camera mounted on their porch roof. My heart beats faster.

Security cameras. Why didn't I think of that?

Something about cameras eats at me, but I can't figure out what the problem is.

But instead of inviting the officer in, Mr. Whitmire gestures back. He shakes his head. It's clear he's explaining something, but I don't know what it is. The officer shakes both of their hands and heads to the next house.

"We need to check our security footage," I tell Theo. "I feel like I should be doing something, and that's it." He hasn't said a word since Julie left him here with me so she could go inside the house. I don't know if he's supposed to guard me to prevent me from doing something stupid or to make sure I don't fall apart.

"Security footage?" He turns to look at me.

Excitement bubbles up in me. "Yes! Look." I point overhead at the camera on the porch. "We have cameras, we have..." My voice trails off when I see the expression on his face. "What? What is it?"

"It looks like a Security Solutions camera."

"It is."

He scrubs his hand down his face. "They've had storage issues for a few weeks. We can see live footage, but nothing is being saved. Trust me, it's top priority."

"They had... what?" I grab his arm and squeeze it hard. "*Storage issues?* You've got to be kidding me!"

"I'm sorry." He doesn't jerk away from me. "I don't know what to tell you."

I moan and let go of his arm. Fear and anger wash over me. "How do you know about that?"

He sighs. "I work for an independent company that handles behind-the-scenes work for security companies. I was there late last night and into this morning working on the coding and back end to get it all back up and running. You should have gotten an email about it."

"Ryan mentioned it." My heart sinks as I remember our conversation this morning. I'd heard what he said, but I was too busy thinking about the email I'd received to pay much attention to him.

"Hey, as hard as it is, the best thing you can do right now is wait at home until Nealie comes back. She could be lost in a neighbor's yard, already on the way to you." He turns and looks at me, his blue eyes bright in the morning sun. "You don't want to have left your home when she needs you."

He's right. It used to drive me nuts when people younger than me were right about things, but now I'm happy to let someone else take control. I don't want to have to make any decisions.

I just want Nealie back.

I swallow hard. The paint on the steps is peeling, wearing away from so much use. I've been on Ryan for a month about repainting them so they match the railing, but he hasn't done it yet, and I pick at the paint with one nail. The movement feels distant, like I'm watching someone else do it.

Behind us, the screen door slams, and Ryan clears his throat.

Theo pulls away from me like he's been burned. "Sorry," he mumbles. "I'll let you two talk." He's up from the step in a flash. Julie hurries past my husband to join him. I watch as he throws his arm around her shoulder and leads her to an officer in the front yard.

"You two looked cozy." Ryan drops down next to me. He's closer than Theo was, but I don't lean into him for comfort. Not when the memory of what happened between the two of us this morning is still so fresh in my mind. "Care to share what you were talking about before we all meet with the detective to learn about the search plan?"

I don't want to answer him, but that's the thing about Ryan. A trial lawyer, he's excellent at getting the information he wants from people. Even if I avoid him for now, he'll wear me down eventually.

It's what he does best.

"Theo and I were talking about the security cameras. He works for the company, or with the company, or something, and they've had storage issues. There's no footage to show what happened last night." I rub my temples. When I'd first laid eyes on Theo, I'd have sworn I knew him from somewhere, but I must be wrong. Julie's never brought him to the house to meet us, at any rate.

"That's not all you two were talking about."

I turn to look at him. His jaw is set, his eyes locked on the mass of officers in the yard. He wants an answer, and soon, but I take a moment and think.

"No, it's not." The words feel heavy. Sun beats down on my bare arms, and I imagine I can feel my skin burning. Thinking about that and focusing on that pain is preferable to thinking about what I'm going to say to him.

"Go on."

"We were talking about me staying here at the house for when Nealie shows up scared. I don't want her to panic if she can't get to me right away."

"Wow. Insightful." Sarcasm drips from his words.

Unable to stand it any longer, I wheel on him. "Are you enjoying this?" My words are a hiss. "Nealie is missing, Ryan, in case you can't seem to get that through your thick skull. And you're acting weird about it. You refused to let me call the cops. *You took my phone.* I still don't know what the hell that was about, but now you're laughing about my friendship with Carrie." My mind races, making it difficult for me to pin down a single thought. "Tell me, Ryan, exactly why you were upset I called the police this morning?"

His jaw tightens. His teeth have to hurt, like they're almost being ground to dust. I watch as he works his jaw, the muscles in his cheeks bunching.

Finally, he's had enough time to come up with a response. "You lost any right to that information the moment you stole your phone and ran from me. We'll get Nealie back, Alison, I'm sure of it. But I don't know how much of a family she'll have to come home to."

I close my eyes and take deep breaths. He stands, and I feel him step past me, but I don't open my eyes to watch him go. It's too painful.

Because he's right. We'll get Nealie back, but Ryan and I... we won't recover from this. We were already falling apart before Nealie went missing. We started falling apart before he twisted my arm and made me do the one thing I didn't want to do. My timeline has changed, but my plan hasn't.

Get Nealie out of here. Single parenting hasn't ever been on my to-do list, but it seems like the best option for the two of us.

I scrub my hand down my face. Roll back my shoulders. But before I can join the officers in the yard or go back inside, the front door slams again, and the detective is sitting next to me.

"I found this photo in the trash." She pushes a photo of Ryan and Carrie in front of my face. "Care to tell me why that's the only one missing from your gallery wall?"

I close my eyes. It takes no effort at all to remember every detail of that night, but I don't want to. When... Ryan and I did what we did, I couldn't have any reminders of our old friends in the house.

"I got tired of looking at it." My voice is flat.

She pulls the photo back to look at it. "But it's a great shot of both of them. They look so happy, don't they? So cozy. Were you not there?"

"I was taking it," I tell her.

"Ahh, that's why you weren't in it. And Daniel?"

"He was in the bathroom." I inhale, count to five, then slowly exhale. "How is this helping you find my daughter, Detective?"

"Right now, I'm just figuring out all of the key players and their relationships." She pauses for a moment. "I'm going to put together a search party for the girls, but you and I have a lot to talk about, Alison. I'd love to hear the real story of why you threw this photo in the trash." She pauses, obviously waiting for me to respond.

I don't.

"Hey, when you get mad at Ryan, where do you take Nealie?"

What?

A chill dances up my spine. "I don't get mad enough at Ryan to *take* Nealie. I don't know what you're talking about."

"Hmm." She taps her chin as she looks at me. "So you and Ryan are solid? No problems there?"

"None." I fix my gaze on her as I lie.

"Good to know." She stands and hurries off, taking the photo with her. I don't move.

I can't move.

What she doesn't know about that night—what she *can't* know—is that it was the last night the four of us were out together. Just a week later, Daniel lost his job. I threw the photo away because of the immense guilt I felt when looking at it.

I'd love to keep all of that hidden from her because as soon as she finds out about Ryan firing Daniel, she'll want to know why. If she digs into that, she'll find out about my involvement.

I did what I did for Nealie. That's what I keep telling myself.

I did what I did so Ryan wouldn't catch on to the lies I was telling him.

SIXTEEN

Anger flushes through me, and I know trying to deal with my anonymous texter right now isn't the best idea, but I don't know what else to do.

There's nobody I can turn to, so I open my texts. This time, the ones from earlier are still there, and I ignore the obvious threat.

I've been running out of time. But did I already? Is it over? For both girls?

Sweat beads on my brow, and I wipe it away before tapping out some words. My hand shakes before I press send.

As I do, I lift my eyes and look around me. It's not like I really believe I'll see someone suspicious looking at their phone at the exact same time as I send the text, but what if that's what happens?

What if it's all that easy?

But I don't get lucky. The yard is full of people. Hell, the entire neighborhood is teeming with residents and police, but nobody looks suspicious.

My phone vibrates, and I jump.

I told you what I want. 250k

Before I can respond, another text comes through.

You didn't ask, but she's fine.

I exhale in relief, but the next text makes me feel like I'm going to throw up.

For now.

SEVENTEEN
CARRIE

11:21 a.m.

I jump a foot when my phone rings, but when I see the name flash on the screen, I swipe my thumb across it to hang up.

Daniel's head jerks up from his phone. He's been scrolling mindlessly for half an hour, his thumb endlessly moving up and down his screen, but I don't think he's actually taking in anything he's seeing. It's just to keep busy, to give him something to do while we wait.

"What was that? Was it the detective?" He keeps a death grip on his phone and leans forward a bit, like he needs to get a better look at me.

"Nothing," I lie. "A scam call."

Daniel doesn't respond. Instead, he sinks back in his seat, his eyes closing halfway. I don't realize he's crying until he reaches up and wipes a finger across his cheek.

It makes me uncomfortable. I know it's sexist, to think that the man always has to be strong, to expect him to remain in control of his emotions all the time, but I need Daniel to pull it together.

His gentle spirit is one of the things that drew me to him when we first met. I loved how he would show up at my place with flowers when I had a hard day at work. How he made me dinner when I was tired. How he knew exactly what to say when my dog died.

He loves to read, loves good wine, and he's loved jazz since he was four. Combine all three and the man is perfect. Well, almost.

That all changed when Ryan fired him. It was one thing for him to be soft and gentle and kind when he was supporting us, but now? Now it just frustrates me. I don't want him to be gentle and kind. I want him to be strong, but I've been the one handling everything since he lost his job, and I'm tired. For once, I want him to comfort me.

"I have to pee," I announce. Before he responds, I turn from the living room and hurry up the stairs. Yes, there's a bathroom downstairs, but I need privacy.

Once the door behind me is closed, I tap on my phone and navigate to my recent calls. I chew my lip, then return the call.

Ryan picks up immediately. "Carrie. How are you?"

Tears burn my eyes, but instead of fighting them back like I might if I were talking to Daniel, I let them fall. "This is terrible, Ryan. I don't know what to do." I hiccup and stop, take a deep breath. "Emma... and Nealie. How are you?" *How is Alison?* But I don't ask that.

"Terrible. We're terrible." He pauses. "Listen, I want to be there for you. I'd come check on you, but I don't know how things would go with Daniel."

I do. Daniel would lose it if Ryan showed up on our front porch. I know he would. After what happened at his work, and what Daniel keeps denying he did, I can only imagine their conversation would come to blows, and that wouldn't bring either of the girls home.

Daniel's so careful. I can't imagine him screwing up at work the way Ryan said he did. He's a good man. Reliable. Smart. But Ryan wouldn't lie like that, would he? He wouldn't hurt Daniel like that because he knows it would hurt me.

And even though we're not as close as we were, Ryan has always been there for me. I've had to try to decide who I think is telling the truth. Is Daniel being honest when he tells me that he didn't make a mistake at work? Or was Ryan correct when he placed the blame directly at Daniel's feet? As much as I hate to believe it, Daniel had to have screwed up. It's the only thing that makes sense. Besides, he's been... different since he lost his job. He draws away from me, goes inside himself. It's entirely possible this side of him has been hidden the entire time we've been together and is just now coming out.

The alternative is too difficult to believe—that Ryan fired Daniel erroneously. Ryan doesn't make mistakes. I don't like to think that Daniel does, but Ryan... anything he does, he does on purpose.

"You're fine. I'd love to come talk to you and Alison, but she doesn't want to see me." My voice trails off. The truth is that I don't want to see her. I'd love to see Ryan, but they're a package deal now.

And I can't go to him, no matter how much I want to.

We're both silent for a moment. I open the bathroom door and lean out to make sure Daniel hasn't followed me up the stairs, but I don't hear him moving around. He's probably still in the living room, stuck in his chair, unable to take action.

"Listen. I know things are crap right now between all of us, but I don't want you to be a stranger. Reach out. I'll support you. This is a nightmare for both of us."

I exhale and turn to lean against the wall. *A nightmare for both of us.* He has no idea. The child I fought for is gone. The child I was willing to do anything to have.

"Thank you," I say. I need to say something, to fill the silence, to show him that I'm not angry at him, because I'm not.

That's the thing about my friendship with Ryan. I might not agree with what he's doing, but that doesn't mean I'm angry at him. We've been friends for so long and have always been there for each other. When my high school boyfriend cheated on me, Ryan punched him in the nose. When his knocked-up cheerleader girlfriend went to stay with her aunt before homecoming, I went to the dance with him in her place. We're each other's rock, but nothing more than that.

All through high school, I never wanted anything more. I loved Ryan as a friend, but I'd seen what kind of a partner he could be. Even now, I know he has a wandering eye and wandering hands. So even though he's there for me and I'm there for him, it's platonic. Nothing more.

And it's worked. We've supported each other. When he met Alison, I stood up for him in their wedding, and she and I quickly became best friends. And Daniel was so close to making partner in their law firm before everything fell apart.

And now I've not only lost Alison, my best friend, but also Ryan, the friend I've had the longest, the one who knows more about me than anyone else in the world. He's like a brother to me, and now we can only talk over the phone, even though he's just two houses down and all I want is to hug him.

"They'll come home," he says, and I think for a moment he's going to say something else about the girls, about how I don't have to worry, about how he won't sleep until not only Nealie but also Emma is home. It's because of how he doesn't cut off his words, how he trails off, like he's gathering his thoughts, but then when he speaks again, his words are hard. Clipped. "I have to go. Alison's coming."

And he hangs up.

I keep the phone pressed up against my ear far longer than I need to. He's gone, and I know he's gone, but talking to him was the first time I've felt any reassurance about my baby girl coming home.

Ryan has never once backed down when I needed his help, and I have no doubt in my mind he won't start now.

Alison's the problem. My ex-best friend. The woman who knows all of my little secrets.

Well, that's not entirely true, is it? There's one secret she doesn't know. One that would destroy everything.

I sink to the floor and drop my head into my hands. It was a secret I swore to keep, one that could ruin everything. But if people knew the truth, would it make it easier to find the girls?

EIGHTEEN
JULIE

11:40 a.m.

I've noticed the way Ryan keeps staring at me while I stand with Theo, picking us out of the crowd gathered around to hear how we can help find Nealie and Emma. I don't think he'll come say anything to Theo and me, but he does seem... hyper aware of where the two of us are at all times.

Does he think I have something to do with the girls going missing?

"We'll be a team," Theo whispers. He's so much taller than me that he has to lean down to put his lips by my ear. We're in a group of two dozen or so people, most of them Blackwood residents, but nobody pays us any mind. They're too busy listening to the woman standing in front of us.

Detective Martin. I noticed immediately how she seemed completely aware of everything at all times. She's the kind of woman who can look at you and tell when you're lying.

She acts like she won't take shit from anyone.

And like she knows exactly what she's doing.

In short: she makes me really, really nervous.

Not that she ever has to know what I know. What we're doing. Because if she found out what Theo and I do, I know what would happen.

As soon as the girls are found, her focus would be on us, and there's no way the two of us would walk free. That just can't happen. I have to be careful, have to give enough information that will help everyone find the girls, but not so much that it backfires and people find out what Theo and I have been doing.

It's a fine line to walk. I have to do it perfectly.

Detective Martin finishes speaking, and another officer walks through the crowd handing out pieces of paper. How someone found the time to map out the neighborhood and delineate various areas to search, I have no idea. I wait until Theo has finished looking at the paper then take it from him.

Ahh, that's what this is. It's the map they give to all residents when they first move in so they can easily find their way around. Not only are the streets labeled and the houses all numbered, but each house has the owner's last name printed on it. It's great if you want to invite someone over, I guess.

Or if little girls go missing and you have to quickly organize a search party.

"Remember," Detective Martin says, getting our attention, "your job is not to go door-to-door and speak to your neighbors. In fact, I strongly discourage you from doing that. I don't want to see you stopping to chat about what's going on. What I do want is you looking in bushes, under decks and porches, and behind sheds. These girls are young, small, and could easily hide in any number of places outside. Let the officers handle speaking to your neighbors and looking in the actual houses, do you understand?"

There's a chorus of affirmation, then Theo takes the map back from me. He turns it around, then finds where we're standing. Not that it should be hard—both the Browns' and Everetts' houses are marked with stars. The section we're supposed to search is clearly marked as well, the line around it drawn in thick black Sharpie.

"You ready?" Theo asks, giving the paper a flick.

I nod. My mouth feels stuffed full of cotton. When I swallow, my throat hurts. Ever since Carrie texted me about Emma, this hasn't felt real. But now that we're here, about to head out looking for the girls, the full gravity of it weighs down on me.

"Great. Looks like we need to head down to the end of the road here where there's a cul-de-sac, then loop around back there behind these houses. I guess we'll cover their front yards too, since that's kinda what the detective said."

I look at the map again.

Oh, crap. I hadn't paid attention to exactly where our section was, but now I see it. Where Theo and I are supposed to be searching is right where the trails I've shown the girls are located.

Sweat breaks out on my brow. Absentmindedly, I reach up and wipe the back of my hand across my forehead. No way they'll find them. They're hard to see, tucked behind a fence. It was blind luck when we found them.

"You okay?" Theo's staring at me. "This is really hard, Julie, and if you're not up to it, I'll take you home."

"No, I'm fine." I glance past him to look at Ryan, but he's no longer staring at the two of us. He's doing the same thing as most of the people in the crowd we're in—studying his map. "It's just taking a toll on me, you know? But I don't want to leave, not until we know the girls are safe."

"Okay. But I want you to tell me if you change your mind, alright? There are enough people here helping—they don't need us." His eyes flick around us, taking in the scene.

"Right." I pause, gathering my words. There's one thing I've been dying to ask him since we found out both of the girls are missing. "Theo," I say, keeping my voice low, although I don't think anyone is close enough to eavesdrop, "how did we screw up?"

"We didn't." He doesn't look at me. Slowly, like he's not sure he's even doing it, he reaches up and covers his mouth before speaking again. "We didn't do anything out of the ordinary. This is a hiccup, but we'll recover from it. Don't worry." His shoulders bunch up.

"A hiccup. Of course." He sounds confident, but I don't feel the same. Theo's never run into any problems with the jobs we do, but he's not the one in the house, not the one digging up dirt on rich families. I am.

I'm the one getting into the homes, under their noses. The one who really sticks her neck out. We're both on the hook for what happens, but I'm the one people recognize, the one who they could point out to the police. Everything he does is behind the scenes, which means he's safer than I am. I'm still watching as Ryan turns and looks directly at us, a frown creasing his brow.

No, wait. He's not looking at me. He's looking at Theo.

It makes me nervous. None of our other jobs have ever gone like this. It was fine, and now everything's gone off the rails.

"Great. Then let's go. We don't want to be the last ones getting a move on, do we?" he asks, his voice rising in pitch a bit.

We should start searching, but my mind is racing with thoughts of Ryan. I know I should focus everything I have on finding Nealie and Emma, but I'm worried about Ryan.

What he might say. What he might *do*.

He's only ever heard Theo's voice once before this, when my boyfriend made the call that set everything in motion. No way would he be able to recognize his voice out here among so many other people.

Sun beats down on the back of my neck. Everyone around us looks sweaty. They look hot and tired, and like the only thing they want to do is escape to the shade with a glass of something cold.

"Lead the way," I tell Theo. He gives me a strange look, and I shrug. "You have the map. I know my way around this neighborhood, but it's probably best if we try to stay within our section."

Theo nods and leads me away from the scattering crowd. What I said to him was true—kind of. But my mind races as we walk, and I don't want Theo to be paying that much attention to me. Giving him the map also gives him something to focus on. There are a lot of pieces to this case, and I feel like I know some of them, but the missing ones leave big gaps.

The sidewalk curves, and we pass house after house, each with a front porch that rivals the square footage of my apartment. When I first started nannying here, I had to fight down the envy I felt every single time I came to one of the houses.

It was hard.

And I'd like to say that it's gotten easier, but that's not entirely true. I've just gotten used to it. It's really difficult to not let it show on your face when you're surrounded by people who take everything they have for granted.

This neighborhood? I'd do anything to live here. But I can't think of any way I could make that happen, not when this job will burn any bridges with the Browns and Everetts. Not when Theo and I have our rules, and one of them requires us to keep moving. That thought makes me look over at Theo. He looks so intent on the task at hand, so focused on finding the girls.

I know he's telling the truth. Theo and I are excellent liars, but we have one rule.

We don't lie to each other.

That's the only way this works. The only way *we* work, the only way we both get what we want. And so far it hasn't been a problem.

He first came to me with his idea a month after we'd started dating. Blackmailing terrible people so they have to pay for being horrible? It's never something I thought I would do, but I couldn't turn Theo down when he suggested his plan.

My dad deserved to be taught a lesson, but nobody ever did. He was rich, or at least well-off, thanks to winning the lottery. His job as the beloved superintendent meant everyone knew who he was. Everyone liked him.

And nobody suspected him of beating his wife and daughter. If someone had stood up to him, maybe drained him dry to teach him a lesson, taken him down a notch, things might have been different. But nobody knew how terrible he really was.

And that was the lesson I learned—rich people hide their crimes. They hide how awful they are. People see the zeros attached to their bank account, and those zeros hide all sins. But a nanny can sneak around, poke around, find out what they're keeping secret. Nobody suspects that the woman taking care of their children might have an ulterior motive. That's what I do, then Theo and I hit them where it hurts, right in the wallet.

In that moment, when Theo and I made a pact to work together, we swore never to lie to each other.

My toe catches on the sidewalk, and I stutter-step to keep from falling all the way.

Theo and I lie to everyone, but he wouldn't lie to me.

Right?

NINETEEN
KATE

12:08 p.m.

The sun's beating down on everyone searching for the missing girls, but that doesn't explain the red flush to Carrie Everett's cheeks. We're sitting on her huge front porch directly under a turning ceiling fan, but the woman looks like she just ran a marathon.

"Mrs. Everett," I say, leaning forward and resting my elbows on my knees, "why is your husband sleeping on the sofa instead of in bed?"

She rubs the back of her neck and glances towards the front door. Her husband is inside talking to an officer, but I wanted to be the one to speak to the mothers. Fathers tend to be all bluster and blowhard, but mothers? They'll crack, no matter what they're trying to hide. As soon as they realize the threat against their children is real, they'll roll over on anyone standing in the way of them getting to their child.

Unless the mother is a psychopath, of course, but Carrie Everett doesn't strike me as a murderer.

She is a liar though.

"Things have been tense around here since Daniel lost his job," she says, spreading her hands wide on her knees. Another glance at the house. "I'm sure we've both said things that we regret, and there's nothing wrong with taking a little space from your spouse. I'm sure you can understand that."

"Sure. Losing a job causes friction in any relationship. But I'm surprised you're not leaning on the Browns for support since you were best friends. Or is it uncomfortable since Daniel and Ryan no longer work together?"

The words hang between us.

"Uncomfortable, yes. That's a good word for it."

"But surely you and Alison can still support each other. Your entire lives don't revolve around your spouses."

She stiffens. "Well, sometimes you find out things that make a friendship unpalatable."

"Such as?"

She scratches her arm and glances at me out the corner of her eye. "Alison isn't what you might think she is."

I mull that over, giving her time to continue, but when she presses her lips together and gives her head a little shake, I push.

"And who is she?"

"Not a friend." She clears her throat and stares directly at me. Her gaze is unflinching. "Is this really helping you find Emma?"

"It is. Usually, in cases like this, the children know their kidnappers." I let that sink in. "Talk to me more about Alison."

Carrie sighs. "She's driven. Focused. Willing to do whatever it takes to get what she wants."

"Which is what?"

A shrug. "I'm sure it changes from day to day." She presses her lips together.

Fine. "Tell me, what other changes is your family going through? Anything else that might cause stress or introduce you to new people who might take an interest in your daughter?"

"Emma switched preschools."

"Because Daniel lost his job? Or was there another reason?"

The pause before she speaks clues me in to the fact that she's about to lie to me. "We just decided it wasn't the right place for her."

"What preschool was she in?" I'm ready to make a note of whatever she says. I'm going to need a list of their teachers, any parents who might have been overly interested in the girls, anyone who could have had contact with them without their parents around.

There are too many people involved in this case, too many people who were close to the girls and might have built up enough trust with them to take them. Every time I speak to someone, the circle of people I need to interview grows. Thank goodness I have Aletha and all of the other incredible officers working on this case.

Carrie clears her throat before she speaks. "Grace Day Academy."

My eyebrow flies up. "That's the best preschool in the area."

She nods.

I lean back in my chair. The cushion is soft, but the wicker bites into the backs of my knees. More than anything, I want to know how much she's willing to tell me. "Daniel lost his job. I'd wager you didn't pull Emma from Grace Day on a whim. But things get expensive without reliable income, don't they?" I wave my hand to the side, encompassing the huge house, the Range Rover in the driveway, the manicured yard.

Her mouth pinches shut. Again, she glances at the house.

"The job change was a surprise, but we pulled together to make it work. He was a junior partner with Brown and Schenk and now doesn't have as much stress. But you know how that can be, when your spouse makes a big change and you have to adjust." Her eyes flick to my ringless left hand.

"I don't," I say, "but I can imagine." She shifts uncomfortably. "He was a junior partner, but what is he doing now?"

She looks away. "He's a paralegal."

Things are making sense. Paralegals don't make nearly as much as lawyers do, not even when they've been in the job for a long time. With Daniel just making the change, it's entirely possible his income was halved, or more.

"Tell me more about your relationship with Alison. You share a nanny with her, so surely you once thought of her as a friend."

Her head jerks back to me. For just a moment, there's a scowl on her face, but she blinks, and it's gone. "Well, both of the girls love Julie. You've met her—I'm sure you understand."

"So you and Alison haven't ever been close?"

She shakes her head, but before she can respond, I pull my cell phone from my pocket and open my messages.

Every moment she spends not telling me the truth is one more moment her child is missing, one more moment something terrible could happen to her.

"I had an officer take a spin through your social media, and he found some interesting photos." I click on one that shows Carrie and Alison side by side in matching T-shirts, matching grins on their faces, both of them holding a glass of wine. "But you said you two aren't friends."

"That's right."

I turn my phone around for her to see the photo. Her eyes flick to it, then back to the house, before she looks at me. "One photo doesn't mean we were bosom buddies."

"You're totally right. Hang on." I flick my thumb, bringing up another photo of the two of them. Then one of Emma and Nealie sitting together eating popsicles on this very porch. The next is a photo of both families at a cookout. "One photo wouldn't mean much, would it? You can definitely take a single photo out of context. But what do you think about the rest of these? Looks to me like you all were really close, so what happened? Was Daniel losing his job too much for the friendship to endure? Or is it because she's... what did you say? Driven? Willing to do whatever it takes to get what she wants?"

She's silent. I thumb off my phone and slip it into my pocket, then glance at my watch. Honestly, I'm surprised more of the search teams haven't made it back yet. Every time someone calls out, I stiffen, sure they must have found something relating to the search.

But so far, nothing.

"We were friends, but now we're not." She shrugs, like that's the end of it. "The girls were in preschool together and we live right down the road, so it made sense for us all to hang out."

"But not any longer? A simple job change shouldn't end a friendship."

Carrie blinks at me. "It's hard to remain close to someone when your husbands no longer work together."

I give her time to continue, but after ten seconds, I speak. "Jealous, huh?"

She lifts her chin.

"I bet that jealousy alone was enough to drive a wedge between your two families, am I right? To go from being a junior partner in a firm with your neighbor and friend to suddenly not only *not* working there but having to take a lower-paying job? Did you and Alison talk about it? Or was it too weird?"

Carrie's silent for a moment, drumming her fingers on her knee. At first glance, I'd thought her nails were just as perfectly manicured as Alison's, but I see now how the polish has chipped, the way the polish paints a few of her cuticles. An at-home manicure then. Makes sense if you're suddenly on a budget.

"Tell me what happened with Daniel at work. I think—"

"Ryan fired him." She cuts me off, leaning forward and

glaring at me as she speaks. "Happy? Ryan fired my husband. Now, you may think we're friends, but friends don't fire each other."

"What was the reason?"

"You'd have to ask Daniel. Or Ryan."

"Or Alison? Since she's so driven, as you said?"

Her face contorts.

"I don't know how worrying about Daniel's job is helping you find our daughter." Carrie's voice is high and tight. She reaches up and scratches the side of her neck, then fixes her gaze on me again. "Shouldn't you be out there beating bushes to find them?"

"I have a team doing that. But if we don't find the girls here, we need to know where else to look for them. And two families that appear perfect on the surface but have deep cracks are worth a closer look, wouldn't you agree?"

She doesn't respond. Another question is on the tip of my tongue, but before I can ask it, my phone buzzes. No way would I ever ignore it in the middle of a big case like this, and I glance at the screen.

What I see there surprises me.

I stand and gesture to the house. "I'm sure your husband will be available for a chat with me later. I'd love to hear all about how he's handling his career change. I'll be by later, Mrs. Everett."

She doesn't respond, and I leave her sitting in the same chair as I hurry down the porch steps and across the driveway. Standing on the sidewalk, a dark expression on her face, is Aletha, an evidence bag in her hand.

TWENTY
ALISON

12:26 p.m.

"They found something," Ryan tells me. He pauses at the front door long enough to grab his keys and slip them into his pocket, although where the hell he thinks he might be going when Nealie still isn't home is beyond me.

He's been perched on a chair he dragged to the front picture window for the past half an hour after we walked around the house and searched the yard one more time. Those three words are the first thing he's said to me since we came inside, and I close my eyes. Force myself to take a deep breath.

They found something.

Could be evidence. Could be nothing.

Could be a body.

"Shut up," I whisper to myself. I'm hot on Ryan's heels as we tear down the porch stairs and meet the detective in the driveway. She's joined by an officer, a tall woman with a strong jaw. Detective Martin holds an evidence bag. Ignoring Ryan, she gestures for me to step closer to her, then hands me the bag.

"Do you recognize this?"

I turn it over in my hands, the plastic crinkling, my heart sinking as I look at what's inside. I don't know if every parent out there has memorized all of their child's stuffed animals, but I know Nealie's.

She's brutal with getting rid of ones she doesn't love anymore. In fact, I think she pared down her collection last year from three dozen to five.

And this is one of them.

"It's Sir Pinky," I tell the detective. The pink bear is smeared with mud, looking more brown and gray than sparkly pink right now, but I swear I'd recognize this bear anywhere. After the drama a month or so ago when she left it in a booth at Smitty's and I had to return the next morning to pick it up, I don't think I'll ever forget it.

Then it hits me what happened. They found this outside, God knows where.

It's filthy. Wet from the rain.

Grief washes over me.

I don't mean to drop the evidence bag, but the next thing I know, it's slipping from my grasp. I fall to my knees, barely registering the way the ground digs into my skin through the soft fabric of my pants, how the grass and dirt will surely imbed in the fabric and become almost impossible to wash out.

I can't breathe. It feels like there's a band around my chest constricting my lungs. Without thinking, I grab my shirt and pull it away from my body. I have to get some air, have to breathe, have to survive this.

"Nealie!" I scream her name, and that's when Ryan finally drops down next to me. He wraps his arms around me and pulls me to him, pressing my face into his chest.

I don't want to be comforted by him. I shouldn't lean into him, shouldn't inhale his expensive cologne and feel a sense of calm wash over me, but that's exactly what happens. My body is a traitor, so used to the familiarity of my husband that even now, when I know I shouldn't trust him, I turn to him.

"Shh, Alison, shh. You're going to be okay. Nealie is going to be okay. I promise, alright." His hands are on my hair, brushing it back from my face, tucking it behind my ear. Another sob escapes me, one I don't try to hide.

"She's really gone!" The words come out in a jumble, but Ryan's gotten me through a lot of sob-fests before, so I know he understands me.

"She's not gone for good. We're going to find her. You saw how many people are out there searching right now, right? No way will she be gone for much longer. Trust me, Alison—Nealie is coming home. I bet we have her home by tonight."

Someone clears their throat. I look up, straight into Detective Martin's eyes. They're sad, downcast, like she's weighed down with the discovery of Nealie's stuffed animal. She looks at me for a moment longer, then tears her eyes away, squats, and picks up the evidence bag.

I can almost feel the sorrow and concern wafting off her.

As bad as she feels, however, I guarantee I feel worse.

"Where did you find it?" I manage the words, then stand up. My legs are shaky, and I feel my knees wobble like they're going to give out, but I refuse to fall down again. Heat burns the back of my neck.

My daughter is missing. If anyone should be allowed to break down, it's me, but I can't. I'm her mother, and because of that, I have to be strong. Nealie needs me to be strong.

"One of our search teams found it dropped behind a bush three houses down. Sergeant Aletha Bradshaw brought it to me." I take in the officer standing next to the detective, but then she points to the left, where the bear was found, and Ryan and I both automatically turn to look in that direction.

Like in doing so we'll be able to make her appear.

"Dropped behind it? Or placed there? Do you think she went that way and accidentally dropped it, or do you think someone put it there on purpose?" Ryan voices exactly what I want to know but am too afraid to ask.

"That we don't know, and until we get the girls back, I don't know that we will. That storm last night washed away any trace evidence we'd normally hope to see in a case like this." She gives the bear a little squeeze. "Of course, there is still evidence to be found; we just have to work harder for it."

"Like the fingerprints you took from Nealie's window," Ryan offers. There's an edge to his voice.

Detective Martin slowly turns and looks at him, then nods. "Exactly. I took those prints and sent them back to the department to have someone in the lab work on them. I don't want to leave the scene unless I have to, while I conduct interviews."

I hear what she's saying, but I can't drag my eyes away from the teddy bear. Nealie was holding that bear last night, and now she's gone. It's silly to think that this stuffed bear is the most recent connection I have to her, but it's true.

A pit grows in my stomach.

Who in the world would want to take my daughter?

"Can I... can I have the bear?" I reach out for the evidence bag, but my fingers fall short of touching it. Even though I'd do anything to have it, there's some part of me well aware that I can't just take it from her.

"Not right now." My face falls, and Detective Martin continues. "It's evidence and has to be entered as such, exactly how it is. But I promise you, when this case is settled, I will make sure you get it back."

"Okay. Right." When I was a child and I would get upset, I'd hear my voice growing smaller and smaller. My mother hated it and always told me to speak up, to speak my mind, not to be a mouse. For decades I've fought against turning back into that little mouse.

But that's exactly what I am now.

The officer clears her throat. "We found one more thing." She holds out an evidence bag, this one with a piece of paper inside. "It's a ransom note."

"Where was it?" I ask, but Ryan's louder.

"How much?"

She glances at him. "Half a million." Then she turns to me. "It was in your backyard. The storm probably blew it back there from wherever the kidnapper put it. I've got officers looking for any sign of someone in your backyard, but they haven't turned anything up yet."

That doesn't make sense. People have already looked back there. How did they miss it?

Was someone recently behind our house? But how did we or the police not see them?

"Fingerprints?" I gasp out, but she shakes her head.

"Nothing. We're keeping it as evidence, of course." She pauses, then continues. "We'll let you know when we know more."

"What else did it say?" I'm dying to get my hands on the note. "There has to be something about getting Nealie back."

The officer winces. "That's all it said—no threat not to call the police, nothing. Just the money for the two girls."

"Half a what?" The words burst from Ryan. "No way. No."

"We have it." I turn to Ryan. My hands claw against his chest without me realizing what I'm doing. "We have it, right? We'll give it to them. I don't care what it takes, we'll find it."

"Alison, we need to let them do their job." He grabs my wrists and squeezes. Hard.

I yank away from him. "No. This is Nealie we're talking about. And Emma." I wipe my eyes, angry at my body for continuing to cry. I need to be strong for the girls, and I can't do that if I keep crying. "I don't care about them *doing their job*. I want the girls back."

"Mrs. Brown." The detective touches my shoulder. "Right now, we don't have any contact information for the kidnapper. The note says how much they want, but it could be a hoax."

"A hoax?" I try to wrap my mind around what she's saying, but I can't do it. The idea that someone might joke about this when my life is falling apart is too much for me to handle. "A *hoax*? You've got to be kidding me. No way can we think this is a hoax when Nealie is missing. We have to give them the money!"

"Alison, stop." Ryan touches my shoulder.

"Not *now*, Ryan. Let me handle this."

"Alison!" He takes a deep breath. When he speaks again, his voice is calmer. "We appreciate all you're doing. Let us know what else you find out." Ryan takes me by the elbow. That's his signal that he's going to lead me away from a situation. That I should shut up and let him take control.

And for the entire length of our marriage, I've done just that. I've sat back and watched as he led the way, I've let him mold me into the perfect wife. I've done what he asked, even when it meant losing my closest friend.

But I'm tired of it.

He's steering me away from the detective, his fingers tight on my skin.

Tighter. *Tighter*.

"Ryan," I say. "Stop. We need to continue this conversation. I'll pay anything to bring Nealie home safe!"

He doesn't listen to me. Instead, his fingers dig in more, like they're going to break through my skin.

"Look at me," I say.

His eyes remain locked past me.

I follow his gaze.

He's looking at Julie and Theo. There's a swirl of emotion across his face, making it difficult for me to tell exactly what he's thinking. Before I can try to figure out why he's frowning, why his jaw grinds together, why his eyes seem to darken, he gives his head a little shake, hiding everything that had been on his face.

TWENTY-ONE
JULIE

12:48 p.m.

Ryan's walking towards us, his jaw working, Alison crying while he pulls her along with him. His eyes flick from left to right before snagging on me.

Something happened. Alison wouldn't be so upset if there wasn't some kind of news. Maybe they found Nealie.

And maybe she isn't okay.

My throat tightens. Whatever it is they know, I need to find out what it is. See if there's anything he needs.

See if I can find out what he knows. If he somehow recognized Theo's voice.

"Hey," I say to Theo, tugging on his arm to get him to slow down, "I'm going to go chat with Ryan really quickly, okay?"

Theo doesn't break his stride. "Ryan? Why?"

"Um, because he's staring at us." Now Alison is looking this way too, but the expression on her tear-streaked face isn't angry. She just looks concerned.

You and me both, lady.

"I'll handle it," Theo announces, stopping dead in his

tracks. "Whatever the problem is, you shouldn't have to deal with it. Not today. Not when we're just trying to help. Let me. Besides, he might have made his decision about what I talked to him about by now. Remember: time's almost up. And he's stressed, which means he's apt to screw up. If he doesn't want his secret coming to light, then it's time to play ball." He shoves what he's been holding into my hands, and I take it without thinking.

Ryan might have decided what he's going to do, but now is not the time to ask him. "No, wait, he'll talk to me, but he doesn't know you. You only called him, right? That's always the way we do it," I say, but Theo's already striding away from me.

Something about this just isn't right, but I can't put my finger on what it is. Theo approaches Ryan and Alison, and after a moment, the two men walk away together.

Why would Ryan talk to Theo and not me? They don't know each other, and I don't think Ryan recognized Theo's voice.

So why is Theo so insistent about being the one to talk to Ryan? None of this makes any sense, and I chew the inside of my cheek as I think.

I'm dying to know what they're saying to each other, but there's no good way to sneak up on them and listen. I'll just have to wait and see what Theo tells me when he returns.

Frustration washes over me, and I glance down at what he pressed into my hands before striding off. The map, of course, which was to be expected. A half-empty bottle of water he'd grabbed from a neighbor who put out a cooler of them by the end of their driveway, and his cell phone.

I freeze.

His cell phone? Theo and his phone aren't easily separated, which tells me he wasn't thinking straight when he pressed his stuff into my hands. In all the years we've been dating, he's never had it out of his sight. No way would he have willingly handed it over.

I turn it over in my hands and glance up. Ryan and Theo are at the end of the block now, still walking away from me.

Guilt washes over me, but before I can stop and think about whether or not I'm going to snoop, I'm turning and walking in the other direction. There's a huge red oak tree about twenty feet away, and I lean against it, casually glancing down at his phone.

Even though there's no way anyone else knows that the phone in my hand isn't mine, I still feel exposed, like I'm about to be caught doing something I shouldn't. I glance up, but nobody's looking at me.

Excitement rushes through me as I slide my finger across his screen to unlock the phone, but I need his passcode. Before I can let myself think not only about if I want to do this but *why* I want to, I type in the first four numbers that come to mind.

His debit card PIN. Most people wouldn't hand theirs out all willy-nilly, but Theo got pretty sick a week ago and asked me to run to the pharmacy for him. I'd offered to pay for everything, but he'd refused, telling me it was best for him to pay for his meds himself. He gave me his PIN and card to make it as easy as possible.

Still, knowing his PIN and knowing his passcode are two totally different things, and I'm not really expecting the phone to unlock.

But it does.

Another glance to ensure he and Ryan haven't looped back around, but I'm still alone. Even Alison has retreated to the shade of her front porch. An officer is talking to her, but there's no way to make out what's being said.

Not that it matters. I have more than enough on my plate right now.

My finger hovers over his messages icon, then, before I can stop myself or really think through what I'm about to do, I tap it.

There, on the top, messages from me. I'm not surprised; the two of us chat a lot. The next messages are from names I recognize as guys he works with, so those aren't interesting.

There's his best friend.

And a friend from college.

I keep tapping, my heart beating fast as I skim his messages. *What am I looking for?*

I don't want to admit it to myself.

At the diner last weekend, did he stare too hard at that waitress? And what about when we were on our last job, and I had to drive him home from the bar more than once because he was drinking with friends from work?

Only the *friends* had all been women, hadn't they?

"Theo wouldn't cheat on me," I whisper to myself. I'm seeing threats where there are none. He and I are keeping a huge secret together. No way would he put that at risk, right?

Guilt weighs down heavy on my shoulders, and I close his messages, turn off his screen, and slip his phone into my pocket. There are more messages to look through, and I didn't even begin checking his call log, but I don't want to.

Theo trusts me. I trust him, and I don't want to allow myself to think of reasons why I shouldn't. No way would he be willing to just... look the other way if he knew I was snooping. That's a given in any kind of relationship—you don't go through someone else's phone unless the relationship is on the rocks. And ours definitely isn't.

Right?

But he'll never know I was looking. Even though I know that's true, and that I didn't find anything that should make me question Theo at all, I can't shake the thought that I just royally screwed up.

How angry would I be if Theo went through my messages? And how hurt?

"But there was nothing to see," I whisper to myself. As I say it, I reach back into my pocket and pull out the phone. Thumb it back on. "You just look for terrible things to happen when things are really going well." As I speak, I navigate to his browser. My finger trembles as I consider tapping to see his search history.

I take a deep breath, and then I tap it, but I close my eyes so I don't have to see what pops up right away. My mind races, uncontrollable thoughts swirling as I try to make sense of the morning.

I don't have anything to do with what happened to them.

What Theo and I do? It doesn't put kids in danger. That's the rule, and neither one of us would ever break it.

I refuse to let anything take the life that I'm building away from me. I want the family Theo and I are making, and my silly nannying job, and late nights singing karaoke and early mornings eating leftover Chinese food.

If I look at his phone, I could throw it all away.

Get it together, Julie.

The girls have to be fine. They went on an adventure, that's all. They wandered down a sidewalk and...

And what?

Probably straight to the paths out of here that I showed them.

Guilt washes over me.

I don't want the blame to land on my shoulders. I might not be a good person, but I wouldn't ever put them at risk. Theo and I don't hurt the kids I nanny. We don't put them in danger.

That's the deal, and we've never deviated.

I open my eyes.

I don't have to scroll, don't have to search for something damning that will make me question Theo, because his search history is riddled with items that make me break out in a sweat.

NCDating

OneHotNight

NamelessConnections

I close out of his browser and turn off his phone. My hand shakes as I shove it in my pocket. With my mind racing this hard, it's difficult for me to take a breath, to calm down, to think about what I just saw.

Fact: Theo's been searching for dating and hookup websites.

Fact: I've already had a strange feeling sometimes about how he looks at other women.

Fact: I can't ask him about what he's doing until we finish this job because I'm terrified what he'll say, what he'll do, how this will end up.

The fluttering of my heart makes me feel lightheaded. I gulp down air, unable to comprehend what to do next.

I don't want to accuse him of cheating on me. Not now. Not with the girls missing and our plan already being put into action.

But the sooner we find the girls, the sooner he and I can have that talk, and it's something we're going to have to do eventually.

So what happens now? Do the police expand the search? Should I tell them about the trails? I could speed this up, bring it to an end faster so Theo and I can talk.

I bite the cuticle around my thumb. When Theo's face enters my mind, I push it right back out. It's not the time. I can't fall apart, not when Nealie and Emma need me.

Or you know what? I bet they start interviews. It's time to bring people in, to see what they might know, to buckle down and find the girls.

Oh! There. Coming around the corner, it's Theo, and I drink him in, trying to imagine him with another woman. Bile burns the back of my throat when I do.

He's not with Ryan, although someone is walking with him. I watch as the detective cuts away from him towards the Everetts' house. Theo watches her, his eyes greedy.

I can't tear my eyes away from Theo's face. I see the way he drinks her in, how he cocks an eyebrow as she goes up the stairs to the porch. I see it all, and my heart hammers faster.

Theo and I are supposed to be a team, but it's becoming clear that he's not as committed as I am.

It hurts, but I make a split-second decision. As much as I love Theo, I have to protect myself. I'll do anything, say anything, to make sure I come out of this in one piece.

TWENTY-TWO
CARRIE

12:49 p.m.

"What are you looking at?" Daniel's right behind me, and he bumps me out of the way with his hip so he can look out the window as well. "Did the police find anything?"

"I don't think so." I swallow hard. "Just that bear, and it was Nealie's, according to one of the officers." Every time I speak, it feels like my throat is about to close up. I can't seem to get enough air in my lungs. There are tight bands of stress wrapped around my chest, and I can't slip free from them.

"Doesn't mean Emma was with her." He drops the curtain and steps away from the window, watching me as he does. "Emma being gone might not have anything to do with Nealie disappearing."

"Do you really think that?" Sarcasm drips from my words, and I take a step closer to him. "Really, Daniel?"

He shrugs but doesn't answer. The doorbell rings, and I jump, but he beats me to it. Holding my breath, I peek around the wall and look down the hall to the front door.

It's the detective. "I spoke with your wife earlier," she says to Daniel. "But now I'd like the chance to talk to you."

I see the way he stiffens. It's such a small movement, I don't think anyone else would notice, but I do. He's a good man, Daniel. He hates confrontation in his personal life, even though he was always a lion in the courtroom. But after losing his job, his shoulders slump forward. He walks with his head down.

He just looks... exhausted.

Daniel clears his throat. "Of course. Do you want to come in?"

I take a step back into the living room. He'll bring her in here, I have no doubt, but I'm not in the mood to talk to her. I do, however, want to hear what she and Daniel might talk about. She didn't see me, did she? No... she was too focused on Daniel. And he's too worried about saying the wrong thing to think about the fact that I might listen in on their conversation.

It's stupid, but I hurry out of the room, into the hall. There, I carefully press myself up against the wall, making sure they won't be able to see me, even if they glance out the door. My heart beats out a staccato rhythm, and I take deep, slow breaths to try to calm down.

Their voices are muffled for a moment, then they get louder. Even without looking, I can tell they're in the living room. There's a pause, then the shuffling of fabric.

They're sitting.

The hair on the back of my neck rises. My nerves feel frazzled, and I have to fight to keep still. I know I need to keep quiet, to ensure they don't know I'm here, but that's hard when they're so close.

"Mr. Everett, first I want to check in with you. How are you holding up?"

Daniel's silent for long enough that I consider peeping around the doorframe to make sure he's okay, but he finally clears his throat. It sounds thick, like he's doing everything in his power not to cry.

"Not great. This has been a nightmare." He sniffs. "And Carrie's handling it the best she can, but we're both really struggling."

"I'm sure. And I want to let you know, we're doing everything in our power to find Emma and bring her back. I wanted to talk to you—see if there's anything you might know that could help us do that. People don't always realize what kind of information can crack a case wide open. So why don't you tell me about what happened at work?"

I stiffen.

"You mean me losing my job?" Daniel sounds exhausted, which is how I feel.

"That's exactly what I mean. Tell me exactly why Ryan fired you."

"I really don't want to talk about it. I don't see how me losing my job could have any impact on Emma going missing." I don't have to look at him to know Daniel is shaking his head.

"Making those connections is what I do. Tell me what happened."

He sighs. "I was let go because of a mistake with a case. It was a simple error, really."

"Most jobs don't fire you over a simple error."

"If you think that, you must not know Ryan very well. Even a simple error is reason enough for him to go scorched earth."

"What was the error?"

"Just something on a case." He shifts position.

"Did Alison have something to do with it?"

"I don't know. Did someone say she did?" He sounds nervous, and it makes me angry. I've always been great at holding things together, but Daniel's soft. He'll crack if the detective pushes him too hard.

She's silent for a while. I can imagine the way she's probably looking at him, her eyes searching his, waiting for him to continue. He doesn't though.

I'm surprised when she changes tactics.

"Is Carrie home?"

"She is." I hear him moving in his seat. He must be twisting around looking for me. "She was in here before you came, but I bet she went upstairs."

"Okay. Tell me, Mr. Everett, what really happened between her and Alison?"

I swear, the temperature in the room drops ten degrees. I feel the hair on the back of my neck stick up, and I shiver, wrapping my arms around myself.

"What do you mean?" When Daniel speaks, his voice is tight. High.

She's going to know something's up.

"Just that. I understand you and Ryan having a falling-out after him firing you. But Alison and your wife? As close as they were? I'm surprised they don't stay in contact, especially now, when your daughters are missing."

I'm holding my breath.

"Detective, you're not married, are you?" She doesn't respond, but she must shake her head or something because Daniel only pauses for a moment before continuing. "Still, you must know that spouses stick together. I'd be shocked and horrified, honestly, if Carrie didn't side with me."

"So their relationship ending had nothing to do with your wife's relationship with Mr. Brown?"

What?

"What?"

More shifting. "Everything is on social media, but I'm sure you already know that since you're a lawyer. And it's not like people are only uploading current photos. I can't tell you how many times I used to get tagged in photos from middle and high school when my old friends would dig up their photo albums and upload everything. Not only that, but I saw a photo of the two of them looking cozy. Dressed up. At some event. It was pretty clear they'd both been drinking."

"Where was that?"

"In the trash at the Browns' house. Care to explain that?"

"The photo or why it was in the trash?"

"Both."

"The photo was at some fancy dinner. Why they threw it in the trash? Probably because they do that with things they tire of."

"Like you."

He doesn't respond.

"Carrie and Ryan have been friends for decades, haven't they?"

"They have."

"And when did they date?"

"They didn't date."

I'm holding my breath, not because I'm shocked but because I'm afraid to make a sound. Afraid that I might miss something being said if I exhale. My lungs ache, but I don't breathe.

"Just best friends then?"

"That's right."

"And you and Alison weren't ever envious of that?"

"I can't speak for her, but I wasn't." He shifts, the sofa grumbling a little as he does. "There's nothing wrong with men and women being friends."

"Nothing at all."

"And Ryan and I worked together—"

"Well, you did, but you don't now, do you?" She gives a breathy laugh. "But you just said it yourself—spouses stick together. And maybe Carrie and Ryan were getting too close. Maybe Alison pushed him to fire you, to take a step back from his relationship with your wife because it made her uncomfortable. What do you think about that?"

"Are you saying that Ryan fired me because Alison pushed him to do so?"

"It only sounds crazy at first. But mull it over. Who's in control over there? Alison or Ryan?"

"She wouldn't. Alison wouldn't hurt us like that. Wouldn't hurt Carrie like that." There's a loud thunk. If I had to guess, I'd say Daniel got angry and stood up, accidentally kicking the coffee table leg in the process.

"Sure, but you just said that spouses will stick together." The detective's voice is light and airy, a sharp contrast to my husband's. "So I'm thinking Alison got angry about Carrie's relationship with her husband and pushed for you to be fired to punish her. Now your two families are in turmoil and your daughters were both taken. Seems to me like things might be related."

"They're not. Carrie and I didn't do anything to cause Emma to be taken. If you want to point a finger at someone, look closer at Ryan."

"And why should I do that?"

No, no, no, Daniel, shut up—

"Because out of the four of us, he's the one who never grew up. Who never learned to be careful. Sure, everyone loves him because he's so great in the courtroom, but they don't know the real Ryan."

"And who is the real Ryan? I'd love to know."

"He's—" Daniel suddenly stops talking. "He's not the perfect, shiny, wonderful man everyone thinks he is. I swear to you, he has everyone duped. He's fooled everyone, and that includes my wife."

No.

I don't think he's perfect, shiny, and wonderful. I'm not an idiot. I know more about Ryan than anyone else, including his own wife. He and I share the biggest secret of all, one that we both swore never to share with anyone.

If Daniel knew that secret, there's no way he'd be able to control himself. He'd tell the detective—I know he would. And then we'd both lose everything.

I can't let our secret come out, at least not yet.

Not until I'm good and ready.

TWENTY-THREE
KATE

1:25 p.m.

The nanny sits across from me in an interview room, her blonde hair in a messy ponytail, her fingers picking at her cuticles. She's been this nervous all day. Only now, she has nowhere to hide. I watch for a moment, letting her nerves grow, before finally speaking.

"I really appreciate you coming in here to talk to me," I say, then push a cup of coffee closer to her. It'll calm her down, make her think I'm on her side, but it'll also give me her fingerprints.

"Of course." She takes the cup and wraps both hands around it. "I want to find Emma and Nealie as much as everyone else does. No way would I sit this one out."

That and she didn't have a choice.

"And I really appreciate that. Now, tell me how you got this job."

She takes a sip of coffee. "I met Alison at the park while I was babysitting a little boy and we got to talking. She said she was looking for a nanny but only needed one a few days a week." Another sip. "I wasn't going to be able to afford to pay my bills if I worked only a few days a week, so I passed, but she took my information anyway. A few days later, she called, telling me she had found another family who wanted to nanny share with them."

"You stumbled upon her? That seems fortuitous. Most people aren't that lucky."

She freezes. Just for a second but long enough to let me know I hit a nerve. "Sometimes things work out in your favor."

"Sure. And sometimes you get lucky because you do your research. So, just between us, did you stumble upon Alison, or did you know who she was?"

Julie closes her eyes and takes a deep breath.

"Because I can tell you, if I were moving somewhere and wanted to ensure I was working for a good family, one that could pay me what I deserved, one without a lot of problems, I'd poke around online. Maybe hang out at the park, ask around, see who's who. So tell me. Did you research the Browns before you ran into Alison?"

She nods. It's a small movement but enough of an admission.

"And how did you do that?"

"Just like you said... asking other moms at the park. And watching." Her eyes flick up to mine. "You've seen how she dresses and the car she drives. There's money there, and I didn't want to nanny for someone who couldn't pay me. I just watched and learned before approaching her."

"So you stalk your potential families?"

She freezes. "No," she says, obviously careful with her words, "I do my research. I don't stalk them. It's not like I follow them around town or look in their windows."

"Sure. I see how you think there's a difference there. Now,

tell me how a nanny share works." I have a pretty good idea, but I want to hear it from her. I want to know exactly how this arrangement was set up.

She visibly relaxes. "I nanny Nealie Monday, Tuesday, and Wednesday. I have Emma on Thursday and Fridays. It used to be I had both of them on Wednesday, but that changed two months or so ago. And then on weekends I'm available if needed, but it's only ever for Nealie." She gives a little shrug. "My rates go up on the weekends."

"And well they should. How much do you make a week?"

"Eight hundred." There's no hesitation in her answer.

"That's a nice chunk of change. You own your home or rent?"

"Rent."

"And you live alone or with your boyfriend?"

"With Theo, yeah."

"Even though he owns his own house?" She freezes, and I smile at her. "Don't be surprised. That was easy enough to look up."

"It's... complicated."

"Sounds like it. Complicated because you two aren't on the same page or because he likes having his space?"

She shifts in her seat. "He likes having his own space."

"Just in case?"

She nods, and I continue. "Okay then. Tell me, how do the two families determine who pays what?"

She puts her coffee down and drums her fingers on the table. We're in the nicer interview room, one with softer bulbs and more comfortable chairs, but she still looks like she's going to come out of her skin.

"Weeellll," she says, drawing out the word, "it was split equally, but that changed. I didn't think much of it at the time because Carrie and Alison were always such good friends, but Alison started paying me extra to cover what Carrie couldn't."

I stare at her, trying to reconcile what she's saying with what I've heard about the two mothers. "But they're not friends. Why in the world would Alison be willing to pay extra for you to nanny someone else's child?"

She shrugs. "I don't know."

"And you never thought to ask?"

"No. I was getting paid the same, so it didn't matter."

Right. In one breath, Daniel told me Alison might have been behind him getting fired, then turned around and talked about how slimy Ryan is. Carrie said that Alison was driven to get what she wanted. Now Julie's telling me Alison is paying extra for Emma to stay with her old nanny?

Something isn't adding up here. I have more information than I started with, but it's not enough. Time to get the last details I need from her.

"Do you think any of the parents would have taken the girls?"

"What? No. Absolutely not." She's shaking her head, her limp ponytail flopping back and forth. "No way. They're all obsessed with their kids. And even if they took the other daughter, why take their own?"

"To throw someone off the scent."

"Not the Browns and Everetts."

"You sound convinced."

"I am." She stops drumming her fingers on the table and fixes me in place with a stare. "I know you're meeting them at the worst possible time, but you don't know them like I do. They wouldn't hurt those kids."

"Right, and you know that because of the stalking you do." She flushes, and I continue. "You said you were home last night, didn't you?"

"That's right." She scoffs, then catches herself. "Wait. You can't possibly think I had something to do with this, can you?"

"Just covering my bases. You just told me the parents

wouldn't hurt their kids, which means I need to look elsewhere. That's what I'm doing. You have access to the neighborhood, do you not?"

"I do."

"And the houses."

This time, she doesn't answer.

"And the girls trust you. They like you. They would probably do whatever you asked them to, wouldn't they?"

No response.

"Answer the question."

"Yes, they trust me, and yes, they'd do what I asked them to, but I wouldn't ask them to do anything bad or dangerous. I wouldn't. I—"

"Do you have anyone who can corroborate where you were last night?"

Silence.

"Your boyfriend?"

She nods. "He was at my apartment until late." I watch as she shifts in her seat.

"He didn't spend the night?"

"No, he had work to do and came over early this morning. I'm sure he'd be thrilled to show you his timecard." She pauses, then the words burst out of her. "Do you think I had something to do with the girls going missing?"

"I think you know more than you're letting on, and you'd better open up to me. Now. The last thing you want is for me to find out later that you've been lying to me." I brace my elbows on the table and lean closer to her. "Trust me, Julie. I'm going to be most helpful to whoever comes clean with me first. Give me something. Anything."

She chews her lower lip, then forces herself to sit up straighter in her chair. When she clasps her hands together on top of the table and forces herself to make eye contact with me, I know I'm going to get something good.

It's about Ryan.

Of course it is. The man acts like he's perfect even though he's rotten on the inside.

Maybe Alison did help get Daniel fired, but there's no way she knows this about her husband.

She'd kill him. I'm sure of it.

TWENTY-FOUR
ALISON

1:50 p.m.

Ryan drops me off at the front of the police station and is clearly about to get back in his car and drive away when an officer stops him.

"If you'll come inside and wait, Mr. Brown, I know Detective Martin would like to have a word with you as well." She rests her hand on his open window, half leaning in it, not giving him an option to drive away.

I should wait for him. We should walk in together, look supportive of each other. It would be the smart thing to do, to show everyone here that we have nothing to hide.

Because we don't.

Right?

Instead, I leave him behind, hold my head high, and march inside alone, following the directions of an officer at the front desk until I reach the interview room where the detective sits. She's looking down at a pad of paper in front of her, clearly going over her notes.

I'd love to know what she has written down.

What does she think I did?

"Hello?" I knock on the door and wait until she looks up and waves me in.

"Mrs. Brown, thanks for joining me. I thought meeting here and getting away from the craziness of your house might be a good idea." She stands and shakes my hand, then gestures for me to have a seat.

I do, but I don't look away from her.

"I'm happy to talk to you again, but I don't see why we couldn't have met at the house. If Nealie shows up—"

"She'll be met by a team of officers who will keep her safe and call me immediately. Don't worry about that, Mrs. Brown—we're not going to keep your child from you once we get her home." She flips her notebook closed and pushes it off to the side. "Now, let's get started. Are you envious of your husband's relationship with Carrie?"

Her question is a punch to the gut. When I don't immediately respond, she continues.

"Oh, I know what you're thinking. *They're just friends*, am I right? But you know as well as I do that the line between friends can get really blurry sometimes. I saw how cozy they looked in that photo you threw away."

Without thinking about what I'm doing, I slam my hand down on the table between us, but she doesn't flinch. "Carrie and Ryan aren't having an affair! And what does any of this matter? I thought you were supposed to find my daughter!"

"I'm working hard to find Nealie," Detective Martin says calmly. "I can't discount the possibility that whoever took her wanted to hurt you. Or your husband. Or your old friends."

I don't know what to say to that. I keep thinking about Ryan this morning not wanting me to call the police. Something had been wrong, but I don't know what it was.

And I'm not sure I want to mention it here. Not when I have secrets I'd like kept hidden too.

"Let's talk about why you're paying part of Julie's fees for Carrie. I already know that you pay six hundred and fifty dollars a week while Carrie pays one fifty. Is it guilt pushing you to pay that much?"

"What do you mean?"

"Simple. When people do something wrong, they often try to overcompensate for it by being really nice, even going above and beyond the call of duty. Now, if you ask me, paying most of the expense for Emma to have Julie as her nanny is going above and beyond."

"I don't feel guilty about anything." The back of my neck itches with sweat, but I don't move.

"Nothing?" She sounds surprised.

I don't know if it's because I'm not giving her what she wants or because I'm holding it together so well. Still, I feel the pressure getting to me. Something is going to have to give soon. I just don't want it to be me.

I have to get out of here.

"Nothing at all." I shove back from the table, the chair legs scraping against the floor. My brain is screaming at me to leave, but won't that make me look even more guilty? I don't know what to do, so instead of getting up, I stay seated but cross my arms.

"So when I ask Ryan whose idea it was to fire Daniel, he's not going to point his finger at you?"

"No." My voice is a whisper. Sour spit fills my mouth.

"Really? Because you're looking a little pale. Let me tell you what I think. I think you pushed Ryan to fire Daniel. Maybe you don't like Carrie's relationship with your husband, maybe you don't like feeling left out of what goes on at the office, I don't know. But you pushed him, and he did, and now your girls are missing. That tells me one thing."

"What?" My lips seem to crack as I speak.

"Someone in one of your families did something. And I think you know what happened with Ryan."

I close my eyes and take a deep breath. She's close, but she doesn't quite know what happened. That's good. We need to keep it that way. I clear my throat.

"Am I under arrest? Or can I leave?" Just asking a question with that word in it—*arrest*—makes my heart beat harder. I feel like I'm going to be sick, and I force myself to stand up.

"You're free to go, but before you do, just one more thing. If you did do something—and I'm not saying you did; you seem very convinced about that—but if you *did*, and that something is related to Nealie and Emma going missing, you'll wish you'd told me. You may think you don't have anything to feel guilty about now, but you will."

Thank goodness this woman isn't a mind reader or she'd know about the waves of guilt crashing down on me right now. I feel like I'm drowning in a combination of it and grief, and there's not a single person right now I trust enough to talk to.

If I hadn't done what I did, maybe this wouldn't have happened. Should I tell her what happened between our two families? Surely she'll interview the Everetts just like she's interviewing us. The woman is thorough and driven, which should thrill me because it means Nealie should be home as soon as possible, but it also scares me.

I don't want my secrets brought to light.

In the end, I choose to save myself. At least for now.

"Goodbye, Detective. Let me know when you find our daughter." I turn away from her and hurry to the door.

"Send your husband in to talk to me," she says.

I pause in the door and nod but don't turn back to face her.

Once in the hall, I stop and lean against the wall, gasping for air. There's not enough oxygen in this building, I'd swear to it. I can't think straight, I can't focus, I can't do anything without knowing where my baby is.

"Alison." Ryan gives me a tight smile as he passes me in the hall. He pauses for just a moment outside the interview room, then ducks his head and knocks before walking in.

Goosebumps break out on my arms.

I wonder if he'll tell the detective I forged Daniel's signature to ensure he'd lose his job. To give Ryan the perfect reason to fire him.

And why.

TWENTY-FIVE
CARRIE

2:04 p.m.

The key Ryan gave me back when our families were close still works.

There had been part of me afraid that he and Alison would change the locks after our families had our falling-out, but they haven't. At least, they haven't changed the back door. No way would I waltz up onto their front porch and in through their front door, not when this place is crawling with cops and the two of them could come back home any moment.

They're at the police department getting interviewed—or at least I'm pretty sure that's where they are. I'd been watching when the detective met with them in their front yard and seen how both Ryan and Alison shook their heads, clearly not agreeing with what she was telling them.

Then she left. And they did too.

I waited for ten minutes to make sure they weren't taking a trip around the block for some reason, then grabbed my key and slipped out the back door. Daniel had been reading in the living room and never saw me go. He said keeping his mind in a book is the best way for him to forget what's going on in real life, for him to pretend like everything is fine.

I hate it. Honestly, I wish he'd man up. Deal with this. Find our daughter. But he's clearly not interested in taking things into his own hands, so I will.

I close the door behind me and stand still for a moment, listening. Ryan and Alison were both in the car that followed the detective out of here, but what if someone else is in the house? Someone else could be sneaking around just like me, maybe taking advantage of security systems being down.

Or the fact that Ryan and Alison have a Ring doorbell on their front door, not their back.

I can't think of anyone else who would have a reason to break into their house. Although, I doubt I'm the only person they've screwed over.

There aren't any sounds, though, and I hurry down the hall to the front of the house. I'll start here and work my way through the first floor, then head up to the second floor if I still haven't found anything. I know there has to be something here that will give me a clue about what happened to the girls.

Ryan and Alison love to act like their hands are clean. Like they never do anything wrong. Unfortunately for them, I know the truth. And if I can't find anything here that will bring Emma home? Maybe I can find something that will prove what Ryan did to my husband. Prove what I'm hoping—that Daniel didn't do anything wrong.

And if not that? Then I'll find proof of what Alison has been hiding from everyone. She told me her little secret in confidence one night when she'd had too much to drink. And I've kept it.

Even when they fired Daniel. Even when Ryan took Alison's side. I kept her secret, knowing full well that she's terrified I won't.

But that's the problem with a secret like hers. I need proof if

I ever need to take her down. I have to be able to show Ryan, Daniel, the detective—whoever will listen—that she's hiding things. And if she's willing to hide something like this, who knows what else she'll hide?

What I'm looking for won't be in the living room or the kitchen. I need access to her computer because I doubt she'll have proof of it printed out. In the front hall, I pause at a locked door, my hand on the knob.

Ryan's office. That's what they told us, but I've never been inside. He's fastidious about keeping the door locked.

But Alison wouldn't keep her secrets hidden in his office, not when she's trying to keep them *from* him.

There's a laptop on the coffee table, and I sink onto the sofa in front of it. Is it Ryan's? Alison's? I need it to be hers. It's one thing to *know* what she told me she was doing, but to have proof? That's real insurance.

I open it, smiling to myself when I see that it's not password protected. The wallpaper is a picture of Alison and Nealie, the two of them with ice cream cones, matching grins on their faces. I ignore it and click on the icon for the internet, then type in the address of the bank I know they use. It's the same one we use; the same one the business uses. Having everything under the same building always made it easy for Ryan to keep an eye on the accounts.

Alison's login auto fills, and I close my eyes, trying to imagine what her password might be.

Nealie0819
RyanandAlison
Nealiebaby

She's always picked stupid passwords, ones with more sentimental value than actual use. Each time I type in what I think the password might be, however, I get a warning that it's not correct. My throat feels tight as I hover over *Forget your password?* and click it.

Now the race is on, and I open a new tab for her email. Two seconds later, the email from the bank arrives, and I click the link to reset the password, then delete the email. I was fast, right? No way will Alison see it on her phone.

And if she does... chances are good she'll assume it's someone phishing and she'll ignore it.

Back at her online banking, I create a new password for her and then log in.

And finally—finally—I get to see all of her accounts. Not the ones Ryan has on his own, of course, but the ones she's on for the business, her joint accounts with Ryan, and her solo accounts.

Those are the ones I'm most interested in.

There's a small checking account, but I don't care about that. My eyes skim over her VISA card and land on the newest account, a money market savings account with a suspiciously high balance.

Over three hundred thousand dollars, to be exact.

"Ooh, you've done it now, Alison," I whisper. I click on the account, not surprised when the transactions load to see that they're all deposits. No withdrawals. Nothing coming out of the account, only going in.

But they're small deposits. None of them are more than a few hundred dollars. She's been at this for two years, slowly building this large account without accidentally letting anyone else know what's going on.

Except she did, didn't she? She told me.

That was a mistake.

I really want to print the page but pause before clicking the icon. I don't know where they have a printer in the house, but I should find it. I'm not going to use this now, but having it will give me security. If I produce it, I can ensure the detective's focus is on Alison, not on me.

Good. Good. I like that idea. I stand, leave the laptop open and walk around the living room, opening the drawers in the TV stand to look for a printer. There's nothing in here, nor in the kitchen, which means it has to be in Ryan's office or upstairs.

At the bottom of the stairs, I pause, tilting my head to listen. No cars in the driveway. No garage door opening. No front door creaking on its hinges.

I have a little bit longer.

Hurrying now, I race up the stairs and turn not towards Nealie's room but into Ryan and Alison's. Their *sanctuary*, she calls it, then nudges Ryan with a grin on her face.

Like I don't know what she's implying.

Even though we've been friends for years, I've never been in this room, and I stop in the doorway for a moment to take it all in. Entering someone else's bedroom is private, and I'd love to have more time to poke around in here. I'm sure there are secrets galore if I were to take the time to dig them up.

But I don't have time.

My eyes drift around the room, taking in the four-poster bed, the matching bedside tables, the closets, the armoire. There's a TV mounted on the wall across from the bed and over it, on the ceiling, a mirror.

I wrinkle my nose.

On the other side of the room, however, is the jackpot. I race over to the printer and press the button to turn it on. Giddy now, I hurry back downstairs, practically racing into the living room. Really, this is working out a lot better than I thought it would. I'll print these off, keep them to give them to the detective, maybe approach Ryan with them if I have to.

Oh, that would be something to watch. Ryan has this quiet anger that builds in him like a volcano, warming and growing and threatening to take everyone down when it explodes. It'll be delightful to see it pointed at his wife.

I'm just walking into the living room, ready to settle back on the sofa and print the account history when the front door slams.

I don't think. I just run.

Through the house, out the back door, as careful and quiet as possible, even going so far as to hold my breath just in case whoever is in the house could hear me panting as I run. I cut through the neighbor's backyard and race into ours, only stopping when I've reached our house.

And then it hits me.

I left the computer open.

TWENTY-SIX
ALISON

2:14 p.m.

There's dirt on the decorative rock I took from our garden, and I pause long enough to wipe it on my jeans before gripping it with both hands and slamming it down on the locked doorknob.

I don't realize I've closed my eyes until I hear the crunch of impact and open them to see the lock doorknob is dented but still in one piece. I swear, bracing my feet before doing it again. This time, the doorknob twists to the side, the mangled metal shifting, and I drop the rock on the floor.

I have to remember to take that with me when I leave.

Ryan would kill me if he thought I'd left him at the police department for his interview, sped home, and broken into his office, but I don't feel like I have a choice. He's lying to me about something, that much is obvious, and sitting in a hard molded-plastic chair in the police department waiting room isn't going to get me any answers about what he's been up to.

I glance at my watch. The only thing nearly as bad as him catching me in the act of breaking into his office would be him seeing me pull back into the department parking lot. I have to hurry, even though I don't know what I'm looking for.

But I'll know it when I see it. That's what I keep telling myself, the only thing that gives me a bit of hope. If Ryan has any information about where the girls are, I need to know it. He's been strange today, not acting how I'd expect him to with Nealie going missing. I don't know what's going on, but if he has a secret he's keeping from me, I need to know it.

It feels like I'm crossing some invisible line as I step into his office and turn on the light. Even though my attention is drawn to the shelves of files and books, to the stacks of bankers boxes, I hurry to his desk. The leather seat sighs a little as I lower myself into it, then I open his laptop and slide my finger across the trackpad to wake it up.

As I wait for it, I glance at the only sheets of paper on his desk. Even though it should be clear what they are, it takes me a minute to realize what I'm looking at.

Information on local nannies. Ryan told me he wanted to hire someone instead of Julie, but Nealie loves her. Besides, he couldn't give me a good reason why we needed a new nanny. The fact that he was looking to hire someone new without my help? Honestly, it burns me up. I have to force myself to drag my eyes away from the stack and look at the laptop. Hope rises in me as the screen lights up, but then the password box pops up.

It's password protected. Of course. As much as I'd love to sit here and try passwords over and over until I gain access to his files, I don't have time.

I close his laptop and yank on the first drawer on his desk.

Locked. What did I expect?

Panic threatens to wrap around my throat, and I swallow hard, pushing it back down. Now's not the time for me to break down. Shoving the chair back, I drop to my knees and look up under his desk. Ryan always keeps his keys in his pocket, so if the desk is completely locked down, I'm screwed. But the door to his office is locked, and if I'm lucky, he might have a second key stashed in here somewhere.

There. Taped up against the back corner of where his knees go. You can't see the key from the other side of the desk, but it's there. I angle my body under the desk and pull it free.

This time, I don't even bother with sitting back in the chair. My hand shakes as I stab the key into the lock and turn it.

There's a loud thunk from inside the desk as all of the drawers unlock.

"Bingo, bitch." A bolt of excitement shoots through me as I yank the top drawer open. This time it slides easily, the bearings well oiled. Something shifts inside, but my heart falls when I see a stack of Post-its, some pens, and other office supplies.

"Second drawer," I mutter, shoving the first one closed and yanking the second one open. This one is packed with files, and my heart kicks into high gear as I riffle through them.

But there's nothing. One more drawer, one more chance.

I glance at my watch before shoving the second drawer closed and opening the bottom one. For a moment, I'm disappointed, convinced that there isn't anything here that will be helpful. There's just one file, and yeah, it's thick, but that doesn't mean anything.

I'm running out of time, but I pull the file out of the drawer and open it on the floor in front of me.

The first piece of paper inside it is a birth certificate, and I feel my heart kick into a higher speed. It's not Nealie's, I'm sure of that. Hers is in the safety deposit box at our bank. It's been in there since she was born, along with her social security card and vaccination information.

My hand shakes as I pick up the piece of paper. It's older than Nealie's and a different style than the kind they issue now.

"It's got to be Ryan's," I say, and a sense of relief washes over me. That's what this is. Ryan has a file of all of his important paperwork in his home office. It makes sense, when I really think about it. He's never been one to trust banks and always wanted to keep his important information close at hand.

Only it's not Ryan's name on the first line of the certificate.

It's mine.

"What in the world?" I swallow hard. The paper slips from my fingers and flutters down to the floor. Without picking it back up, I grab the next document in the file.

It's also about me, only this isn't something I could explain away. The birth certificate... that's weird, especially because I thought I'd lost it, and Ryan hadn't corrected me when I told him that.

But he's been charting my period.

Icy fear sneaks down my spine as I turn the pages in the file. This isn't something recent he's been doing either. From the looks of things, Ryan's been keeping tabs on my period from when we got married.

No, that's not right.

From when we first started dating.

I drop the pages and sit back, trying to distance myself from the file. Even when I close my eyes, however, I can still see his handwriting, the little red check marks he's made, how meticulous he's been in tracking my cycle.

What is he doing? Why would he want to know this?

I take a deep breath, then another, trying to calm down, even though the only thing I want to do is get up and run. Hide.

No, not hide. Flee.

It's been my plan for months now, but I can't leave without Nealie.

So instead, I look back at the file. It's thick, thicker than any other one I've seen in his office, so what else does he have in here?

I turn the page and am greeted with a DNA test. A swear word slips past my lips, and I grab it to look closer at it. Did

Ryan really think he might not be Nealie's dad? That's insane! Was he testing to see if I'd cheated? And if so, why wouldn't he come talk to me about it?

It makes no sense, and I flip the page to see what else he has in the file.

Photos of me. My work schedule for every single year I worked at his law firm. I was just a secretary, a glorified one actually. I ran copies, answered the phones. Monica was the real brains behind running the office, but I needed a job and Ryan liked having me around.

But now I wonder if he wanted me in the office just so he could keep an eye on me.

My heart starts to beat faster. There's no way he knows what I've been doing. If he did, he couldn't keep it quiet, I know it. Ryan isn't able to keep his mouth shut when he feels like someone has wronged him.

I glance at my watch.

"Oh, crap." There's still at least a hundred pages to go through in this folder, but I don't have time. I close it and toss it back in the desk drawer, then close it.

Lock it.

Pocket the key.

In the hall, I stop and pick up the rock. I'm proud of myself for remembering that it has to go back in the garden. If Ryan were to see it here... well, he'll still notice that someone broke into his office. But I'm not going to leave the evidence here on the floor for him to stumble over.

I pause in the hall.

Something isn't right.

Slowly, I turn, taking in the photos on the wall, the broken lock on Ryan's door, the living room. I'm almost able to convince myself that nothing is out of place, then I see my laptop on the coffee table.

I never leave it open.

I drop the rock and hurry into the living room. The screen is dark, and I touch the trackpad to wake it up. A moment later, light shines in my face, and I blink.

Not because of the light.

But because of what website is loaded.

It's my online banking. And it's open to the account I set up when I decided to leave Ryan.

Someone was in here. Someone saw it.

My palms prickle with sweat, and I wipe them on my pants before closing my laptop.

I have to hope whoever saw this doesn't tell Ryan.

He'd kill me.

TWENTY-SEVEN
KATE

2:15 p.m.

Ryan is a liar. I have to keep that in mind during this interview. No matter what he says, no matter what lies he spins or how he tries to charm me, at his very core, the man is a liar.

And I don't only mean it because he's a lawyer, although percentage wise, I honestly believe most lawyers are liars. No, Ryan's lies run deeper than simply doing his little dance in front of the courtroom.

Heaving a sigh, I glance at my watch. I want to get this over with.

I don't want to believe Ryan had anything to do with Nealie and Emma going missing, but I can't rule it out, especially not after talking to Julie. And who's to say he doesn't have something to do with all of this? He's good at circumventing the truth. He knows how to twist his words to make you believe something you shouldn't.

Ryan sits across from me, his head turning this way and that. As if there's anything to look at in here. I don't speak right away, allowing the silence to grow as he throws me a cautious smile.

He's the one to break the silence, which is exactly what I wanted.

"How is the investigation going?"

I pin him in place with a stare before answering. "As I'm sure you know, we've canvassed the entire neighborhood, only finding your daughter's pink bear left behind. There haven't been any sightings of her, although my team did release a press release on social media with both of the girls' photos."

"So you're now on the interview stage."

I nod. "You're obviously aware I've already spoken to your wife, but I want to hear in your own words what happened last night and this morning."

"Of course. Well, we had a preschool party last night to celebrate the end of the year." He rolls his eyes. "It was a blast, believe me. Sweet punch, tons of cotton candy, no adult food to speak of. I didn't really want to go, but you know Alison."

There's nothing I can say to that because I don't know his wife. Not before today anyway.

"So we went to that and got home late. Nealie was all kinds of riled up, but Alison calmed her down pretty quickly." He reaches up and runs a hand through his thick brown hair.

"How did she do that?" I scratch a few notes in my notebook.

"Warm bath. Lavender essential oils."

"And the bottle of melatonin I found in Nealie's room?"

He stills.

"Yeah, I missed it my first time through, but I saw it when I went back up. You giving your daughter a little something to help her sleep?"

"Melatonin isn't a crime."

"I didn't say it was. I simply asked you a question. Who gives Nealie the melatonin?"

"Alison."

I make a note. I'd thought about asking her when I was interviewing her, but I wasn't sure how much they would be able to talk to each other in the hall before Ryan came in here for his chat. From the expression on his face, Ryan is telling the truth.

But then again, I've fallen for this same expression before, haven't I?

"Moving on then. After Nealie went to bed?"

"Alison and I did too." He pauses, thinking. "Well, no. She stayed up a bit later than I did watching TV or scrolling TikTok or something. But I was exhausted. *I* worked all week. Since she quit working at the law firm, she doesn't have to worry so much about getting up early."

I ignore the pointed barb about Alison currently being a stay-at-home mom and hide the surprise I feel at finding out Alison used to work with both Ryan and Daniel.

"She worked at your law firm? What did she do? And when did she quit?"

"She was a secretary, and she quit a few months ago."

I pause. "A few? So, right around the time Daniel lost his job?"

Ryan doesn't respond. He scratches his chin and stares over my shoulder, but I know I'm right. The pieces are starting to come together. If he's like anyone else sitting across from me, he's going to start scrambling.

"I know you think I'm some terrible guy, but I wonder if the Everetts did something and that's why our girls are missing. If they pissed someone off, someone who retaliated."

There it is. The scrambling.

"Or it's because you fired Daniel."

Ryan's mouth snaps shut. "What? No."

"Don't sound so sure. Why did you fire him?"

"I'm not at liberty to discuss that."

"Please. It's not like it's a HIPAA violation. I want to know why you sacked him, not his medical history."

"I don't see how that has anything to do with Nealie going missing."

"Really?" My voice is getting louder, but I can't seem to stop it. "Maybe because your two families were connected at the hip until you suddenly weren't. And now everyone's being really secretive about what happened. Have you spoken with either of the Everetts since Emma went missing?" He shakes his head, and I continue. "Yeah, I didn't think so! Someone targeted your two families, and I want to know what the hell is going on!"

I'm furious. Waves of anger wash over me.

Ryan's eyes are wide. His mouth drops open. "I promise you, if I knew who would take the girls, I would tell you." A tear runs down his cheek, and he angrily flicks it away. "I don't know what happened. But I swear to you, I didn't do anything that would put Nealie in danger."

I doubt that. Out of all the parents, Ryan is the one putting himself in a position to be hated. The way he carries himself as a blowhard lawyer, the arrogant way he walks over people, the lying to get exactly what he wants.

"Tell me why you fired Daniel." My voice is steady, and I don't look away from him.

Ryan runs his hand through his hair as he stands. "He screwed up at work. We lost a case."

"It was personal then."

"It was business." Now he stares me down, crossing his arms and drawing himself up to his full height.

"So Alison didn't push you to fire him?"

There. In his eyes. The realization that he had a perfectly useful exit to this conversation, and he missed it. If he'd thought about throwing his wife under the bus, he would have. I know it.

"No, she didn't."

"It's strange that the fathers of our missing girls worked together. Anyone in the office you pissed off? Any client who might have a vendetta against you?"

He's shaking his head before I finish speaking. "No, nobody. We've never had a problem like that before."

"Great." I grab a folder and flip it open. "Found this under Nealie's mattress. Care to explain it?" I turn the papers so he can see them, although it's not hard to tell what they are, even from the other side of the table.

He sighs. "I was going to ask Alison for a divorce."

"I can tell. But why hide the papers under your daughter's mattress, Ryan? That's messed up, even for a lawyer."

He sighs. "I was going to talk to her about it last night when Nealie went to bed, but Alison told me she was tired and went to bed at the same time. I panicked and stashed them under the mattress."

I narrow my eyes at him. "I'm going to find out the truth of what happened here," I tell him, standing and gesturing at the door. "I swear to you, I'll uncover every skeleton you're trying to keep hidden. You think you can lie your way through life? You can't. Whatever information you're hiding about those girls, I'll find it."

He doesn't respond, but I don't need him to. This is over. I'll talk to everyone who's so much as looked at those girls before if that's what it takes. Their teachers, the other staff at the school, private chefs, housekeepers, piano teachers, I don't care. I'm going to find them.

But before he leaves, I ask one more thing.

"How many women have you been sleeping with?"

His mouth drops open, and his brows crash together. "Are you asking me for the investigation or because *you're* curious?"

"Answer the question."

He sighs. "Three."

"Names?"

Ryan closes his eyes, and his shoulders collapse in before he rattles them off. I compare them to the ones in my notepad, the ones Julie gave me, then rip the page out. As much as I'd love to check into these women's alibis myself, I'll send an officer to handle it for me.

It's better that way.

"How did you... how did you know about them?"

"It's my job to know these things. Don't act surprised that I'm good at it." No way am I throwing Julie under the bus.

Ryan scoffs and shakes his head. "Am I free to go?" He stands, resting his hands on the back of his chair.

"Go. I know how to reach you."

He dips his chin and hurries out the door to Alison.

His *wife*.

The wife he told so many women he was separated from.

Lies. All of it. Ryan will say anything to get what he wants. He fired Daniel, but I think there's more to it than what he's saying.

Now the question remains: is he lying about Nealie?

TWENTY-EIGHT
JULIE

2:20 p.m.

I've called Theo five times since leaving the police department and each time my call goes to voicemail. My stomach rumbles, but instead of going home to grab something to eat, I turn into Blackwood, carefully parking as close to the Everett and Brown houses as I can.

If Theo and I thought there were a lot of police here earlier, they seem to have doubled. I swear, I didn't think there were this many cops in town, but I guess I was wrong.

Now's the time to rob a store and have a good chance of getting away, I guess.

I shake my head to clear the thought. It was weird seeing the Browns pull into the police department parking lot as I was leaving. They'd been stony-faced, staring straight ahead, and I don't think either one recognized me. Yeah, I know the detective wanted to talk to them, but to leave their house when Nealie wasn't home yet? I don't think I could do it if it were my child that was missing.

My stomach drops when I think about the parting information I gave to the detective. Will Ryan be angry if he ever finds out that I was the one who revealed his multiple affairs? Undoubtedly. But I had to give her something, especially when she was looking at me like I was her prime suspect.

I still might be, for all I know. But the information that Ryan can't keep his pants zipped around anything with a nice pair of legs should at least give her something to dig into.

There's a bench in Alison and Ryan's front yard half hidden among some red Japanese maples, and I sit there, grateful for the shade, waiting for Theo to call me back.

It feels good to stretch and sit for a moment. My body has been on high alert from the moment Alison and Carrie texted this morning. Never in my wildest dreams did I think this was how the day was going to go. I'm starving and would love a nap, but how would that look if I disappeared?

Someone would get suspicious. And if they get suspicious, they start digging. And if they start digging, it's entirely possible they might find out what Theo and I are really doing here.

My teeth find the edge of my thumb's cuticle, and I nibble on it while waiting for Theo. The sound of the Browns' front door slamming shut makes me twist around on the bench. For a moment, I can't see who's on the porch, so I shield my eyes with my hand to get a better look.

It's Theo.

Are you kidding me right now?

He walks to the edge of the porch and does the same as I do, shielding his eyes before carefully looking from left to right.

Goosebumps break out on my arms when I realize he's looking for me.

As I watch, he grabs his phone and types on it. A moment later, mine buzzes in my lap.

> *Sorry I missed your calls. Just heading back towards the house now. Where are you?*

I stare at him, unable to believe what I'm seeing. My hands shake as I respond.

Down by the entrance. Meet me?

You got it.

He pockets his phone and wipes his hand across his forehead, then hurries down the porch steps, cuts across the lawn, and beelines for the front entrance. I sit in the shade, mostly hidden by the ornamental trees, and try to think things through.

Fact: Theo is lying to me.

What else could he be lying about?

Fact: He doesn't want me to know he was in the Browns' house.

Why would he break in there? What could he want from inside?

Fact: I have no idea what's going on.

I lean to the left and look after where he walked, but he's already out of sight. Once he gets down to the main entrance, he'll probably mill around for a while looking for me before he texts again. Now that he knows I'm looking for him, I doubt he'll do anything shady.

Like poke around in an empty house.

Resolution flows through me, and I stand, practically running to the house. I fly up the steps and through the front door, quietly closing it behind me. The foyer light is off, but light streams in through all the house's front windows, so I don't need to turn on a light to see.

Where would Theo have been?

I trail my hands along the wall as I walk down the hall, my head on a swivel, looking for anything that might be out of place.

There.

The third door on the left, right past the craft room and the bathroom, is Ryan's office. I've only ever been in there once, when the door was left open by accident. And that one time I was in there? I learned the truth about the girls. The truth Ryan and Carrie are obviously keeping hidden from everyone else—and exactly what we'd been looking for to take our plan to the next level.

But the door is unlocked and wide open right now.

My breath catches in my throat, and I throw a hurried glance over my shoulder at the front door. It's probably paranoid of me to imagine Alison and Ryan pulling up right now, the two of them wondering what I'm doing in their house, but the sight of the unlocked door is too much to ignore.

I can't help myself.

Instead of turning and leaving the house, which would be the smart and responsible thing to do, I follow the siren's call of the open door, pausing outside it for a moment, my hand out, my heart slamming hard in my chest.

My eyes fall on the lock. It's not *unlocked*. It's broken.

Theo. What did he do?

I take a deep breath. Steel myself.

And then I step inside and am immediately disappointed.

Whatever I was thinking I would find in here, I doubt I'm going to be able to. Not without an uninterrupted week of digging through paperwork, that is. There are stacks of it, with bankers boxes three high on one wall, each of them bulging and groaning with papers.

In the back right corner, a filing cabinet. Even without walking over to it and trying a drawer, I already know it's going to be locked. I walk into the middle of the office, studiously not touching anything, and turn in a slow circle.

Law books are loaded up on one bookshelf. There are a few awards Ryan won decorating the top of the shelf. Then the bankers boxes, a small window with a dark curtain, and the filing cabinet. There isn't any art on the walls, not with so much space taken up by a credenza and yet another bookcase. This one has files, and I take a step closer to see what they are.

Cases, I guess. I frown and a lightbulb goes off.

Of course he had to keep his office locked. If he has always had case files and personal information in here, it makes sense he'd need to keep it safe and protected. I've never once even considered law school, but I'd be shocked if lawyers weren't held to some kind of standards regarding client information.

There's still an unsettled feeling in the pit of my stomach. I don't know what it is, but then I look closer at some of the files on his shelf. And I recognize some of the names. A few of them are the same ones, in fact, that I just gave to the detective.

And there, right next to those files, is another, with a name I know really well.

I reach out to take it, even though my brain is screaming at me to stop, when I hear the front door slam.

Every hair on the back of my neck sticks straight up. I stiffen and whip around to look at the door, already praying Alison and Ryan will stop off in the kitchen before walking through the house, but before I turn all the way, I take that last file, pulling it free from the bookshelf and tucking it under my arm.

I know stealing it is wrong and I could get in a lot of trouble, but I don't feel like I have a choice.

It's got Theo's name on it.

TWENTY-NINE

The text that comes through doesn't have any words.

It's a photo of both girls, but Nealie's the focus of the shot. She's turned towards the camera, but she's not looking right at it. Her face is tilted up like she's watching whoever's taking the photo.

Emma sits next to her, but she's staring off to the side. She holds something in her hand—half of a muffin? It's hard to tell.

My breath catches in my throat. I know the girls aren't there, but I still reach out and lightly touch the screen. Just as I do, my phone vibrates.

They're innocent, but that won't matter in the end. Don't keep me waiting.

THIRTY
ALISON

2:25 p.m.

The detective knows I did something; she just doesn't know what.

I put my purse on the kitchen counter and sink into a stool, dropping my chin onto my hand. My stomach had started to gnaw on itself when Detective Martin called me for a meeting, but our conversation drove any thought of food from my mind.

Ryan has his back to me and is rummaging through the fridge. "You want something to eat?" he asks without turning around.

"No. I'm not hungry," I lie. My stomach rumbles in opposition, but his head is surrounded by cold cuts and leftovers, and he can't hear it. The thought of eating anything when we don't know where Nealie is or if she's okay makes me feel sick.

"I'm famished." Ryan turns around, a slice of cold pizza in his hand. I can't even remember when we had pizza. Two nights ago? Three? Or maybe Julie ordered it for her and Nealie. Whenever it was, the pizza looks disgusting, but that doesn't stop my husband from taking a huge bite.

"How was your interview?" I ask. We didn't speak in the car on the way home, both of us sitting in our own fear over what the detective had to say to us, but here, in the comfort and safety of our home, I want to know what happened.

Although, if Nealie could be taken from this house, it isn't as safe as I thought, is it?

"Fine. She doesn't know anything and is grasping at straws by having us in." He takes another bite and speaks around his food. "I wish she'd spend more time interviewing neighbors and other people who spend time around Nealie instead of focusing on us."

"We *are* her parents," I counter. "It makes sense to want to know what we know."

He doesn't respond.

Guilt over my conversation with the detective weighs on me. She's right—I should tell her anything I can that would help her find who took the girls. It's insane to think that I might be holding that information back.

The problem is: I don't know that what I could tell her would help bring them home. If anything, it would drive a wedge even deeper between Carrie and me and could result in me getting in trouble later.

Nealie needs me at home, not paying for what I did. That's what I keep telling myself, and it's why I decided to keep my mouth shut.

"Ryan," I say, ignoring the fact that he's chowing down on a second piece of pizza, "what did the detective want to ask you?"

"The same as you, I bet. If I knew anyone who might want to hurt Nealie. Where we were last night and this morning."

"Did she ask you about Daniel?"

He nods. "Did she ask you about your friendship with Carrie?"

"She did. What did you tell her about Daniel?"

"That I couldn't give her the exact reason why we fired him, that it was between us and the company. She backed off then."

No, she didn't. She may have seemed like she backed off, but I highly doubt Detective Martin would actually back off if she thought there was some information there she needed to get.

"Do you think..." I let my voice trail off as I gather not only the words I want to ask him but also the courage to put them into the world. "Do you think Carrie and Daniel had something to do with this? That they're getting back at us?" I swallow hard. "At me?"

He eyeballs me over his crust, then slowly puts it down on the counter. "Emma is missing too, Alison."

"I know." Tears well up in my eyes. My entire face feels puffy from all the crying I've done. Still, there's no way to fight them back, not when there are questions I need answered.

Not until Nealie is home.

"Then why are you asking?"

I bite my lower lip. Not hard enough to bleed but hard enough to hurt. "Because I don't know how angry they were about what happened."

Ryan plants both hands on the counter, the pizza crust ignored. All of his attention is now focused directly on me. "And what, pray tell, do you think happened?"

I wipe my hand across my cheeks to clear the tears. "I think that Daniel lost a high-paying job and, with it, the chance at making partner anytime in the next century. I think there's a lot of stress and anger there, especially because we were once so close to them and now we've moved on and they haven't."

"We didn't move on," he corrects. "They fell behind, and that's not our fault."

But it is.

I don't say that though. Ryan hates being argued with. He's honed his sharp tongue in the courtroom and slices neatly to the bone when he wields it. I've gone up against it before and never once have I walked away feeling like I came out on top.

"You're a part of what we did to Daniel," Ryan tells me, stabbing his finger through the air at me. "But that doesn't mean he would do anything to harm Nealie. He loves Nealie."

"You didn't give me a choice but to forge his signature so he'd take the fall. And then hiding evidence? Planting things in the files that didn't belong?" I'm breathing hard, and I should shut up, but my plan is falling apart, and I can't help myself. "You could have done it yourself, but you had to tie me up in it, didn't you? You couldn't handle the thought of getting caught and going down by yourself; you had to make sure you took me with you!"

Ryan looks like he wants to scream.

"Don't act like I held a gun to your head. And what, you think that's tied to Nealie going missing? Do you think they kidnapped Nealie and then pretended like Emma also went missing? What do you think their master plan is? That they'll pretend to find Emma and kill Nealie, ensuring a miraculous recovery for one child and a funeral for the other?"

I want him to shut up. His cheeks are red, the cords in his neck standing out. It's not uncommon for Ryan to get this upset, but it is rare for his ire to be directed at me. Not since I did what he asked anyway. Not since I made sure we wouldn't *fall behind*.

He'd made it so I didn't have a choice. I hadn't wanted to; that's what I keep reminding myself. I love Carrie and wouldn't ever do anything to hurt her.

Except I did, didn't I?

Yes, but Ryan told me I had to. He didn't threaten me, not exactly, but I knew what he meant when he told me what to do. That if I didn't help him, didn't place the blame where *he* thought it deserved to be, that all of this—the house, the yoga, the nice car and fancy clothes, Nealie—it would all go away.

After all, what judge in their right mind would reward full custody to a mother who didn't have a job? Or a home? Or a car?

"I didn't—" I begin, but he's not finished, and when he isn't finished, he'll steamroll right over anyone interrupting him.

"We'd never hurt Emma like that. I'm shocked you think they'd hurt Nealie like that. Maybe if you'd focus more on what could have actually happened to our daughter and not your hare-brained concerns, we'd have a better chance at bringing her home today!"

The front door slams.

I whip around, unwilling to listen to one more moment of Ryan's yelling. He's just getting started—I can tell by the way he's standing, how strong his shoulders look, how he's bending forward, his hands wide on the counter. He could pontificate for the next twenty minutes if I were willing to take it.

But I'm not.

Because that slamming door? Either someone just walked in and is going to hear everything going on, or someone just left.

And I don't like either option.

I reach the front door at a skid, ignoring Ryan calling for me to come back and continue the conversation. Taking a deep breath, I wrench the door open and stand out on the porch, immediately shielding my eyes from the sun.

But it's impossible to know who was in the house. Officers mill around in the yard. Neighbors stand in clumps, talking to each other while they try to avoid looking at our house. I see the glances they cast up here, the way they turn their heads just a little and peek from the corners of their eyes.

And I know I must look a mess. I want to peel my face off, it feels so puffy and tight. My stomach cramps and twists with hunger and fear. My hair was in a cute ponytail this morning, but now it's sagging, drooped over my shoulder, the baby hairs around my face all frizzy.

I'm falling apart. And while that may be true, there's something else I know to be true too.

Someone was in my house. They rushed out, unwilling to let us know they were there.

Which means they were listening.

Which means they know I'm the reason Daniel lost his job.

THIRTY-ONE
KATE

2:39 p.m.

"Carrie went for a walk then locked herself in the bedroom," Daniel tells me. He holds his hands out to the sides, his eyes downcast. He looks repentant, about to pray for forgiveness. "I'm sorry, she's not normally like this anymore. I wouldn't hold your breath on interviewing her though." He runs a hand through his thinning hair and sighs.

I'm frustrated, sure, but refuse to show it. "Anymore? She used to be like this?"

He nods. "Before Emma was born. She just... shuts down."

"Is she on medication for it?"

He shakes his head but won't look at me. I watch his gaze flick to a stack of papers on a table in the corner.

Without asking, I cross the room to them. "What are these?"

"Nothing." He's next to me faster than I would have thought possible. "I was just going through some filing earlier. Trying to stay busy."

"Bank documents?" I flip through them. "And ooh, these

aren't yours. How did you get your hands on them?" I stack them into a pile but don't put them back on the table.

"I had them. They're old."

"They're not," I tell him. "The most recent transactions are from yesterday, so try again. How did you get these?"

He stares at me but doesn't answer.

"I'll answer for you, and you tell me if I'm on target. You still have access to the law firm's online banking." He nods, and I continue, picking up steam. "You're checking in from time to time to see what you're missing out on. What you *could* be making."

He shakes his head. I frown and look back at the pages, flipping back a few months. Some of the withdrawals are highlighted. They're not for huge amounts, not by a long shot, but they're regular.

"Are these statements from different accounts?" I ask, flipping a few pages. A moment later, I answer for him. "Yep, I see the account numbers. So you're interested in these withdrawals, and they're coming from all over the place. Why? What's going on with them?"

"I don't know what they are."

"And why would you? You don't work there. You shouldn't even have access to this information."

"Look at them," he says, coming to stand next to me. "They're coming from all of the accounts, all in little amounts, and they all have the same code on them, like they're all going to the same place."

"Does Ryan know about them?"

He shrugs. "Ryan was never big on keeping up with the banking. He hated it. I don't know how far back they go, but they suddenly stop." He points, and I nod.

"They stopped just a few months ago." I glance at him. "When you were fired."

He flushes. "I—"

I'm not finished speaking, and I cut him off. "And when Alison quit her job."

We stare at each other.

"Are you the one stealing this money?"

I wouldn't have thought it was possible for Daniel to blush more than he already is, but his cheeks burn hotter. "No! I'm not. I wouldn't. I can't believe you'd even think that." He rubs his hand over his forehead and takes a deep breath, but he won't look me in the eyes. "It had to have been Alison."

It *could* have been Alison. But the way he's acting?

I clear my throat. "I need you to go get Carrie right now. I know she's struggling, and I want to respect that, but I need to talk to her. Your daughter is missing, Daniel. And so is Nealie. Not to mention, there's weird stuff happening with the business account. You both need to come clean. Now."

For a moment, he doesn't move. His eyes are locked on me, and his breathing is shallow like he can't quite catch his breath. Finally, he nods, and I feel the stress in my shoulders relax.

"I'll go, okay? I'll go get her. But don't get mad at me when you can't get anything out of her. I told you—she's a mess right now. She's not thinking straight. She keeps talking about Emma and saving her, but it's not like she has a plan; she's just rambling." He holds his hands up and takes a step away from me.

"Now, Daniel."

The man nods and turns away from me. While he's gone, I pull out my phone and fire off a text to Aletha.

Nanny's name is Julie Staton. I need her address.

Finding an address when someone owns their home? A piece of cake. Finding an address when they're renting an apartment? That's a bit trickier. Luckily, her response is almost immediate.

On it.

I nod and pocket my phone before turning and leaning against the wall. Carrie might think she can avoid being questioned, but she can't hide from me forever. It's so quiet in the house that I can hear Daniel's voice.

It's raised, but not by a lot. Carrie responds, but even though she's talking louder than normal, I can't make out the words.

I take a step forward, away from the wall. Daniel disappeared down the hall, and I start walking in that direction, my ears pricked for any sound. They're arguing again, their voices louder than before, and I walk faster, my eyes locked on the stairs ten feet in front of me.

"Daniel, no!"

My heart kicks into high gear, and I move faster, wanting to get to the bottom of the stairs, wanting to see what they're doing, make sure nothing is happening, but there's a moment of silence and then everything speeds up.

There's a gasp and a thud, and although I'm not close enough to the stairs to see what happened at the top, I do see Carrie fall, her arms and legs windmilling, her head thunking into the stairs before she lands on the floor, sprawled out, her eyes closed.

THIRTY-TWO
JULIE

2:52 p.m.

I know I shouldn't have taken the file on Theo, but I couldn't help myself. Once I heard Alison and Ryan enter the house and argue, I knew I needed to get out of there. I'd waited until I could sneak down the hall, but then, because I have no luck, the wind caught the front door in my hurry to escape and slammed it shut.

They had to have heard it. I'm lucky they didn't run outside and catch me, because if they caught me in their house, they'd be livid. No way was I going to let that happen, especially not when it's obvious something weird's going on. Possibly something more than just the girls going missing.

This day has me questioning everything I've ever thought to be true.

The file sits, a silent accusation, next to me on the gazebo bench, but I can't make myself open it. It never once crossed my mind that Ryan would know Theo, but there his file was, sitting right next to the files of women he'd had affairs with. Yes, Theo called him to blackmail him, but that's the only contact they've had. Even when he drops me off to nanny, we make sure he never runs into Ryan.

So how does Ryan know him well enough to have a file on him? It's not possible.

We thought we were in control. But it looks like he's on to us.

And there was one for someone I never would have expected. I need to remember that, and I need to figure out what it means.

Why would Ryan have a file on her?

"Oh my God," I say, wrapping my arms around my stomach and rocking back and forth. If Theo finds me with this file, what will he say? Would he know why Ryan was looking into him? Will he tell me the truth?

I have to remember that he's already lied to me once today.

Do I even want to know the truth?

My fingers trace the edge of the file, and I consider flipping it open, but instead I put my hand under my thigh to prevent myself from doing just that. I don't know what I'm going to find in there, but I doubt it'll be anything good.

It feels like an hour that I sit here, staring at the file, but it can't be that long. Outside, people walk in groups, almost as if they're afraid they'll get taken if they're alone.

But they're not little girls. They don't need to worry.

Finally, I can't stand it any longer. I flip the file open but close my eyes. It's silly, but I feel like I need to do whatever it takes to protect myself from what's inside. After a moment, I open them.

There are only a few sheets of paper in the folder. My hand trembles as I pick them up, and for one wild second, I consider ripping them into confetti. Throwing them into the wind. Pretending this didn't happen.

But it did. And now that I've come this far, I have to know what's in here. How much does Ryan know about Theo? Theo never gives our marks his name. Beyond being my boyfriend, how does Ryan even know Theo exists?

And does that mean he's researched me as well?

That could make sense. Like maybe he looked into my boyfriend to make sure I'm safe.

Yeah, right.

"Theo Jackson Roberts," I whisper, reading his name at the top of the first sheet. Directly underneath it is his birthday, which I knew.

There's also his address, with information on when he bought his little starter home as well as how much he paid for it. There's a note with the names of past cities we've lived in. Again, this is nobody's business.

But Ryan wanted to know it all apparently.

Next there's a photo of Theo, but it doesn't look like he knew it was being taken. He's turned slightly away from the camera talking to...

Me.

Bile burns the back of my throat. I swallow it down, closing my eyes and forcing myself to take a few deep breaths. Someone took this photo without the two of us knowing. But who? And why? I force myself to look away from the smile on my face as I talked to Theo and pay attention to where we were.

Downtown. At a café—just last month. I remember this! I remember it was a little chilly when we went, like spring mornings weren't willing to cede their grip on the world to summer, so I'd had a light cardigan with me. Theo had been dying to try this place since it had just opened up, and while we don't usually go out for breakfast, there's a chocolate croissant on the plate in front of me next to a steaming mug of coffee.

We'd been talking about our future. Theo doesn't know this, but I've been wondering if a ring is ever coming my way. I love him, love being with him, love what we're doing, how we're making the world a better place, one family at a time.

But I wouldn't mind settling down. Or I wouldn't have before I found out that he was willing to lie to me. Before I found those websites in his search history.

Fear grips me as I look at the picture. Just the thought of someone being that close to me, watching me, and me not having any idea makes me sick. Neither of us are looking at the camera, which makes me think neither of us had any idea someone was there, focused on us.

Or he knew and didn't say anything about being watched. But that doesn't make sense either. Why would he hide that?

My eyes drop to the text below the photo. It's very clinical the way it's written, like someone did a report on Theo and turned it in for college credit. I read it, my eyes flicking faster and faster across the page as I drink it in.

> Theo Jackson Roberts is employed by On-Screen Security, where he has worked without incident for the past two years. His employer describes him as punctual and reliable. They say he's never missed a day of work and is always willing to work late to help when needed. When his current job was posted, the starting salary was $55,700. With cost-of-living raises and presumed raises due to his work ethic, it's assumed that he's currently making around $58,000. He drives an older Subaru that is paid off.
>
> Theo bought a house in Rockridge two years ago but only recently started living in it part-time. Before this, he's moved from apartment to apartment across the country with his girlfriend, Julie Staton. He owns a small single-family residence off Whitted Street where he lives alone. When he's not working, he spends a lot of time outside, often meeting up with friends to play basketball. While he does frequent bars with friends, he never has more than one beer while out. His driving record is clean.
>
> While Theo owns his own home, he usually spends the

night with Julie at her walk-up apartment on Eighth Avenue. There are no children or pets in the relationship. Theo and Julie are cinephiles and prefer to rent movies and stay in for date night, although they do like to hike on weekends when she's not working.

He does not have a close relationship with his mother, and it was difficult to find any information about his childhood. Theo has not been active on social media, and his profiles are private.

That's it.

I turn to the next page, fully expecting there to be more about Theo and his mother, or his job or friends, but there isn't any more text. The only other things included in the packet are copies of his driver's license, GIS information on his house purchase, and more photos of him.

I close the folder and lean my head back, my mind racing.

There are so many questions that I want answered, and I don't know where to start with them. Why would Ryan want this information about Theo? Who would he pay to get it for him? Did he hire someone to get this information for him before or after I started nannying for the girls?

How much does Ryan know? Or suspect?

I groan, closing my eyes and pressing my fingers hard into my temples. If this were a normal day, I'd go to Theo with any questions I had, but now I'm beginning to doubt everything.

The fact that Ryan has this file on Theo tells me he's more careful than I thought he would be. I bet he started the file after Theo approached him, not before. But how? Theo doesn't give his name to our marks when he talks to them. He does everything possible to ensure they can't ever connect the two of us and hasn't ever given a mark his personal info. He uses a separate phone for all of our jobs and tosses it once we've been paid.

None of this makes any sense.

But still, why would Ryan be the one to catch on to what we're doing? Why this time, when so many times in the past people have stayed clueless? We've been so careful choosing who I nanny for. It's never blown up in our face before, so why is it now?

When Theo told me we could make a difference, could get back at the upper class for being assholes in fancy suits, I'd thought it sounded great. Every job so far has been the same. I take a nannying position, find information that would ruin the family, and we blackmail them. These families have terrible secrets. Affairs. Child abuse. Hard drugs. The marks remind me a lot of my dad, if I'm being honest. Their wives and children are at risk, and that's not something I can live with. I can't walk away from children who need help, not when I know firsthand what it's like to live with an abusive liar for a dad.

I find the blackmail, then Theo contacts them. Never in person, of course—we're not stupid. He reaches out to them using a burner phone and makes his demands. They panic. They pay. We move. Rinse and repeat. It's never been a problem.

So why is this job the one that might ruin us?

Theo called Ryan, right? He said he did anyway, and he said that Ryan wanted to think about it, which doesn't make any sense. I mean, come on. Look at their house! They have money. The only time a mark needed *to think about it* was when we screwed up and chose someone so in debt they couldn't buy a fast-food burger without a credit card.

But we've gotten better since then. No more mistakes.

Still... did we screw up? Does Ryan not have the money we think he does?

The sound of a siren stirs me to move. The last thing I want is to get caught with the file, especially when I'm sure Theo will be looking for me by now. When I tap on my phone to make the screen light up, I'm not surprised to see a handful of missed calls from him. I'd turned my phone to silent so I could have some time to think things through.

The siren comes closer. It sounds like an ambulance.

I need to move. What if they found one of the girls?

Without a pillow on the bench, there's no good place to hide the file in the gazebo, so I move quickly, tucking it behind a large hydrangea right outside the gazebo. I'll have to remember to come back and get it later.

That done, I wipe my hands off on my jeans. Just as I'm about to call Theo back, the siren stops.

I glance up and spot it. When I do, my stomach drops.

The ambulance is parked right outside the Everetts' house.

THIRTY-THREE
ALISON

3:08 p.m.

Sirens fall silent right down the road from us, and while there's a voice in the back of my head telling me I should check on Carrie and Daniel, I can't tear my eyes away from Ryan.

He's standing in the door to his office, breathing hard, his stance wide, his hands on his hips.

"Did you open my office door?" There's a low rumble to his voice that reminds me of how angry he was this morning.

"What? No." I'm half-distracted. Even though I want to know what's going on with Ryan, I'm concerned about what could be going on down the street. I know Carrie and I aren't friends anymore, but I still want her to be okay.

I don't wish her harm. I just... well, I did what I had to in order to keep my family in one piece. To make sure we weren't the ones who lost everything. It was us or them. I chose us.

Still, she might be the one who needs the ambulance. I did what I had to, but I still care for Carrie.

Or maybe the ambulance is for Emma. Or Nealie.

Oh God. Nealie.

I take a step towards the front door, the desire to know if my daughter was found spurring me away from Ryan. At the same time, I pull my phone from my pocket and thumb it on.

No missed calls. No messages.

Still. I have to know. *It could be Nealie.*

"My door. The lock was messed up: look!" Ryan pulls me out of my thoughts and steps to the side, angrily gesturing at his doorknob. "Look, Alison!"

I barely glance at the lock I broke. What would Ryan say if he knew I was in his office and I left the door wide open for whoever else was just in our house? And what about whoever had my laptop open?

I swallow hard. "What would someone want in your office?"

"I don't know." He runs his hands through his hair. "Case files? Could it be a disgruntled client? Shit!" He turns and leans against the wall, taking deep breaths to try to calm down.

"It could have something to do with Nealie going missing."

He doesn't immediately respond. He's worried about his office. I'm worried about my laptop. The banking. What someone might have seen, what they might have pieced together. But if they pieced it all together, why haven't they said anything?

"Ryan. Do you think—"

"I don't know! Let me think, Alison, God. If you would shut up for just a moment, I might be able to figure this out." He slams one hand onto the wall behind him, and I jump.

He stares at me. For a moment, it's almost like he doesn't recognize me, then he gives his head a little shake.

"I'm sorry," he says. "That was uncalled for. It's just Nealie going missing and then this. I mean, who would want to break into my office? And why do it now?"

"Because you're distracted. Because they think you did something." I answer without thinking, but I'm sure I'm right.

Ryan and I have been in and out of the house all day. There's been a steady stream of officers looking through here for any sign of Nealie or who might have taken her. That means anyone could have walked right into the house and helped themselves to whatever they wanted. So who was in his office after I broke the lock? There's no way to know.

"I'll have to see if anything is missing." He turns from me and stalks into his office, but he doesn't close the door behind him.

I know I should leave him alone. The thought of what those sirens mean eats at me, but if it had something to do with Nealie, the police would have come let us know. No way would they have any sign of her and not tell us immediately, right?

Maybe this has to do with his most recent affair.

That thought is on a loop in my mind as I watch Ryan walk to his desk.

Will he be able to tell I was in his desk?

He stands, his hands planted on his hips, and stares at his space. No way can he tell I was poking around in there, right? He'd have to open his desk and check the file he has on me to see if anything is out of place. And although he looks nervous, maybe even paranoid, right now, I don't think he'll do that.

I take a deep breath. Hold it. Release it. From where I'm standing, nothing looks different, but it's impossible to tell.

Slowly, he loops around the room, taking his time, pausing and squinting, obviously mapping out his office and where everything is. As well as where something might not be.

He makes it to the last bookshelf and pauses. Leans closer. His fingers dance along some files, and I lean forward, my heart in my throat.

I didn't look there. I'd been so interested in getting into his desk and then ran out of time.

All the signs that he's figured something out are there. His shoulders slump forward. His head drops just a bit. I take in the way his hands open and close like he's imagining grabbing something.

"Ryan?"

He whips around, his eyes wide. His mouth is stretched funny, and he stares at me, but then, like magic, he seems to relax.

No, he's *forcing* himself to relax.

"Everything okay?"

"Fine. It's completely fine." *He's lying to me.* "Nothing's missing."

I didn't ask him if something is missing, but it's clear something is. Something major. Something Ryan is obviously really upset by. Something he doesn't want me to know about.

"Great." I force myself to smile. "If nothing's missing, then it's just some vandalism, right? Nothing to worry about?"

He nods, but the movement is slow. Reluctant. "Right. That's exactly what I'm thinking." He gives his head a little shake like he's clearing water from his ears or getting rid of any other thoughts he might have. "Those sirens," he says.

I nod. "I'm going to go check. Do you want to come with me?"

Please say yes. If he says yes and agrees to come with me, then I'm going to be able to convince myself that maybe things aren't all bad, that this is a misunderstanding, that I read him wrong like I do sometimes when I'm a little stressed out.

He shakes his head. "I'm staying here. Someone should be in the house in case whoever vandalized my office thinks it would be a good idea to come back and try again. Just because they didn't take something the first time doesn't mean they won't try to in the future."

"Smart," I lie. "But I bet it's over. Whatever they tried to take or thought they'd find? It's done." I pause, thinking. "This place is crawling with cops. Why don't I grab one or talk to the detective? Surely they can figure out who was in the house." I'm talking quickly, desperate to say anything that will ensure he doesn't suspect me.

"No." His voice is sharp, but when he speaks again, he's tempered it some. "No, Alison, that won't be necessary. Don't worry about that."

He glances at a few files on his bookshelf. They're the same ones he was looking through when he suddenly acted like he'd seen a ghost.

"You head down the street," he says. "I'm going upstairs to get a Tylenol."

"I will." I pause. "Love you." I should do what he wants me to—find out what those sirens were. There's no way they weren't related to the girls going missing, but I also have to find out what's going on with Ryan.

It's too much. One thing at a time, right?

Right.

"Love you." He watches as I leave his office and walk slowly down the hall to the front door. I feel like I'm moving stiffly, like I'm on stage and am not quite sure what to do with my limbs.

When I reach the front door, I open it. Step outside. Count to twenty.

The hall is empty when I poke my head back inside the house. I hold my breath as I scurry down the hall to his office.

Empty.

A floorboard creaks upstairs.

I need to be fast, but of course I feel like I'm fumbling my phone when I pull it out and open the camera. Moving faster now, I hurry to the bookshelf.

Look at the files.

There are half a dozen or so, and I fan them out so I can see the names written on the tabs. What I'd give to take them with me, to have time to really look over them, to see who it is that Ryan wants to keep hidden.

Even though, in my core, I know exactly what these files are.

I'll have to do with taking photos of the tabs so I can research them later.

My hand shakes as I take them and upload them to my cloud, but that's nothing compared to the sick feeling I get when I see the name written on the last file.

Detective Kate Martin.

THIRTY-FOUR
KATE

3:16 p.m.

Alison runs down the street breathing hard, pumping her arms like she's training for some kind of race. Her eyes are wide, her mouth tight. She looks like she's been through hell and back. She races onto the front porch, then sees me, pulling up short, her eyes landing everywhere but on my face.

"Mrs. Brown," I say, giving her a nod. "Came to see what was going on?"

"Is it Nealie?" A pause, then she adds: "Or Emma?"

"It's—"

"Please tell me you found the girls." She's clutching her phone and holds it up for me to see. "I wondered why you didn't call, but I won't even be angry if you found them and hadn't managed to reach out. Please, just let me know what's going on. Say you have them!"

"Mrs. Brown," I say, but I'm interrupted by the front door opening. Daniel walks outside, then stands at the edge of the porch, his head hanging forward.

"Carrie? It's Carrie, isn't it?" Alison takes a step forward like she's going to rush to the house, but then stops, glancing at me.

"I'm not going to stop you," I say, gesturing for her to continue. "Go to her."

"No." She chews her lower lip. Glances at me. Looks away. "I don't want to get involved if she doesn't want me there."

"Oh, but you two are friends. Or you were." I'm worried too, but she was moving by the time I reached her at the bottom of the stairs. Her eyes were open, and she was talking.

Well, she was saying one thing. *Daniel pushed me.*

EMS is with her now and will take care of her. This might be the breaking point that pushes Alison to tell me exactly what she's been hiding from me.

"We were friends," she agrees, then gives a little nod like she's talked herself into something. "You're right. We were friends. I should go to her. Maybe she—"

But she's too late. Aletha stalks past us, leading Daniel, his hands cuffed behind his back.

"Daniel?" Alison sounds pained, like she can't believe what she's seeing. He turns and looks over his shoulder at her, his mouth already opening like he's going to say something, but Aletha must stop him because he turns back, his head drooping, his feet shuffling forward.

"What happened to Carrie?" she asks. She turns to me, then leans to the side, trying to look through the Everetts' front door. "Why are you arresting Daniel? Did you find something tying him to the girls? Is he the reason they're missing?"

"We're taking care of it," I tell Alison. I'm going to continue, but she cuts me off.

"*Taking care of it?* You're arresting Daniel and an ambulance is here! Is Carrie okay? Or is it the girls? You have to tell me!" She reaches out and grabs my arms, sinking her nails into my skin. I'm suddenly hit with the memory of the nail marks in Ryan's hand this morning.

"Alison, you don't need to worry about what's going on. Let us handle it." I pause, debating how much more to tell her. "We have no reason to believe Daniel did anything to the girls. I'd tell you if we had more evidence regarding their whereabouts."

"So he hurt Carrie! That's why the ambulance is here!" She takes a step closer to me, then seems to realize how close we're standing. She lets me go, steps back, brushes her hands together.

I take a deep breath. "Why don't you go home? Unless there's something you want to tell me, there's no reason for you to be here if you're not going to talk to Carrie. Go be with Ryan so you two can support each other."

It's the first time she looks me in the eyes. There's anger there, a dark expression I haven't seen on her face before.

"You think I want to support my husband when he's been running around on me?" Her words are a hiss. Now that her concern over the ambulance has been allayed, she's free to attack me.

My breath catches in my throat.

Alison's anger only grows at my silence. "What? Got nothing to say? What do you think the chief would say if he found out that you'd been sleeping with my husband and are now investigating our missing daughter?"

"I didn't know," I whisper. The word is quiet like all the breath has been sucked out of my lungs. "How did you find out?"

"I saw the file on you. Sick, isn't it? For him to keep files on the women he sleeps with? It's messed up, but there you were, right in his little stack of trophies." She gestures angrily at me. "Ryan's a collector. Always has been. Watches. Cufflinks. *Women.*"

"He told me he was single. That you were separated. I ended it months ago."

"He told you what?" She looks like I slapped her. "That he was single?"

I swallow hard. Nod. No matter what she thinks, I'm not the bad guy here. I'm not the married man sleeping with numerous women.

"And you believed him?"

"Why wouldn't I?" I feel my chest puff out. It's one thing to know I screwed up, to berate myself for what I did. It's another entirely for Alison to call me out when all I've done today is try to find Nealie.

"I don't know—because you're the police and people lie to you all the time?" She presses both hands into her temples, her teeth gritting together. "You didn't look him up online?"

"No."

"You didn't ask his friends?"

"Like who? Daniel?"

Her mouth slams shut. The anger in her eyes? It's not gone, but it's disappearing. I stare at her, trying to see what she's thinking, what she's feeling.

Scared. She's scared.

I get it, I really do. The rage she's feeling right now? And the fear? It's no wonder she—

"If it makes you feel any better, you weren't the only one." She spits the words at me like they're a weapon she has to brandish before it turns on her. If she hurts me with her words, then maybe she won't be hurt herself.

I ignore what she said, not only because Julie already gave me that information. At this point, it doesn't matter to me if Ryan was sleeping with everyone in Blackwood. What matters is that we find the girls, and we're no closer to accomplishing that than we were a few hours ago.

"You weren't the only one," she repeats, taking a step back from me. "You may have thought you were special, but you weren't." Huge tears run down her cheeks, but she doesn't move to wipe them away.

"I know."

"You're nothing!" Another step away from me. "You know that? Nothing! Find my daughter! Can you do that? Or is that too much for you?"

Still, I don't respond. A few officers nearby are whispering to each other, their faces close together, their eyes locked on me. The back of my neck burns, but I don't want to give them the satisfaction of knowing I'm aware they're talking about me. This is humiliating. I never... I never would have been with Ryan if I'd known the truth. That's not who I am, but it's who everyone now thinks I am.

I take a step closer to Alison and grab her by the arm.

She gasps when I yank her closer to me. It's only when my lips are right by her ear that I speak. What I have to say is for her ears alone.

"I messed up when I slept with your husband, but only one of us knew you were still in the picture. I understand that you're angry at me; really, I do. But your anger is misplaced."

She's breathing hard. Her skin is warm under my grip, and I think about loosening up a little, but I'm afraid she'll try to slip away from me, and I'm not finished with her.

"You're angry with him, and you should be. You're angry that someone has Nealie, that they might hurt her."

She jerks but doesn't try to pull away from me. I'm surprised when, instead, she turns so she's staring me in the face. I'm not speaking directly into her ear any longer, but my words are still only for her.

"I know you want to defend Ryan. It makes sense, really, it does. He's your husband. Your partner. Your rock. Am I right?"

She doesn't respond.

"When you said your vows, you meant it. You thought you'd be together forever, that nothing could tear you apart." I debate whether or not to continue, to tell her the thing I know. In the end, I decide that pushing her closer to the edge might be exactly what it takes to get an answer from her.

"He was planning to divorce you," I say, speaking slowly so she can't miss a single word. "I found divorce papers hidden in Nealie's room."

"You're a liar," Alison says, but she doesn't sound convincing. She doesn't look it either, not the way her eyes are darting back and forth. She chews her lower lip and doesn't seem to notice when I let go of her arm.

"I'm not. I know you don't want to hear this, Alison, but you need to listen to me. Ryan wanted out of your relationship." I pause, letting what I just said sink in before continuing. "How far would he have gone to make that happen? What if he thought Nealie was in the way of him getting his freedom?"

"He wouldn't hurt our daughter."

"Even if he knew she was standing in his way of a clean divorce? An easy divorce?"

"No." Her response should have power, but I hear the doubt in her voice.

I'm close. I can feel it, like all I need to do is pry a little bit more, and she's going to pop open and tell me all her secrets.

"Ryan never threatened Nealie? Never made comments about how much easier life would be without her?"

"God, no." Her cheeks are flushed. Her nostrils flare.

"Listen, right now is not the time to stay loyal to someone who isn't loyal to you," I tell her. "It's time to tell me everything, even if what you're thinking is only a concern, not something you know to be true. Don't protect Ryan if it means Nealie stays in danger."

Alison doesn't respond.

"Why did you leave the law firm? Was it because you did what you needed to and made sure Daniel got fired? Are you the one skimming money out of the accounts?"

"No!" She takes a step away from me. "I needed to spend more time at home. With Nealie. And I wouldn't take money like that. Why would I hurt my husband?"

"Because he wants to divorce you. Because you'd do anything for your daughter."

"Not that."

"Okay, sure. But I've heard how you take her when you're upset. How you just... leave without letting anyone know what you're doing, where you're going. And the melatonin at night? Is that because she has problems sleeping or because you want her quiet?"

"What are you implying?"

"That your family isn't as perfect as you'd like to pretend it is. That both you and Ryan could be the reason Nealie's missing."

Alison doesn't immediately respond. She keeps looking around, her eyes darting from left to right. She's keeping tabs on who might be listening to us.

Or making an escape plan.

After a moment, she takes a deep breath and draws herself up. "Ryan and I are happy. Very happy. I know you wouldn't understand what it's like to be married, but his dalliances don't mean he'd hurt Nealie. We're solid. Nothing can come between us."

Liar.

But I don't say it, no matter how much I'd like to.

"Great. You don't have to tell me." I spot someone behind Alison. Someone I'm dying to talk to again because every time I do, she gives me little bits of information. Someone I'm sure Alison would love to keep me away from. "I think I found someone else who will."

THIRTY-FIVE
JULIE

3:23 p.m.

I should have known that being nosy about the ambulance would come back to bite me in the butt. What I should have done was reach out to Theo, let him know where I was, and got out of here before anything weird happened.

But I didn't, and now the detective is making a beeline for me. Again.

Honestly though? The thought of being alone in the car with Theo is enough to make my stomach turn. *He's a cheater.* I don't think I can do it, at least not until I know exactly why he was in the Browns' house and then lied to me about it. And I need to know why Ryan had a file on him in his office.

As well as the photo of me.

Yeah, I can't forget that. Can't forget the sinking feeling I felt when I saw it. How did he catch onto us?

I thought we had Ryan pinned down. No, I never get close to our marks, and I never trust them, but I usually rest easy that we have them under control. Backed into a corner. It's never crossed my mind to worry that one of our marks might turn it around on us.

Did he hire someone to follow Theo when I first started nannying for the girls? Or was it after Theo called him? Ryan's ballsy if that's what happened. Most people hear what Theo has to say and turn tail. They don't dare push him, not when we're always so careful. So prepared.

But that doesn't make sense either, unless Theo broke protocol and approached Ryan in person. He always calls our marks so they don't see his face, making it almost impossible to identify him. But it seems like that's exactly what Ryan did. Somehow.

Did we pick the wrong family?

That's the question I need answered. Theo's always done thorough research. He's great with computers and looking people up online. He's always found the perfect mark. People with more money than they know what to do with. People who have secrets they're willing to pay to keep private. Then he finds the perfect way for me to run into them. Every part of this is orchestrated. We don't leave anything to chance.

I've never known Theo to make a mistake when choosing a family, but what if he did this time?

What if Ryan's just a little bit smarter than the two of us?

"Julie, do you have a moment?" Detective Martin stands with her feet wide, her hands on her hips. She looks like every PE teacher I had growing up; mainly in the way that she could chase me down and tackle me to the ground if I thought it was a good idea to run away from her.

I stare at her as I try to get my mouth to work, and as I do, I think about the other files I found in Ryan's office.

Hers. Along with the ones from women I know he was cheating with. Nannies see everything, we know everything, but the one thing I don't quite have figured out is if she was also having an affair with Ryan. She didn't react during my interview when I told her about the affairs he's been having. Was it because she already knew about them?

If she was having an affair with him, it explains the file on her.

If she wasn't? It means he wanted to keep an eye on her, like he did on Theo. But why?

"I was actually about to head home," I lie.

"Ahh, yes. Well, the ambulance showing up certainly did bring everyone out of their houses to see what was going on, didn't it?" She gestures at the neighbors clustered on the streets. Most of them are staring openly at the Everetts' house, like it's suddenly going to start speaking and tell them all of its secrets.

"I guess." I take a step away from her. Even though I know there's no way she can tell what I've done, I still don't want to spend any more time with her than I need to.

"Since your boyfriend isn't here, why don't you and I talk for a few minutes? It'll help pass the time." She smiles at me, but it's tight and barely stretches her cheeks.

"Of course." In an attempt to appear like I don't have a care in the world, I roll my shoulders back. My smile is much larger than hers.

"Great. You know, I used to babysit when I was in high school. It was the en vogue thing to do when you weren't skilled enough to get a real job, and I wasn't keen on one that would have me flipping burgers all afternoon."

I don't respond.

"So I know how much you learn about a family when you're in their house. Not that I was in a family's house nearly as much as a nanny is, so I never learned nearly as much information about the families I worked for as you do. Private stuff. Personal stuff."

I've never been great with letting silence stretch out

between me and another person. When the detective finishes speaking, she stares at me, obviously waiting for me to respond.

My throat feels thick, so I clear it. "I guess. Maybe."

"Oh, I don't have to guess. I know I'm right, and you proved it when you told me Ryan was having so many affairs. Out of everyone here, it feels like you're the one who really knows what's going on." She blinks hard, her mouth tight. "So why don't you tell me, Julie, exactly what happened between Alison and Ryan?"

When I open my mouth to lie, to tell her I don't know anything, she holds up a hand to stop me. "Enough dancing around it. I'm not interested in hearing you lie to me or try to convince yourself that you're clueless. I want the truth. You told me the truth earlier. Tell me more."

At least she doesn't know what I've done. She's not asking about any of that.

"Julie. Today. I don't think I need to remind you what's at stake."

She doesn't. Whenever I have a moment of free time, my mind instantly lands on Emma and Nealie. I can't handle the thought that they might be hurt, that someone could take them like this. I know that I need to speak to this woman and tell her what I know, but that's not how I was raised.

I've always been taught that you have to protect yourself. That the best way to live your life is keeping yourself safe, that you can't take care of anyone else until you adjust your own oxygen mask.

But they're so young. They can't help themselves. Can't protect themselves. And what if Theo and I somehow set this into motion?

"Am I under arrest?" I should be. If she knew what I've done, she'd slap those handcuffs on me so fast my head would spin.

She cocks a brow. Her pistol is on her right hip, and I watch as she adjusts her weight to the side before gently resting her hand on its butt. It doesn't look like a threatening motion, more like she's trying to get comfortable, but I still don't like it.

"No, you're not. I have no reason to arrest you at this point, but I will as soon as I think I need to. You don't like me breathing down your back, but you know what I bet you'd like even less?" She opens her phone and shows me a picture of Emma, then scrolls to one of Nealie. "What do you think? Do you think they're still alive? Or are they dead?"

"Stop it."

"Because, realistically, if we're looking at stats and figures and how long kids survive after they're taken, it's not looking so good for the two of them. Or, and this might be worse, you let me know what you think: they may be alive. But they might not wish they were."

"Please." I take a step away from her, but she closes the gap immediately. "I didn't do anything."

"But you know something. And inaction is action—you know that. Tell me what you know. Help me bring the girls home because right now nobody can find them."

"I don't know anything."

"Bullshit. What happened with the Browns? Is it his affairs? Is that why he's filing for divorce?"

Ryan's filing for divorce? My head spins. I had no idea he was going to do that. Sure, I've felt the tension in the house, but I thought it was because Ryan fired Daniel and made Alison help him. But why is he the one wanting a divorce?

I close my eyes and picture the files in Ryan's office. I thought he was having an affair with the detective, but the way she's talking, how she's laser-focused on finding the girls, makes me think maybe I was wrong. Although, did she wince when she mentioned his affairs? Just a little? Like maybe she couldn't believe his dirty laundry would get aired out like that?

My stomach rumbles.

"Let me buy you something to eat," she offers, but I shake my head.

"No, I just want to go home." I take another step away from her and look around. There are so many people out, but very few of them are looking at me.

"Emma and Nealie need you."

I nod. My tongue feels thick and furry and stuck to the roof of my mouth. I swallow hard. "I told you he's having numerous affairs. And now Carrie and Alison aren't friends any longer because Alison got Daniel fired, but Ryan asked her to. No, he *told* her to." She looks like she's going to respond, so I speak faster to cut her off. "But she did it. She forged his signature so he'd lose his job. Maybe Alison hates him for that and he doesn't want to stay married to someone who loathes him? Or maybe Ryan wants to distance himself from what they did. He's the mastermind, but she's the one who pulled the trigger."

If Alison were divorcing Ryan, this would all make sense. But the other way around? I can't wrap my head round it.

"You should have told me this already. You just keep hindering this investigation, Julie."

Behind her, Theo's walking towards us. He starts waving. For some reason, I don't want him to come over here, so I try to wrap it up.

"I know, I'm so sorry! You don't understand what he's like." I pause, thinking about how to lay it on as thick as possible, how to make sure she sees Ryan as the bad guy and doesn't focus on me. "Please don't let them know what I told you," I tell her. "I don't want any of this to blow back on me when I didn't do anything." I don't give her a chance to respond before I cut around her, walking as quickly as possible.

Theo sees me coming and smiles, but then he looks past me and his face falls. His brows crash together, a furrow appearing between them as he sees who I was talking to.

Yeah, the detective.

This has gotten out of control. The girls were never supposed to be a part of this.

And now we have to fix it before we both go to jail.

THIRTY-SIX
ALISON

3:41 p.m.

There's no way to get my car out of my driveway, not with so many cruisers parked in and around it, but I have to get out of Blackwood. Ryan may have pushed for us to live here, saying it was the best way to let people know we were on the up, that we had money, that we were of the upper echelon, but I'm the one who really fell in love with the neighborhood.

Now, however, it feels like it's choking me. The walls are closing in, the cloudless sky seems to hang low, pressing down on me. I have to get out of here, away from everyone watching me.

And away from my husband. Away from the knowledge that Daniel was arrested for... something. It had to do with Carrie, and there was an ambulance, so I think I can fill in the blanks, no matter how much I don't want to.

Clutching my phone in my right hand, I power-walk away from the house, keeping my head down. Normally, I'd never consider cutting through someone else's backyard, but I do that now, pushing through hydrangeas and stepping over lilies so I can break out on another street, one with fewer people on it.

There. I slow down on the sidewalk, but my heart still hammers in my throat. It's nice to be away from the hubbub for a moment, but I still feel trapped. As much as I'd love to get out of here completely, I'm not going to be able to do that without a car. I'm going to have to be happy with putting some distance between me and the house.

Up ahead is the gazebo. I've never actually spent any time in it, mostly because I've always believed gazebos will be crawling with spiders, and I hate anything with more than four legs. Right now, though, it looks inviting.

It drips wisteria, and there are thick hydrangeas planted around the entire thing, giving it more privacy than I've experienced since the morning. I hurry to it and step inside, instantly relaxing in the shade.

Turning so I'm facing the door, I sit, then exhale hard, lowering my head into my hands. The tears start as soon as I think about Nealie, about how scared she must be right now, about how much I'd love to have her home.

Last Christmas I talked to Ryan about getting a kid's tracker watch for her just in case. She's going to kindergarten in the fall, and even though she'll be at a private school, I know how dangerous schools can be for kids.

I thought a tracker watch would be a great idea. It would make it easy for me to double-check her location during the day. I wouldn't have to worry about where she was because I'd always know. Besides, a tracker watch is a better option than a phone. The school wouldn't have a problem with it since it couldn't make phone calls or text.

Of course, Ryan shot it down, telling me it was silly, that she would only go to the best and safest school, that any concerns I had over her getting lost were ridiculous. In the end, he bought her a programmable robot she was supposed to use to practice coding. I'm pretty sure it's still in its box in her closet.

"Nealie," I whisper. I picture her at the party last night, how excited she was to see her friends. How excited she was to see Emma. That starts the tears flowing harder, and I know I need to pull myself together. Falling apart when she needs me the most won't do a bit of good.

So I steel myself and pull out my phone. Flick to the photo I took in Ryan's office. There's no way for him to know what I did, that I found these files, that I'm going to look these women up. Especially the detective. What do I know about her besides the fact she was sleeping with my husband? Was it her lipstick I found on his collar just this week? She acted like they ended it a while ago, but how am I supposed to know if I can believe her? I have to find out, have to know everything I can about her.

But not yet. I'll end with her, once I've researched these other women. Opening Facebook, I type in the first name. *Gabby Wright*.

I can honestly say I've never seen this woman before, but I feel like I have because she looks a lot like me, only fifteen years younger. Safe to say, she's Ryan's type, and my stomach falls at the thought of what that means.

On to the next woman. *Tara McKenzie*. Same thing. Me but younger. Prettier. With fewer smile lines and bigger lips.

One more before the detective. *Lora Hahn*.

All three of these women are Ryan's type. Vapid. Pretty. Young. Probably huge hot yoga or Pilates aficionados, if I'm being honest.

But what about the detective? I weigh my phone in my hand for a moment before finally typing her name into the search bar. I know what she looks like and, while she's pretty, she doesn't have that model look to her that Ryan definitely prefers.

What was it about her that made my husband fall for her?

That made it worth staying late at the office, sneaking out to be with her, spending time with her instead of Nealie and me?

Detective Martin doesn't have a public Facebook profile. That or she has it hidden away under a fake name. That's an option that's growing in popularity as more and more people want to keep their private lives... well, private.

"Come on," I say, tapping faster. I navigate to the local police department's page, looking for any photos she might be tagged in. There are a few pictures of her, but none of them are linked back to her personal page.

My finger flicks across the screen, sending blocks of text and photos zipping by. When I've scrolled as far back as December, I stop.

There. The police had had some holiday event downtown, and I remember Ryan going to it. He'd made a big deal about not wanting to go, about how it was a waste of time, about how he'd be much happier staying at home with Nealie and me.

But in this shot, he looks pretty happy. He's in the background of a young couple who posed to have their photo taken, and I would have missed him at first if he hadn't worn that stupid Christmas tree tie he has. I've always hated it, hated how it stuck out like a sore thumb, but now I'm glad he had it on because it helps me pick him out of a crowd. Using two fingers, I zoom in on the photo to see who he's talking to, whose elbow he's holding, who he's leaning closer to like he wants to tell them a secret.

The detective.

Even though it's exactly what I expected to see, I yelp and drop my phone. It clatters against the wood floor and skids off to the side under another bench.

"Shit," I mutter. My mind races, trying both to remember and erase what I just saw on my phone. I need to get a closer look at it.

I drop to my knees, then crawl halfway under a bench to

grab it. But as I do, my eyes catch on something outside the gazebo, something light tan tucked under a bush. It takes me a minute to realize what it is, but then it hits me.

A manilla folder. Just like the ones in Ryan's office.

After I grab my phone, I shove it into my pocket. There will be time later to have a closer look at that photo. Right now, I need to see that folder.

Someone broke into Ryan's office, but he didn't want to tell the cops. Why not? What if they'd taken something? He'd acted like they hadn't, but there are so many files in there, he could be wrong.

Or he could have realized what was missing but not wanted to tell me.

I barely notice that I'm outside the gazebo, or back on my knees, or the way the bushes scratch my bare arms. Even before I open the folder, I know my suspicions were right.

This came from Ryan's office. I recognize his writing on the tab.

THIRTY-SEVEN
JULIE

3:56 p.m.

"How are we going to get out of this?" I take a huge bite of my sandwich after I ask the question to give Theo time to answer. Even though I'd originally told him I didn't think leaving Blackwood and grabbing something to eat was a good idea, he'd pushed for it, and I'm glad.

Honestly, I had no idea just how hungry I really was. I've been so focused on finding the girls—*and looking at Ryan's folder on Theo*—that food hadn't crossed my mind.

And it feels good to be away from the stress of the search, even though that thought instantly fills me with guilt. Nealie and Emma can't escape the stress, can they?

I still have to figure out when I can get that folder back.

"We have to hope the cops find the girls." Theo closes his eyes for a minute. "She's digging into everything, and I'm worried she's going to figure out what we were really doing with the Browns." He puts his sandwich down and stares at me. "Especially if you let something slip."

"I haven't. You think this is a joke? That I'm not being careful? *You* didn't get interviewed. She's all over me, and I keep having to give her bits of information about the Browns so she'll leave me alone. I don't want her to get too close, but she keeps coming back to me."

"How many times has she talked to you?" He pushes his plate away from him and locks me in place with a stare. "How can you be sure you've been careful enough?"

"I don't know. A few? I am a connection between the families, but don't worry. She has no idea what we're really doing here." A wave of frustration washes over me, but I push it away. I can't let what I just learned about him cloud my judgement. I still need him to make sure the two of us get out of this in one piece.

He shakes his head. "No, you're not listening to me."

I'm pretty sure I am, but I put my sandwich on my plate and stare at him to make sure he can tell just how focused I am right now.

"Okay. Tell me what's really bothering you."

Theo nods and rakes a hand through his hair. "She keeps talking to you, and you're right: you're a connection between the two girls. What if you slip up? We'll be screwed."

"I'm not going to slip up. That's why I told her about Ryan's affairs. And I've clued her in about Alison's involvement with Daniel getting fired. I have this under control."

Right? I do have this under control, don't I?

"I don't want her to think she can blame you for something you didn't do or figure out what we *have* been doing and try to use it against us." He pauses. "What we do? It isn't this. You can't slip up, let her think we're involved in the girls going missing."

The words fall like stones on my ears. I blink hard, a dull roar in the back of my mind making it difficult to concentrate. As long as she doesn't find out what Theo and I are really doing here, no way can she try to blame the girls going missing on us, not when we didn't have anything to do with it.

But, yeah, he's right. We're safe as long as she doesn't know the truth. But as soon as that comes out… let's just say we have to find the girls before anyone finds out what Theo and I are really doing here.

No wonder Theo looks nervous. He doesn't want me to take him down with me if she tries to pin this on me.

But he's the one who is always in charge.

My palms feel sweaty, and I wipe them on my napkin. Even though I've only eaten about half of my sandwich and was famished when we sat down, I no longer have an appetite.

"Theo," I say slowly, my mind racing, "you don't think that would happen, do you? We're innocent. At least of this. And besides, they could arrest me or charge me, and it's not like I'd be able to produce the girls. I don't know where they are any more than the detective does."

Right? He wouldn't throw me under the bus to save himself, would he?

I'm getting loud. The couple sitting at the table next to us turns to look at me, and I feel my face heat. Even as I say it, I have to admit that I've been worried about this exact thing. It's been a worry in the back of my mind, one I've wanted to ignore, but I can't any longer. Not when Theo's incised it, brought it out into the open.

"I know you didn't do anything," Theo says, reaching out for my hand. I pause, then take his, but I don't return the squeeze he gives me. How dry his skin is only highlights how much I'm sweating. "But I don't want you to get caught up in something terrible."

No, he doesn't want to be caught up in something terrible.

The more I think about it, the more terrified I am, and the more convinced he's hiding a lot from me. "Theo," I say, leaning forward and lowering my voice. "Why this time? We've never had a problem like this before. Never! It's always been in and out. Why did it all go south?"

How did Ryan know enough to make a file on Theo?

"I don't know." His voice is just as low as mine. Believe me, I wish I knew. But it's all going to work out." He glances quickly to the side like he can't keep looking at me.

He's lying to me about something. Why should I trust him?

"I was planning on going back to Blackwood after we ate," I tell him. "I thought we could help look some more."

He's already shaking his head. "I don't think that's a good idea. I know you want to keep helping, but it might be smart to take a step back. Let the detective and her team work the case without you there for her to look at as a possible suspect."

"Out of sight, out of mind?"

"Yes, thank goodness you get it." He gives me a smile. "I know this isn't want you want to hear, Julie, but I'm worried. This case is a nightmare. Don't get caught up in it, okay?"

Yeah, right. We're about as caught up in it as possible.

I take another bite of my sandwich as I think. The only things I know about missing persons cases is from TV, and from what I've seen, police officers aren't kind to people they think are lying to them. And the detective has come on really strong. I thought telling her about Alison getting Daniel fired might be enough to get her off my back, but maybe I was wrong. What if this was just the beginning with her? What if it's only going to get worse?

"Hey, you okay?" Theo reaches across the table and lightly touches my arm. "You look terrified, and I didn't mean to do that to you. I just wanted to make sure you were seeing things the way I am. You're really involved, and you might be missing some details, but I don't have a dog in the fight. Trust me, Julie, this doesn't have anything to do with our plan. Nobody's going to find out what we do."

"I'm fine," I lie. "Just... yeah, I'm glad you mentioned that.

You're right—I think I'll go back to my apartment this afternoon."

"I think that's a good idea."

"You want to come with me?" Hope rises in me. As much as I love spending time alone, I don't want to be by myself right now. If he comes home with me, I can pretend like none of this is really happening. If he doesn't... should I go back to Blackwood? Keep looking for the girls? If I do that, I won't let him know.

He sucks his teeth, and I already know what the answer is going to be. "I have a little work to do today. I didn't want to mention it, but it's best if I take some time to handle it."

"Of course, you have to do what you have to do." Guilt presses down on me. I've been so wrapped up in my drama that I didn't think about what Theo was putting to the side to support me.

"No big deal." He smiles at me. "Hey, I'm going to run to the bathroom before we go. I'll be back."

"Yeah, of course."

He pushes back from the table, and I watch him weave his way across the restaurant. I know I need to talk to him about the file I found in Ryan's office, but I don't know how to bring it up. Maybe it would be best to talk to Ryan about it first.

But then I'd have to admit to him that I took it, and I can't see that going over well.

There's a soft beep, and I reach for my phone before realizing Theo left his on the table. Without thinking, I grab it, then hold it in my lap so he couldn't see it.

When I glance up towards the bathrooms, I can't see him.

Should I look? A good girlfriend wouldn't look, but I have to know why he was in Ryan's house and lied to me about it. If Ryan is going to go to the police about what we did... or tried to do. No, I didn't find anything before, but that doesn't mean I shouldn't look again, right?

I slide my thumb across the screen and tap in the code I used earlier to unlock his phone.

The screen shakes. Frowning, I tap it in again.

But the phone doesn't unlock.

"He changed it this afternoon?" I ask. I'm not expecting a response, of course. I'm just confused.

I close my eyes for a moment and think, then try the PIN one more time.

No dice.

Does he know I was poking through his phone earlier? Is that why he changed his PIN?

I force myself to slow down and really look at the phone, and that's when it hits me.

This isn't the same phone I was looking at earlier.

Panic grips my throat before I realize it must be his burner for this job. I don't handle communicating with our marks once I've found the blackmail to use against them. Theo buys a new phone, saves our mark as the only contact, and deals with them. I heft it, thinking. A text came through, and since this is his burner, that must mean Ryan is willing to play ball, right?

Something isn't right. I chew the inside of my cheek while I think, and then it hits me. Theo doesn't text our marks because he doesn't want to leave a paper trail. He calls them. If they respond in a text, he calls them again. It could still be Ryan texting, but what if it isn't?

I can't unlock the phone, but at least I can read the text that came through. Before tapping on the screen again, I glance up at the bathrooms.

Still no Theo.

I tap the screen on, revealing the text. It's from an unsaved number, and I frown. If it's Ryan texting him, his contact info should be saved in this phone.

How much does she know about me?

She? Is this text about me? I feel my blood chill. Desperate, I stab at the screen, hoping I'm going to be able to unlock the phone, but, again, no dice.

The words stay there, an accusation. I try to take a deep breath and ignore the growing pit in my stomach, but I can't.

How much does she know about me?

Ryan wouldn't text something like that. They're not in cahoots, not when one of them is the mark.

So who the hell sent this?

THIRTY-EIGHT
ALISON

4:01 p.m.

I don't even go back inside the gazebo. Desperate to find out what's in the folder, I sit on the ground and flip it open on my lap. And then I read everything there is to know about Julie's boyfriend. It's clinical, like doctor's notes, and even though I read through it three times, I still have no idea what I'm looking at. Why would Ryan have this? What's the point?

But then there are pictures. My heart beats in my throat, and I feel like I'm going to be sick, but I force myself to go slowly and look at every single one. Julie's in a ton of them, and I try to be observant without letting my feelings get in the way.

She's attractive. Her jaw is strong, her breasts are perky, her eyes are big, and she always wears the right amount of mascara to really make them pop. If Ryan had had a file on her, I don't think I'd be as surprised as I am right now.

But one on Theo? That doesn't make any sense.

A laugh threatens to bubble out of me, and I clap my hand over my mouth. Now is not the time to crack up, not when everything is falling apart and Nealie needs me. I don't know what her father has done, how many affairs he's had, but I do know that I have to put this behind me until I get her back.

I stand and brush off my pants. For a moment, I consider putting the folder back where I found it, but I change my mind.

I was right before—someone stole it from the house and brought it out here. Someone who didn't want anyone else to see it. I'd had an inkling that it might have been Julie sneaking around in our house, but now I'm not so sure.

It could have been Theo, right? There's no way anyone would be willing to leave a file about themselves just sitting out where anyone could pick it up. Except that's exactly what happened. Whoever took the file brought it here. Left it here.

But why? Why not destroy it? Unless they needed it, or... unless they were interrupted. Hid it. Vowed to come back later for it.

What if a neighbor had found it? That thought is terrifying.

At least they wouldn't have immediately known where it came from, right? It was only luck that Ryan wrote on the tab and didn't use his label maker. If he hadn't, I'd never have been able to recognize his handwriting and know for sure that this came from his office.

I have to think this through, make connections, but the longer I spend in Blackwood, the harder it's getting. For a moment, I consider going back to the house, locking myself in the bedroom so I can be alone, then I think about what it will be like seeing Ryan face-to-face.

No, that's not what I need to do. I need to see Carrie.

Going to visit her is dangerous, all things considered, but it suddenly takes priority over me fleeing the neighborhood. Still, I have to know why the ambulance was at her house. I have to know if she's okay and if she knows the truth about why Daniel lost his job.

More importantly, I have to know if she's going to tell Ryan or the detective what I did.

Ten minutes later, I've crept through backyards, looping around houses to avoid walking down the sidewalk where Ryan might see me. This is insane, going to visit Carrie like this. I don't even know if she's at home still. While I walk, I think about what to say to her.

I'm sorry?
I didn't mean for this to happen?
It was my family or yours?

No, none of those would work. I have to avoid apologizing at all costs. Apologizing will mean I'm guilty, and the only thing I'm guilty of is protecting my family. Everything I've done... to Ryan, to Daniel and Carrie... it's all been for Nealie.

I reach her house and pause. Instead of waltzing in through the front door, which is what I would have done months ago, I duck my head and hurry around to the back. The drive to see Carrie is stronger than ever.

But at least I don't have to worry about seeing Daniel.

I haven't seen him since Ryan fired him, and I can't imagine he'd be very pleased if he rounded a corner and we ended up face-to-face. My heart beats faster as I step onto their back deck, scoot around a yoga mat and some yoga blocks, then hurry to the door.

My hand shakes as I reach for the knob. I hold my breath as I take it, saying a little prayer that it will be unlocked, then slowly turn it, giving the door a gentle push to open.

It squeals a little on its hinges, and I freeze, holding my breath. I count to ten, then push it open a bit more.

So where is Carrie?

I'm in the kitchen, and I take one step forward, then another. When I reach the island, I pause, debating if I should go into the living room or leave the house.

Coming in here to try to talk to Carrie was the dumbest idea I've ever had. If I really wanted to talk to her, I should have called her, I should have—

"Alison?"

I whip around, fighting the urge to flee.

This is the closest I've been to Carrie since... I screwed over her husband.

She has a bandage on the side of her head. Her eyes are wide, her cheeks bright red. For a moment, I feel the same compassion I've always felt for her, and I want to rush to her, pull her into a hug, but then her jaw tightens, and I stay rooted to the spot.

"Carrie." Her name catches in my throat, and I clear it. "How are you? I wanted to check on you when I saw the ambulance." She doesn't respond when I pause, so I keep talking, faster now, the words flowing. "I'd wanted to come by and check on you before to make sure you were doing okay with everything, but we've been so busy at home, and I didn't feel like there was ever a good time to—"

"You only thought to come by after my husband was arrested."

I glance up at the ceiling, as if answers are going to be written there. "I'm sorry," I whisper. "I should have come sooner."

"You should have. If you'd cared, you would have." She takes a step closer to me. "You did this, you know."

I nod, unable to speak.

"I was making tea." She sweeps past me to the pantry, and I follow. It feels like I have no control over my body, like I've fallen back into the pattern of how I acted when we were still friends, helping her, getting things out of her pantry, grabbing a snack without feeling like I had to ask.

The overhead light clicks on automatically, and I blink at its intrusion before looking around. Her pantry has always looked like mine. Perfectly organized. Shelves loaded down with name-brand food.

But some of the shelves sit empty, and I see a lot of store

brands. I drag my gaze away from them when she turns around, a box of tea bags in her hand.

"It's hard to keep the pantry stocked now that Daniel makes so much less than he used to."

I swallow hard. "I'm sorry."

The pause before she speaks is so long I feel uncomfortable. "I wondered when you'd come by." Her words have bite.

Shame washes over me, but I can't defend myself. It was crazy of me to think Carrie would welcome me into her house with open arms, but that's exactly what part of me hoped would happen. We used to be close enough to be sisters.

"I wanted to," I tell her. "But Ryan thought I should stay home. You know what he's like, how he's always worried about what other people will think of him. I had to listen to him. I didn't have a choice."

"Does he know you're here now? Or are you sneaking around?"

I shake my head.

"Afraid to tell him?"

"He's scared," I whisper. "Just like you and me and Daniel." It hurts to say her husband's name. "Are you okay? Did he hurt you? I saw he was arrested, but..." My voice trails off when I clock the expression on her face.

"You're here because you're nosy. I knew you didn't really care about me."

"No! I had to see you, Carrie. Nobody else knows what the two of us are going through."

"You're kidding me, right? You ruined my life, Alison, then you creep over here like you think I'm going to tell you everything is fine?"

"I'm sorry." The words hurt. My throat feels ragged from crying so much. I don't know how to make her see how terribly sorry I am about everything. I never should have chosen Ryan's side, but I had to keep him happy just a bit longer so I could finalize my plan.

"You're sorry for ruining my life." She scoffs. Shakes her head. When she looks back at me, her gaze is bright, and she pins me in place with her stare. "Are you why they were taken?"

No. "What?" I take a step back, but the door keeps me from putting any more space between us. Taking a deep breath, I stare at Carrie, willing her to look at me, but she doesn't meet my eyes as she speaks.

"But you're why Daniel was fired."

I don't answer. I *can't* answer.

"Get out of my house, Alison. Out of my life. I want my daughter back. I want her father. And I never want to see you again."

"Carrie, please." Tears spring to my eyes. "Ryan's filing for divorce."

There's something there, some spark in her gaze, but then it's gone. "That's what you wanted."

"Not like this." I reach for her but let my hand fall back by my side. "Not without Nealie. Not without you. You're my friend."

"I *was* your friend. Friends don't do this to each other." She waves her arm, encompassing the half-empty shelves.

I wince. "Carrie—"

"You. You did this." She's getting louder and louder, and she catches herself, lowering her voice again. "You got greedy, and this is what happens. It's always been all about you, Alison."

She's not talking about me getting Daniel fired.

I know she's not.

She's talking about the other thing I did. The money. I told her about it when we were still friends, when I needed her moral support that I was doing the right thing for me and Nealie. But if she wants to hurt me, why hasn't she told Ryan or the police when she knows it would destroy me?

THIRTY-NINE
CARRIE

4:23 p.m.

"Get. Out." I hiss the words in Alison's face. "You think I want you over here? You think I want you anywhere near me? You're the problem, Alison. You're the reason this is happening." I have to clench my hands at my sides to keep from slapping her smug face. How Ryan can love her, can kiss her, can roll over in bed in the morning and see her and not want to scream, I don't know.

"No. I didn't do anything. I promise you—I have nothing to do with the girls going missing!" She's whisper-yelling, hyper aware that she shouldn't be here.

"You may not have taken them yourself, but you can't deny the fact that you screw everything up." I take a deep breath to try to calm myself. "Leave. Now." My head hurts. The meds the EMT gave me haven't kicked in yet, but no way was I going to the hospital, not while Emma's still missing.

Alison's face is pale. She opens her mouth like she's going to argue with me but must see the expression on my face, because she turns and scurries out of the pantry without another word.

She's a rat, she is, always sneaking around where she isn't wanted, always screwing people over.

I should tell Ryan about the money. It would be the smart thing, to point a finger at his wife and show him who she really is, but up until recently, she was my best friend.

And, besides, if she gets what she wanted, then I'll finally get the one thing I want. That's the reason I've kept my mouth shut about what she's done, even though I thought for a bit about turning her in.

I'm suddenly grateful I wasn't able to print off her bank records. I might have done something I'd regret. It's in my best interests to let her sneak around, to keep working on her own little plan. If I wait long enough, things will work out.

I step out of the pantry and slam the door closed behind me. Alison has already left, probably fleeing through the back door and scurrying back to her house.

That *bitch*. Thinking she could waltz into my house and be welcomed. Thinking that just because our daughters are missing we'd suddenly be friends.

At the sink, I fill an empty glass and drain it, then do it again. My head pounds. It took a lot of lying to ensure I could stay in my house. The EMTs wanted to pack me up, strap me down, ship me out. I told them over and over that I'm fine, that nothing really hurts, that I got lucky.

I passed their little tests and stood my ground.

Rolling my shoulders back, I step outside into the backyard. It's still hot out here, and sticky, and I walk to my favorite place in the yard. Daniel has his oversized deck and fancy grill, his gorgeous custom-made teak furniture, his firepit.

But I have my weeping willow.

It's tucked back in the corner of the yard, far enough away from the deck that even when Daniel's sitting out there, he can't see me standing by the tree. The long branches brush the ground, swaying with the breeze, creating the perfect spot for me to be by myself.

I've cried over all the babies I've lost under this tree.

I cried tears of joy when I found out I was pregnant with Emma.

When Daniel lost his job, I sat out here on the ground and sobbed.

I've rejoiced under here. Mourned under here.

Before having Emma, I've thought about ending it all under here.

I'm barefoot, and the thick grass tickles my feet. Moving quickly, I brush the leaves out of the way and step closer to the trunk, allowing the branches to fall like a living curtain behind me.

Last summer, I put a small stool under here, and I sit on it. Lean forward. Rest my head in my hands.

I'm barely settled before I hear someone approach the tree. I stiffen and sit up before wiping my cheeks.

Daniel never comes back here. *Never*. Nobody knows about my little spot. The thought of Alison finding me here, intruding on my private spot, is enough to make me grind my jaw. She's always sticking her nose in, always poking around. I hate her, not only for what she did to me, but what she has. And now she followed me here, and I can't stop her from reaching through the willow branches, brushing them aside, and stepping through.

But it's not her.

"Ryan? What are you doing here?" I'm suddenly aware of how pale I probably look, how my eyes have bags from crying. The shirt I have on is faded, the stripes so pale they hardly resemble the bright colors they were when the fabric was first made. I shift, tugging it into place so I look a little bit more presentable.

"I needed to check on you." He pauses, half through the

branches, half not. After a moment, he takes a step closer. The branches fall into place, blocking out some of the sun and throwing dancing shadows across the ground. "I wanted to make sure you're okay."

"I'm fine." *Fine.* Like there's any word in the English language that can fully encompass how I really feel. My brain is a jumble of words and emotions, and I can't seem to focus on any long enough to make them make sense.

"You're really fine?" he asks, and I blush. That's Ryan, though, always calling me out when he knows I'm not telling the entire truth. "That's why there was an ambulance here? Because you were fine?"

I'm silent, unwilling to form the words I need to, unwilling to tell him what happened.

"Daniel pushed me."

He stills, his eyes locked on me. "What?"

"I deserved it," I cry. "We're both under so much stress, and he came to get me to talk to the detective, but I just wanted to lie down for a second, wanted to rest. I should have just gone with him, but I didn't want to, and I made him angry." I close my eyes as I picture the scene, how it happened. And how I'm painting it for Ryan.

He approaches me, and then he's there, next to me, squatting on the ground, his arm around me. I lean on his shoulder.

It feels good. Safe.

"I screwed up," I whisper.

"We both did."

That's the closest he's ever come to apologizing or owning up for what he did to my husband—to me. I know I should be angry, should kick him off our property, refuse to talk to him, but he's been part of my life for so long. It's impossible to be angry at him.

"What do we do now?" Our faces are inches apart; I could kiss him. That's the thing—Ryan and I have never kissed. Oh, sure, when we were in middle and high school I might have thought about what it would be like to feel his lips on mine, but it's never happened. That's not the relationship we have, although anyone who walked in on the two of us right now might think otherwise.

His gaze flicks to my mouth, and my heart stills, but his eyes lock back on mine before he speaks.

"We wait. We keep thinking about who might have taken the girls. We take care of ourselves." He reaches up and lightly touches the bandage on my temple.

My breath catches in my throat. "So the same thing we've been doing all day."

"Yes." He gives me a squeeze.

"Right." The word sounds thick. There's been something I want to ask him, but now that he's here and I can talk to him, I'm afraid. And that's new. I've never been afraid of Ryan before. Not all through school, not when we were adults. Not even when he fired Daniel, changing everything.

I should tell him Alison came by. I should tell him what she's doing, how she's planning on screwing him over, but I won't. Not when keeping my mouth shut means I'll have a chance to get the one thing I've always wanted. If I didn't think I'd get something out of this, I'd throw her under the bus. It's hard to sit back and let things play out knowing full well that Ryan will get hurt, but I have to remember that it's going to work out for me in the end.

"Are you sure you're okay? They said you're fine to be at home? You don't need to go to the hospital?"

"I'm fine."

"Okay. Good. In that case, I'm going to get out of here. I need to be at the house in case they find anything." He stands, and I feel my chance slipping away along with my resolve. I've played this conversation in my head half a dozen times, but now that it's time to ask it, I'm afraid.

I just want to make sure he'll take care of Emma if something happens to me.

He's at the branches, walking faster now, not looking back. With a flick of his wrist, he knocks them out of his way, then keeps going, not pausing, always walking with the confidence of someone who hasn't done anything wrong.

He breezed through high school. College. Law school. Ryan's Teflon—nothing ever sticks to him. He can get into the worst, messiest situations and walk out unscathed.

Just like he is now.

I open my mouth to call to him but just as quickly press my lips together. I didn't do it. Sighing, I bring my knees up to my chest and wrap my arms around them. Even if I had asked him, would he have told me the truth?

Would he even consider that what he did so many years ago might come back to haunt him like this?

FORTY
KATE

4:24 p.m.

So Alison forged Daniel's signature at work, and that's the reason Ryan had for firing him? I keep turning that thought over and over in my mind as I hurry back down the sidewalk to the Browns' house. It's starting to cool off, the sun slowly dipping lower and lower, and we're no closer to finding these girls than we were when we got called out here this morning. But these secrets everyone has? They're tied to the girls going missing.

Just as I'm about to turn up Ryan's driveway, Aletha approaches me.

"Got a second?" she asks.

I pause, looking at the house. I'm dying to get in there and find out its secrets, but they can wait another minute. I completely forgot to check in with Aletha about Carrie.

This case is a nightmare, with so many moving pieces it's hard to get a handle on them. Even coming from LA, I didn't have cases like this. There were kidnappings and murders, sure, but they were all straightforward compared to this.

It feels like everyone here is lying to me.

Hopefully, Aletha will be able to clear some things up for me. "First tell me the status on Daniel Everett."

Aletha pulls a face. "Daniel said he didn't push her, but as you saw, she's adamant he did. The entire way to the police department, he kept saying he was innocent, but then he got angry at the end."

"Angry how?"

"At her, for putting him in this position in the first place."

"He could be talking about him pushing her. Or what happened at work."

"True. How's Carrie?"

"Says she's fine. When I got to her at the bottom of the stairs, she sat up and immediately pointed the finger at Daniel, then she refused medical treatment. EMS said they had no good reason to take her."

"A fall down the stairs would kill some people."

"And yet others walk away from being hit by a car. Who knows?" I pause. "What else do you have for me?"

"We've talked to the preschool teachers. They're clean. One is still out of town—she left after the party last night—the other was with her husband. He's a solid alibi. So it's a dead end there, although I have found something else I thought you mind find interesting."

"Which is?"

"First, understand I pulled some strings to get his information. Monica Allman works at Ryan's law office. She got me some information on contentious cases the team had been working on."

"Please tell me you went through the correct channels to get this information."

"The paperwork is in progress; I just did it backwards. Time is running out—you know that." She fixes me in place with a stare and only starts talking when I wave her on.

"Continue. But you need to get your paperwork in order."

She grins. "I will. Apparently most of the cases there are pretty cut and dry. I don't think Ryan would take one if he didn't think he could win it. But there was one a few months ago that fell apart, and a client went to jail."

"Seems like a lot of things fell apart a few months ago."

"That's what I thought. Daniel messed up, and that's when dominoes started falling."

"Ahh, but Daniel didn't mess up. Alison forged his signature, according to the nanny," I say, glancing back at the house. The windows are dark, the door shut tight. It feels like the house is hunched on the property, a living thing closed tight to protect its secrets.

Aletha's eyebrows shoot up. "What? How?" She pauses, considering. "And why?"

"You forgot *when*, and the answer to that is a few months ago, maybe right around the time that one case fell apart. Seems like Alison's been hiding a fair amount from us, and we can't allow that to continue."

I swallow hard when I think about what it will be like to push her for more information. The wife I didn't know Ryan still had. The one he promised me was out of the picture. Of course, I've never met Nealie, not because I didn't want to but because of what Ryan told me.

That he wanted to keep her safe. Not introduce her to anyone until he knew for sure his date was the one.

He lied about being married, so what else could he be lying about?

More and more, I can't help but think he knows who took his daughter.

Or maybe he took her himself.

He is planning on divorcing Alison. Why not pave the way? Make it as easy as possible? And it's clear he's not afraid of hurting Daniel and Carrie, or he wouldn't have thrown Daniel under the bus at work.

"Hey, you okay?" Aletha touches my arm, bringing me back to reality. "Lost you there for a second."

I nod, forcing a small smile. "Yeah, sorry. There's a lot to this case."

"There really is. I'll take you out for a beer when we bring them home." She jerks her chin at the house and adjusts her duty belt. "Good luck in there. Let me know what else I can do, but right now I'm going to follow up with more neighbors. We're expanding our search area from the neighborhood to include others right around here. Since we found the teddy bear outside, I'm going on hope the girls walked away and weren't taken in a car. I got Julie's address and sent it to you—"

"I've been slammed. Drive out there, will you? Poke around and see what you can. If you find the landlord, ask about her."

Aletha nods. "You got it."

"Thank you. Also—I was working on a press release. It's in our shared file. Will you please check it over and send it to the news stations? I know we released the photos of the girls, but I want to keep everyone in town aware of what's going on. We can't let people get complacent."

"On it." She spins away from me, already pulling her phone from her pocket to check the press release draft I wrote. Time is of the essence, but we also have to keep people interested, keep them invested so everyone has an eye out for the girls.

Aletha has it under control. I've seen her on cases before pulling long hours, skipping meals. She's always taken missing children's cases personally, although we don't have that many. Not ones like this nightmare anyway. That thought races through my mind as I roll my shoulders back and walk up to the house. I ring the doorbell and step back.

And wait.

After a minute, I knock hard, pounding my fist into the door to get Ryan's or Alison's attention. It doesn't matter who I talk to: I have no doubt that if Alison got Daniel fired, Ryan pulled the strings to make it happen.

After a moment, I hear footsteps. Stepping back from the door, I cross my arms on my chest and wait.

Alison? Or Ryan?

Ryan's scowling when he opens the door but immediately tries to fix his face. He doesn't let go of the door and almost seems to brace himself against it.

"Detective. What can I do for you?"

"I was hoping to talk to you. Is Alison home?"

"She's not." He doesn't offer where his wife is. "Did you find more information about Nealie? Do you have any idea where she might be?"

I pause for a moment before answering. Ryan has deep lines on his forehead. His skin is ashy and dry. The man looks like he hasn't slept in days. Even this morning he looked like the Ryan I dated—handsome and in control, but Nealie going missing has not only finally sunk in but heavily affected him.

"We don't have any more information on where Nealie is," I tell him. "But I did just learn something interesting about your law firm. Sounds like you and Daniel lost a pretty big case a few months ago, and shortly after that, Daniel lost his job."

"Coincidence."

"I don't believe in them. You fired Daniel to take the heat off you. Someone in your law firm screwed up, and it was easy enough for you to point the finger elsewhere. But you needed help, and Alison just so happened to work with you. It was easy for her to get involved, wasn't it? You pushed her to do something she didn't want to, to forge his signature, but she did, and then she quit. And now I find out you want to divorce your wife, after she so kindly helped you out. And then your daughter goes missing." I take a deep breath. "Everything's lining up. Whatever happened at your law firm resulted in Nealie going missing."

"You're insane! You can't try to make connections where there aren't any."

"Except for the fact that Daniel's daughter, Emma, went missing at the same time." I stare at him, trying to wrap my mind around him being so bull-headed. "Don't think for a second that parents' actions couldn't have resulted in what happened to your daughters. Now, Mr. Brown, tell me exactly what happened, what Alison did—*what you made her do*—before I charge you with obstruction and take you to jail. It would be a lot harder to help find Nealie from a cell, wouldn't it?"

He's breathing hard. I watch as his chest rises and falls erratically. If he's trying to get his emotions under control, he's really not doing a very good job.

"Mr. Brown—"

"You were right that Alison got involved when we had a problem with a case," he finally says. He's speaking quickly, practically spitting the words at me like he has to get them out before he changes his mind. Before his body physically prevents him from continuing. "*She* made sure blame fell where it was deserved."

He can't make eye contact with me. From the moment he started speaking, he's done everything in his power to avoid looking directly at me.

"She only did it because you made her. Stop trying to dodge accountability for your actions. You need to let me in the house right now, Ryan. Because whatever you're hiding is putting your daughter at risk. You and I have a lot to discuss, and we can do it here or while you're in handcuffs."

He winces. Nods. Steps aside.

Before I can walk past him, his phone beeps, and he freezes.

"Need to get that?"

His expression goes blank. Slowly, like that'll keep me from seeing what he's doing, he moves his hand to cover his pocket. "It's nothing."

"You're not acting like it's nothing." My heart beats faster.

There's another ding. And another.

Ryan looks like he's going to throw up.

FORTY-ONE
RYAN

4:29 p.m.

Tick tock.

Want to see another picture? I want 500k.

I know where you bank. They're closed now, but online banking is always open.

I can't respond right now, not when Kate's staring at me like she's going to rip my head off the moment she catches on that I've been delaying telling her the truth.

I shouldn't have checked the text to be honest. I should have ignored it, but I've been on edge, waiting for the next one, waiting for this unknown person to reach out, to ruin everything, to drive me one step closer to madness.

"Friend of yours?" Kate crosses her arms and jerks her chin at my phone.

I mumble something. Shove it back into my pocket.

We should have the money to pay the ransom. I could get

Nealie back, but when I checked our online banking after the threatening texts started, it wasn't there.

It was supposed to be in our business accounts, but it's gone. Skimmed off the top of every account for months. Years. My hands sweat, and I wipe them on my pants.

Someone took the money I need to save my daughter. Some asshole has been swiping money from our business account. I've been trying to track it down, trying to figure out who it was, but they're good. Smart.

Hell, I'd admire them if I didn't want to kill them.

And then it stopped right when Daniel left the firm.

Even though I should ignore these texts, I can't. Kate's breathing down my neck, and it's dangerous, but I yank my phone back out of my pocket and fire off a quick response.

I need more time.

The text is desperate—I know it. But I say a little prayer that it will work, that I'll be able to buy enough time to find the money.

But first I have to find who the hell took it.

Was it Daniel?

FORTY-TWO
ALISON

4:31 p.m.

I watched from the road as Carrie hurried to the willow in her backyard. A moment later, Ryan followed her. My stomach clenched as he pushed his way through the branches to join her.

He left a moment later, but I'm still stuck here, still watching like something's going to happen. Carrie's hidden by the tree. She still hasn't moved. By now, Ryan's in the house, maybe settling on the sofa, maybe wondering where I am.

Now's my chance.

I feel conspicuous as I glance left to right, checking the road to see if anyone's watching me. Nobody seems to be, and I take a deep breath and steel myself before striding around the side of the house. I'm getting closer and closer to Carrie's tree. If she were to pop out now and see me, what would she think?

I can't worry about that.

The hair on the back of my neck prickles as I hurry through the side door and into their house. It's cool in here, and quiet, but I don't linger in the kitchen. I try to keep as quiet as possible as I race up the stairs, beelining to the bedroom.

Once inside Carrie and Daniel's bedroom, I stop. What am I doing here? What am I hoping to find? I... don't know. I hate the knowledge that someone broke into our house, that they were poking around, and I'm driven by the desire to do the same to someone else, even though I don't think I'll find any secrets here.

Still, I walk around the bedroom, relying on the fading light through the windows instead of turning on the overhead light. If Carrie were to walk around the front of the house, look up, and see the light on in her bedroom, she'd freak.

There are matching bedside tables. One is free from everything but a lamp. I'm sure it's Daniel's since the other holds hand cream, ChapStick, and a glass of water in addition to a matching lamp.

I sit down on Carrie's side of the bed, which is still unmade from the morning. My hand trembles as I slide open the drawer on her nightstand. Inside is a pen and notebook.

She'd lose it if she caught me snooping.

But she won't. I don't plan on being in here long, and if she comes in, I'll hide.

There's a voice in the back of my head telling me that this is a stupid idea, but I do my best to shut it up, then lift out the notebook. The cover is a swirl of pink and gold, and I flip it open, turning pages to get to the most recent entry.

It's from yesterday. Before I start reading, I hold my breath, listening for any sound in the house. There's nothing, and even though I know I need to be careful, that I tend to lose track of time when I'm reading, I can't stop myself.

Daniel doesn't see that what he's done has ruined our family. I'm not sure how I'm going to handle this, how we can come back from—

I lean back on her bed to keep reading when something falls out of the journal. "Crap," I mutter, putting the notebook down next to me on the bed and dropping to the floor to pick up the pieces of paper.

Only they're not just pieces of paper—they're photos. An involuntary smile curls my lips as I flip through them, but it quickly slides off my face.

I'm not in any of them. But Ryan's in all of them.

The sound of the front door closing makes me stop. As carefully as possible, I put them back in the notebook, close it, and slip it into the drawer. It's silly, but I say a little prayer as I push it closed.

It's silent, thank goodness.

I stand, well aware that most houses have a spot on the floor that creaks and I don't know where it is. I can't very well hide up here, not when Carrie's bound to come upstairs eventually. I have to get downstairs, have to get out of here. Tiptoeing so I make as little noise as possible, I work my way to the bedroom door, then out into the hall.

Once in the hall, I pause. The stairs are enclosed, which means I can't see down them without actually going down them. The feeling is claustrophobic, like the hall is suddenly narrowing in on me.

I reach the top step and pause.

Nothing.

The next step. Still nothing. A trickle of sweat races down my back as I squat to try to see the first floor of the house. There's no sound, no movement that I can see. Carrie must be in the kitchen or living room. I don't have a way to tell where she is.

I take a deep breath. Hold it. Exhale and count to three, then I hurry down the stairs as quickly as possible, grateful for the thick carpet runner racing up the middle of the stairs. In the hall, I don't pause, I don't slow down. I race for the front door, the skin on the back of my neck crawling as I throw it open and step outside.

Instinct tells me to slam the door so it's closed as quickly as possible, but I force myself to slow down and carefully close it behind me. The long sidewalk stretches out to the street, and I take a step towards it, but then stop.

No way will I make it all the way to the street without being seen. Someone, probably Carrie, will see me running like a fool away from her house and put two and two together. It's stupid to sit here on her porch, but it might be the better option. Even though it goes against everything I want to do, instead of making a run for it, I walk to the side of the porch and drop down onto the swing.

My heart hammers in my chest. On the street, cruisers glide slowly back and forth. Uniformed officers are still combing the neighborhood, but it feels fruitless at this point.

I drop my head into my hands to think. The only contact we've had with the kidnapper has been via the ransom note, and I swear I would have seen it in the backyard. It's so wild to me that it just... showed up.

Before I can think too much on that, the front door opens. I stiffen, then slowly lift my head to face Carrie. She's going to be pissed—I know she is. I'll have to explain my presence, but I can tell her I came here to sit and think after talking to her. I can deal with her anger; I'm sure of it.

But it's not Carrie. It's that officer, the one who's been attached at the hip with the detective. She closes the door carefully behind her, then exhales hard. I'm staring at her profile, taking in her strong jaw, the slight bump in her nose. She gives her head a little shake, then turns and hurries down the stairs.

She didn't see me.

It seems hard to believe, but she was so focused on getting out of the house and hurrying to the street that she didn't look at the porch. She never saw me sitting here, thank goodness.

I stand and force myself to follow her. She's on the street now, going to talk to a handful of officers. I keep my eyes locked on her before cutting across the yard towards my house. As I walk, I think and pull out my phone.

She could have been in Carrie's house on official business. Maybe she came to interview Carrie again after what happened with Daniel. Maybe she was looking for some kind of evidence, or taking photos of the crime scene, but I don't get the feeling that's what she was doing.

She looked... furtive. Like she was there for the same reason I was—to snoop.

No. Stop. I'm exhausted, and my imagination is running away with me. There's no reason why she'd be snooping. She's a police officer. They don't *snoop*. They gather evidence.

I pause and tap the Uber app. The drive to get out of Blackwood, to find out what's really going on, is so strong I can't avoid it any longer. I'd thought that taking a walk and getting away from the house would be enough, but I was wrong. The file on Theo only makes me more unsure of what's going on. I enter the address and turn to walk towards the entrance. I'm taking action. I'm *doing* something.

Still...

There's something about the officer that feels familiar. Something I can't put my finger on.

FORTY-THREE
KATE

4:37 p.m.

I study Ryan for any signs that he might snap. Whatever those texts were, they seemed enough to put him over the edge. He's doing everything in his power to avoid making eye contact with me. It's clear from the expression on his face that he's barely holding it together.

I have to remember: he's a liar. He could be dangerous. Just because we used to have a relationship, have a close connection, doesn't mean I can trust him. It doesn't mean anything.

Not now. Not ever, if I'm honest with myself.

He stalks back and forth across the living room, his hands alternately perched on his hips and running through his hair. He wears a scowl on his face, the same one I've seen when he's losing a case, which isn't often.

Finally, he turns, his eyes dark, and stares at me.

"It was all Alison's idea."

Does he think I'm an idiot? "Yeah, I don't believe that," I tell him. "I need you to tell me the truth. I want to know exactly what happened."

"This has nothing to do with Nealie going missing."

"Oh, please." I straighten up. As nice as this sofa looks, it's uncomfortable. In fact... I glance around the room, not really surprised that everything looks like it was chosen for its aesthetics, not for its practicality or comfort.

That's the way Ryan has always presented himself—aloof and untouchable. He's not the type of man you joke around with after a case. He's the person who handles what needs to be done, puts people in their places, and deals with problems.

This is the first time I've ever seen him so upset. He's unfocused, flighty. Never in his life has Ryan not been in control of a situation, and it's wearing on him.

"Listen, Ryan," I say, and he stops pacing to look at me, "I know you want to think you're untouchable, that nothing bad could ever happen to you, but look at what's going on right now. Nealie is missing. What you and Alison did to Daniel isn't worth keeping hidden any longer if it means we can bring her home. You made Alison forge his signature."

That gets his attention.

"I didn't do anything. It was all Alison." His eyes are wide. Desperate. Like he's actually going to be able to convince me of his innocence.

I know how men like Ryan work. They make the decisions. They come up with the plan. Then, when they have a woman in their life ready and willing to do whatever it is they want, they step back and watch all the pieces fall where they may.

No way do I believe Ryan's hands are clean of whatever happened with Daniel, but I can play this game.

"Ryan, I don't know how to get through to you on this. Alison may have screwed up big time, but at least she seems to understand the severity of the situation. Nealie is missing. She may be dead, injured, tortured. We don't know." I pause to let that sink in. "So whatever you're trying to keep from me right now? It's not that big in the grand scheme of things. Tell me what happened."

He stares at me, our eyes locked. It would feel intimate, but I'm past that.

We both are.

"I was going to lose my job," he finally says, and I'm so surprised that my jaw drops open a little. "Shocking, right?" He nods at me. "I screwed up a case. You know the Fred Alan embezzlement?"

"I do." I didn't work it, but I still know about it. Everyone in the department does.

"Right. Well, I screwed up, and Fred went to prison."

"He's an embezzler," I point out. "Prison is what he deserves."

"You'd think that, but he was innocent." I roll my eyes, and he shakes his head. "I'm serious, Kate. He was innocent. I knew it. Alison knew it. She knew all the details of the case..." His voice trails off, a fleeting expression on his face. There and gone, like he just realized something.

I want to know more, to know what he just thought of, but I don't want to interrupt him, not when he's finally starting to talk.

He clears his throat. "It wasn't Fred. It was his partner, Luke. Luke's the one who was taking all that money, and I screwed up. I failed Fred, and he's locked up now."

"You can fix it," I tell him.

"Luke's gone. In the wind. He took all the proof I needed. Burned it or buried it or stuffed it in a safety deposit box somewhere and threw away the key. I don't know. Point is, it's gone. And without it, Fred's in prison."

"*You* screwed up, but Daniel got fired."

"Right." He exhales hard and drops into an overstuffed leather seat across from me. "The family was out for blood thanks to my screw-up. But Alison is great at signing other people's signatures, and—"

"You were more than happy to let someone else take the fall for you..."

He hangs his head. He's not ashamed—Ryan Brown has never been ashamed of anything in his life. But he's finally being honest with me.

I think.

"That's... not all we did. We adjusted some evidence. Lost some things. Alison helped with everything; she ensured it was airtight when we were finished."

"Why would she willingly do that?"

He pauses. Shakes his head.

Because he made her do it.

It's written on his face, clear as day. Just like Julie said.

"Alright. Good. Thank you for coming clean with me about that." This is something I'm going to have to handle later, when the girls are found. Ryan must know it because he rubs his eyes and looks at me.

"Is Alison going to get in trouble for what she did? Or am I?"

"Both of you are." I let that sink in and watch as his face falls. "But I'm not worried about that right now," I tell him. "What I'm worried about is how your actions are related to the girls going missing."

He's already shaking his head. "I don't think they are. I know you're looking for any connections that you could find, and that's a good thing, but I don't think there's one here. We don't need to grasp at straws."

"Ryan." I'm speaking as gently as possible, especially because he looks like he's about to come out of his skin. First Nealie going missing, and now this with Alison? The man isn't stupid, and I'm sure he's aware that there are going to be severe consequences for what he and his wife did, and for the fact that he hid the truth, putting an innocent man in prison. "Right now, I don't have anything but straws. There aren't any signs of the girls. You two screwed up and placed the blame on Daniel. Don't act surprised that I think what you and Alison did is the reason your daughter is missing." I pause, thinking. "Unless there's someone else out there who also hates you this much?"

He shakes his head. "No, nobody. Quit trying to blame me for this!"

"I'm not blaming any of you. You didn't kidnap the girls," I say, but I'm watching him for any sign that I'm hitting close to home, for any sign that he might be involved in them going missing. "But you might be the reason this all happened. We're digging into everyone who interacts with them, everyone who might have so much as *looked* at them, and you know what we're finding? Solid alibis. For every. Single. Person. That means we have to look closer to home. It's our only choice."

"Out." He stands, pointing at the door behind me. "Get out of my house."

"Ryan, listen." I don't want to leave, but I stand as well, if only to placate him. "I know you're upset. This is a nightmare. I'm not saying you *did* anything to your girls, but someone did, and it might be because of you."

Fear flashes on his face, then another emotion takes its place, but it's quickly overshadowed by rage.

"How dare you come into my house and accuse me of having something to do with Nealie and Emma going missing? This isn't on me!"

I don't respond.

"I want you off the case."

"Not going to happen." I turn away from him and walk towards the front door, but before leaving, I face him again. "And do you want to know why that won't happen? Because I'm the best, and the chief wouldn't dare remove me from a case where we have to make sure two girls are safe. Be angry at me, I don't care. But don't fight this. Come clean with me about what you know."

"I don't know anything." He reaches past me and flings open the front door. "Out."

"Going," I say, and I step out onto the porch. The afternoon was painfully hot, but the sun is finally starting to cool. I feel like I can breathe out here, away from Ryan's rage.

And his guilt.

That's what I saw on his face. A mixture of understanding, like something finally clicked, and guilt.

I don't think Ryan took his little girl. But I'd bet anything he knows who did.

FORTY-FOUR
JULIE

4:52 p.m.

Before I became a nanny, I was really good at cracking people's passwords. It comes in handy when finding information to blackmail the families I work for.

Even though I'm good at it, I'd never use my skills in my personal life. Sure, sometimes I wish I could read Theo's mind to know exactly what he thinks about our future, but I wouldn't ever put myself in a position where I'd have to lie to him about reading his texts or emails.

Until now.

He pulls up to my apartment building, and we sit in silence for a moment. I don't know what he's thinking about, but I can't stop going over and over what I just saw on his phone.

The mature thing to do would be to ask him about the text. But I can't do that. Not now. Not when it's clear he's been lying to me.

Who is he talking to about me? And what do they know?

"I'm sorry you have to work," I lie.

He shrugs. "Me too. But I like having a paycheck. And I

need to keep an eye on the Blackwood security cameras. Make sure we don't miss anything, anyone coming in and out today who looks suspicious."

I freeze. "The security cameras! That's it! Is it possible—"

Theo's already shaking his head. "I wish, but no. Everything was down last night. I already explained this to Alison."

"They were down for everyone?"

Theo sighs. "I know you don't understand how this all works, but I do. Trust me, okay?"

Jerk. He's lying to me. Possibly cheating on me. And now treating me like an idiot?

I murmur my assent, force myself to lean in for a kiss, because that's what I'd normally do, then get out of the car. I slam the door. Throw him a wave. I feel incredibly self-conscious as I enter the building and walk up to my apartment. It's only when I'm inside that I don't feel his eyes on me any longer.

I sigh as I close and lock the door. Theo has a key to my apartment, has had one since I signed the lease on this place, and I slide the security chain into place.

Am I afraid of him? No.

Then why did I use the chain?

There's probably a simple explanation that, if I knew it, would make everything make sense. Maybe the burner is for work. Maybe it's so he can keep in touch with old friends without letting them bleed into his everyday life. Lord knows we don't try to make friends when we move to a new city. It's best to blend in, be forgettable.

But who was texting him? It didn't sound like a friend.

I don't remove the chain.

"I'm being ridiculous," I say to myself, but my voice sounds small and unsure in the silence of my apartment. In the entire time that I've lived here, I've felt like this place is tiny, like I bump into the walls and furniture anytime I move around.

But now the space feels cavernous. Grabbing my laptop and phone, I hurry to the sofa and wrap a blanket around myself. It only takes me a moment to log out of my Facebook account and into his.

He didn't change the password.

That means he has nothing to hide, right?

My gut twists and my hand shakes as I navigate the mouse over to click on his messages. I've already breached his trust twice today. I've always trusted Theo with everything.

But I don't right now.

"Right." I exhale hard and click, causing all of his most recent messages to appear in a drop-down. Some of them are older, and I recognize most of the names, but the few newest ones are unfamiliar to me.

I hesitate, then click on one from Hunter Saltz.

Thanks for the heads-up about Vinnie's.

Vinnie's is a sandwich place in town, and a quick click on Hunter's profile tells me the two of them must have met in a bar. Nothing to see there.

I click on another unfamiliar name. Tabitha Gray.

Their conversation is longer, and the more I read back in their messages, the more curious I become.

I hope we can meet one day.

That one was from him by the way. She gave it a heart. When I see that, I almost close the laptop and put it away, but instead I keep scrolling back.

And back.

And back.

Their conversation began before the two of us moved here.

Does Theo have an online girlfriend?

I... guess that makes sense. He couldn't very well start dating someone in the towns we go to, not when we've been together as long as we have, and not when we spend all of our free time together. But online you can be whoever you want to be. And I have to remember the websites I saw in his search history.

"Wait," I say, forcing myself to slow down and read some of their messages. The tone is overly friendly, like they've known each other for years, but then I see something that pops out at me.

FamilyDNA.com.

My heart starts beating faster.

Looks like Theo went digging and found some of his family, but he never told me. All he's ever said about his family is that he was raised by his mom and that she struggled to make ends meet. It always killed him that he never had a father figure in his life and that he had to work to contribute to the house as soon as he was old enough to get a job, scanning groceries at the local grocery store.

His dad? Deadbeat.

Grandparents? He only knew the ones on his mom's side. They lived halfway across the country, and he only saw them three times before they died when he was a teen.

Any other siblings? Just the possibility of half-siblings he doesn't know.

Now my head really is swimming as I try to think through the implications of this. He obviously wanted to know about his dad and his side of the family and turned to spitting in a tube to do that.

Thousands of people do that every year. Millions maybe. This isn't anything out of the ordinary, not when you consider how many people find unknown family all the time. It even makes the news! More than once, I've read articles about people finding out they have dozens of siblings because their biological dad didn't abide by sperm donor rules.

Not that I think Theo suddenly has a family the size of Connecticut, but it looks like it's bigger than he thought it was.

But then why hasn't he ever told me about her? *Tabitha*. I say her name out loud, but it's as unfamiliar to hear as it was to see.

When I click to her profile, I'm sorely disappointed. While I didn't think there would be all of her personal life history on display, it's so locked down I can only see her profile picture.

Which, of course, is the tree of life. It seems ironic, and a sneer curls my lip.

I don't have any problem with Theo digging into his family tree and finding family. That would be insane of me to take issue with. What I do find frustrating is that he never once told me about what he was looking for—or what he found.

I don't even know what relation Tabitha is. He knows his mom's side of the family, but his dad has always been a mystery. He must have gone looking for him and found... a cousin? An aunt? A *sister*? With a few flicks of my finger, I scroll through their chat, but they moved it offline shortly after connecting.

Strange that I didn't see texts from her when I went through his phone. Unless he deleted them. Or she's who he's texting on his burner.

A chill races up my spine.

Besides dropping by to send memes to each other, they don't use Facebook messenger to keep in touch. Hope rises in me when I see a phone number in the chat, but it's Theo's, not Tabitha's.

I log out of his Facebook and chew on my cuticle before closing the laptop. Snooping was supposed to make me feel better. It was supposed to remove any worry or concern I had over what Theo was doing, but it did the exact opposite.

Somehow, I know both more and less about him than I ever did before.

I could ask him. I *should* ask him. But in order to find out the truth, I'd have to come clean with him about snooping in his Facebook, and I can't do that.

My thumb bleeds along the edge of the nail, and I absent-mindedly suck it as I think.

I can't ask Theo.

But what else is he hiding from me?

FORTY-FIVE
ALISON

5:06 p.m.

The tires catch in the gravel on the side of the road, and the steering wheel jerks to the right. My Uber driver swears, slamming on the brakes and pulling the wheel back as hard as he can. With a groan, the car centers in the lane, and he presses his foot all the way down on the brake. To the right of the road is a drop-off, one that leads down into a deep ravine. There was a guardrail here, but a semi took it out a few months ago and the state hasn't replaced it yet.

It's only when we come to a complete stop in the middle of the road that I realize what just happened.

I almost died.

Right here, just a mile from home. But isn't that the statistic? That most people will die within three miles of their home? It's something like that, but my body is flooded with adrenaline, and it's too difficult for me to think straight.

"Did you fall asleep?" I screech the words, unable to keep the anger out of my voice. "What were you doing?"

"I'm so sorry!" The kid driving looks about nineteen. He has shaggy bangs that he keeps pushing out of his face. "I'm sorry!"

"Oh my God." I lean back in my seat, my heart still going a mile a minute.

I'd been so engrossed in my own thoughts that I'd forgotten I was even in the car. Now, though, a slick of sweat blooms on my skin. I feel hot and cold at the same time, like I'm going to throw up.

I'd been thinking about Nealie. Of course. Wondering where she could be. Wondering if she's okay.

And I was thinking about Carrie.

She knows what I've been keeping from Ryan. And since getting in the car, I've pictured us alone together in her house.

She'd been in my face. Rude. What would have happened if she'd gotten aggressive? If I'd pushed her.

If she'd hit her head on the way down?

She already had a bandage there. It would be impossible for doctors to tell that she was hit again, right?

Nobody knew I'd even been there.

It would have been so easy. Shove her. Trip her. Knock her over.

Nobody would know what I did. I imagine how her head would snap to the side when she hit it, how blood would ooze out and leak down her temple, how she might reach for me, her nails raking down my arms, how muffled her cries would be before they just... stopped.

Shaking my head, I push the thought away. Carrie used to be my friend. I wouldn't hurt her.

But why hasn't she told anyone what I did? Not what I did to Daniel—that's between Ryan and me, and I hope she never finds out—but the other thing, the one I thought I'd hidden so well.

I never should have told her.

I can beat myself up over that all day long, but it doesn't

matter. What matters is that she doesn't seem interested in throwing me under the bus.

She's keeping my secret.

For now.

But I can't figure out why or what she might be planning.

All I know is that I had to get out of there. Out of her pantry, out of her house, out of Blackwood. But I wasn't just running away. I'm going somewhere important. Or... I hope I am, or I wouldn't dare leave Blackwood while Nealie was missing. Maybe it's silly to go there, but I can't help myself. Why in the world does Ryan have a file on our nanny's boyfriend? There has to be a reason, and I'm going to find it.

Someone behind us honks.

"Get me there. In one piece." I dig my nails into my thighs as the kid nods and presses down on the gas, slowly coming back up to speed. From my position in the backseat, I can see how flushed his neck is. He's embarrassed.

He sniffles.

And he's crying.

But I don't care about him. I can't, not when I have so many other thoughts racing through my mind. What I should do is go home and wait for the cops, but the thought of being in the same house with Ryan right now makes me sick.

So does the thought of the detective hanging around.

Ten minutes later, we pull up in front of a small house. "We're here," the kid says.

I hear him but don't respond. I don't know what's come over me. Instinctively, I know I should go home, should be there for Nealie, should not do what I'm about to. But I have my phone with me. If the cops find anything or have to get in touch with me, they can do that. And really—what's more useful? Sitting at the house hoping someone will have information and bring it to me, or going out and trying to get it myself?

I used to sit around, wait for other people to take control, but not anymore.

After slipping my phone into my pocket, I ask the kid to wait for me, then hurry up to the front door. It's a small house, more of a bungalow, with lanky grass and plenty of weeds in the front. I ignore all of that, and I ignore how my stomach twists as I step up onto the small front porch.

Raise my hand.

Knock.

There's no bell, so when nobody answers right away, I knock again, really pounding the side of my fist into the door. I hear the way the sound reverberates, then it dies away.

Still nobody answers.

"Please," I say, hurrying to a front window and cupping my hands around my eyes so I can look inside. "Please, I need to talk to you."

I have to know why Ryan would be so interested in this person.

The glass is cleaner than I would have thought it would be, and I can see right inside, but it doesn't look like anyone is home. The living room boasts a small sofa and coffee table, both free of any clutter.

There's a blue rug on the floor, the edge of it turned up, but that's the only sign that this space isn't magazine-ready. I let my eyes drift around the room, taking in unsurprising beige art on the walls. Try as I might to see into whatever other rooms are off this living room, I can't get the angle right.

Without thinking about what I'm doing, I walk around back and try the door. To my surprise, it twists easily under my hand. I hesitate for a moment, then push it open and step inside, quickly closing the door behind me.

It smells good in here, like lilacs. Room spray, I'm sure of it, since I don't see any flowers on display. I take a step across the floor, then another, and then it hits me what I just did.

Breaking and entering.

Sweat breaks out along my brow, and I wipe it off. What would the detective say if she pulled up here and saw me? If she knew I'd broken in? I can't imagine being in jail when they bring Nealie home.

Turning, I reach for the front door, but something stops me. I've already screwed up. Running out of the house right now won't undo what I've already done, so I might as well keep looking.

I walk through the bathroom, but my eyes don't focus on much. A blue toothbrush, a pink one. No surprise there, not when he's dating Julie.

The kitchen then. Going into the bedroom feels so much more intimate, and I don't think I'm ready for that yet.

I ignore the voice in my head as I stand in the middle of the galley kitchen. Just like the living room, everything is neat and put away. I take in the knives hanging on the magnetic strip by the stove, the kettle pushed to the side, the wooden cutting boards leaning in the corner.

Without thinking about what I'm doing, I walk to the fridge. Ours is covered with family photos and Nealie's artwork, but this one is mostly bare. I glance at the monthly calendar stuck right at eye level, but that's it. There's one magnet holding it in place. A second magnet sticks to the fridge, but whatever it was holding there is gone.

"Or it fell," I mutter to myself. I drop to my knees and run my fingers under the fridge, but they come back empty. Shifting to the side, I grab my phone and switch on the flashlight, angling it along the side of the fridge where it meets the cabinets.

There.

It's almost out of reach, but I grit my teeth and shove my hand harder into the little space, gasping with excitement when the tips of my fingers press together, the corner of the paper between them.

It's a photo of two people.

I drop my phone to the floor and look at the photo, trying to make sense of what I'm seeing. I know the man, even though this is an older photo and he's aged a lot since then. He has his arm slung around a woman's shoulders, a huge grin on both of their faces. They're standing close together, like they couldn't be happier to be in each other's company.

What I don't understand is why this old photo of Ryan fell next to someone else's fridge.

FORTY-SIX
JULIE

5:22 p.m.

My mind spins with thoughts of the woman Theo's been in contact with.

Tabitha.

I'd do anything to know her relation to him.

The only way for me to get to the bottom of this now that I can't trust him to tell me the truth is to do my own research. But I have to be careful—there is so much on the line. Not when I don't know if anyone is going to find out what Theo and I did.

The last thing I want to do is throw him under the bus, but how do I know he's not planning to do the same to me?

Instead of calling him, I glance around the apartment parking lot, then unlock my car. It's dark unusually early, thick gray clouds bunching up and covering the sky, blocking out the sun. Normally, I'd be thrilled at the thought of a stormy night, of the way the sky will crackle and light up, how thunder shakes my apartment. But I can't enjoy it now, not when Emma and Nealie aren't home.

Without knowing where they are, if they're under shelter or if they're out in the open...

By the time I reach Blackwood, it's starting to rain. Huge drops spatter on my windshield, my wipers thumping hard as they rise and fall. It falls faster, sheets of rain hitting my car, and I double-check my lights. As dark as the sky is thanks to the heavy rain, you'd think it was well past sunset. I make a few turns, slowing down when I pass police cars, then park on the side of the road.

The smart thing to do right now would be to go to the detective. Tell her everything. Try to get ahead of this. Maybe, if I came clean, she'd treat me with leniency. A lighter sentence would be wonderful. But that'll never happen, and I know it, not when I keep lying to her and to so many other people. If I'm honest with myself, no jury would hear what Theo and I have done and look the other way.

Which is why I'm here.

It's stupid, I'm sure of it, but finding the girls might be the only way to avoid getting in trouble for what Theo and I have done. I don't know if it'll really work the way I want it to, but it's the only chance I have.

For another minute, I consider trying to find the detective. I could give her one more bit of info that might help her find the girls. At the very least, it would point the blame away from me. But instead, I'm going to try to handle this myself, even though there's a voice in the back of my head screaming at me that I'm making a terrible mistake.

When everyone has a garage, it's impossible to know who's home. I don't want to run into Alison. Ryan's the one I need to talk to if I'm going to get the answer I want.

He's also the one I'm most afraid of right now.

Taking my phone from the cupholder, I turn it over and over in my hand. The smart thing to do would be to call him and ask him if he has time to meet. But I don't want to show my hand if he doesn't know what I know.

Snooping has consequences. I know that now. I never should have gone poking around where I didn't belong.

This is our last job. I'll never blackmail someone again. Theo and I are over—he's been lying and cheating, and I'm done. But I can't walk away until we find the girls.

My mind spins.

Theo and Tabitha.

Nealie and Emma.

I don't know what to do, who to turn to. I don't know how to handle any of this.

Whatever. I can't wait any longer. Getting out of my car, I flip my hood up over my head and race up to the front porch. The lights inside are all on like a beacon on this gloomy evening, calling Nealie home.

If only it were that easy.

Overhead, the sky opens up, the dark clouds releasing more rain. I blink against the drops, relieved when I finally make it to the porch.

I press the doorbell and step back, my hand slipping into my pocket to finger the house key tucked there. I'll handle this. Then go back to the gazebo and retrieve the folder on Theo. Nobody has to be the wiser. Normally, nobody would bat an eye if I let myself into the house, but tonight's not normal.

And I don't know if I'll ever let myself in again. I'm overcome with the desire to take the key and throw it as hard as I can into the yard, but the grass is perfectly manicured and cut short. It would only be there a day or so before the gardener found it, and that's not nearly as final as dropping it into a river or a lake.

The door opens, and I spin back around. Ryan seems to fill the frame. He's hunched over more than I've seen him in the past, but his shoulders are wide. *He was a linebacker in college.* I remember him telling me that once, then Alison had laughed and said he'd been really popular with the girls.

He'd blushed. She'd laughed.

But now I wonder.

"Julie. What are you doing here?" He doesn't move to the side. Doesn't invite me in. He looks past me, just for a second, like he's checking to see if anyone else is there, then his eyes settle on me again. "Did you need something?"

"Just to talk to you." The wind shifts, and a mist blows up onto the porch. I shiver and wait for an invitation that clearly isn't going to come. "Can I come in?"

He pauses, his face tight, then he nods. Finally, he steps to the side, and I follow him into the foyer.

It's muscle memory that causes me to kick off my shoes, leaving them by the runner. I follow him to the kitchen and watch as he takes a beer from the fridge. He pops the cap and holds it out to me. When I shake my head, he shrugs and takes a long sip.

"What did you need?"

I exhale hard. "First, I wanted to see if you'd gotten any updates about Nealie." And Emma, but I don't say her name. Not yet.

He shakes his head. "Nothing. I wouldn't be here if I knew where she was."

"Right."

"What do you want, Julie?" Another long sip, but his eyes never leave mine. I wanted his attention, I got it, and now I wish I didn't have it.

"The detective thinks there's more connecting you and the Everetts."

He nods but doesn't respond.

I swallow hard and continue. "And she keeps interviewing

me," I tell him. I'm backed up to the counter, and I reach back, grabbing the edge of it and squeezing. The marble is cold and hard. Grounding. "I worry that she thinks I'm the link, that I had something to do with the girls going missing. She might focus on me so much she misses the truth of what happened to the girls."

If she finds out what Theo and I do, she'll use it as ammo to bury us both. The blame for Nealie and Emma will land on our shoulders. Somehow. I have to make sure we find the girls first. Getting Ryan on board is a better option than putting myself back on the detective's radar.

He looks at me. *Really* looks at me. "And are you the link? Would she be right to point the finger at you?"

I shake my head. "No. There's something else tying the girls together. Something bigger than the fact that I nanny both of them." I take a deep breath. Once I continue talking, there's no going back. "And you know it."

"And why are you here telling me this?" He waves his hand at the large windows that cover one entire side of the kitchen. Normally, the view is gorgeous, but now it's dark. Rain lashes against the panes. "Shouldn't you be home where it's nice and dry?"

I should. This is stupid.

He finishes his beer. Thunks the bottle on the counter. Pulls another from the fridge and cracks it open. This time, he doesn't offer me any before he drains half of it.

"I wanted to know if you'd told the detective the real connection between the two girls. It may help them find them faster." I say the words slowly, trying to gauge his mood. Ryan normally wears his emotions on his sleeve, but not when he's been drinking.

When he has a drink in his hand, his emotions get locked up in a little box deep inside him where nobody can get to them.

I've seen it before but have never had to worry about what he was thinking.

Now, though, I'd give anything to be able to read his mind.

"Come on, Julie. Get to the point. What are you trying to say?"

I saw the letter on his desk weeks ago. It was stupid, going into his office, but I'd worked here for months, trying my best to dig up some dirt on him, and it had always been locked. Then, one night, he and Alison went out for dinner, which wasn't unusual. What was strange was that he'd popped back into the house, hurried into his office, left something there, and hurried out.

And he'd forgotten to lock the door.

Of course I was going to snoop. That's why I'm here in the first place.

I saw the letter.

I read it.

Over and over.

The only thing I didn't do—which now I'm thinking I should have—was take a picture of it so I could refer to it again. But the words seared into my head, and I haven't been able to get them out since then. And after that? I had to know the truth to make sure our blackmail would stick. That's why I took Nealie and Emma out of the neighborhood via the back paths. I had to test something, and I couldn't do it here, not when someone might see what I was doing.

"Ryan, I know the truth."

"Of what?" He finishes the beer, but this time he doesn't put it down and get a new one. He stares at me, twisting the bottle around and around.

"Nealie. And Emma."

His eyes darken. "And what truth is that?"

I swallow hard. *This is a mistake, I've really screwed up*

now, I should just leave, pretend this didn't happen, let him think I lost my mind for a moment, run, run, run run runrunrun—

    I take a deep breath.
    "That they're sisters."

FORTY-SEVEN
JULIE

5:31 p.m.

Ryan advances towards me.

He's still got his empty beer bottle in a death grip but is no longer paying any attention to it. His entire focus is on me.

My breath catches in my throat, and I take a step to the side, then another, then another. I'm trying to get away from him, to put some space between the two of us, but he keeps advancing.

And he's moving faster than I am.

"Ryan. What are you doing? Ryan!" I yell his name in his face when he's only a few feet away from me, and that seems to work. He stops, blinks. It's almost like he's coming out of some fugue state and now that he's seeing me, he's not sure what happened.

But his eyes are still dark. His brow is still furrowed. He may be able to hear me now—to listen to me without blowing up—but I don't in any way think that the danger is over.

"How did you find out?" His voice is flat. Low. There's anger there, so much pent-up rage just waiting to be released, and I shiver. The room feels electric, like the storm has moved inside.

I'm afraid to answer, but I don't have a choice.

I did this.

Coming here was stupid. Going to the detective, even if it meant I'd be punished, would have been smarter than this. I've been so desperate to avoid any suspicion, to prevent her from having any reason to look closely at me, that I just did the single most stupid thing I possibly could have.

My mouth is dry, and I have to swallow hard to speak. "I saw the letter." I don't mention that after seeing the letter, I immediately DNA tested the girls. Just to double-check.

He'd kill me if he knew—I honestly believe he would.

"The letter."

It's not a question, but I nod and respond like it is. "From Carrie."

"The letter I put on my desk. In my office."

"Ye-es." My voice falters.

He takes another step towards me.

Without thinking, I throw my hands up between us. "I didn't mean to. I'm sorry! It... was there, and the door was open after you ran back into the house from the car, and I looked." My heart hammers, and I swallow hard again. "I didn't mean to do it, and I didn't mean to find something out like that."

Ryan closes his eyes. He's breathing slow. Hard. Like he can't quite get himself under control. I watch as his hand squeezes the beer bottle so tightly I swear it could shatter.

Finally, he exhales, his eyes locking on me. "You're how he found out. Theo. You're the reason he knew about the girls. It was you. You greedy bitch."

"I'm sorry! It was stupid, and I made a mistake." I take a too shallow breath. "But we didn't take the girls. We wouldn't. I promise!"

He groans and scrubs his hand down his cheek.

He might have enough self-control not to hurt me, but that doesn't mean he doesn't want to.

"I'm sorry."

"Carrie's always been a romantic," he says, his voice soft. His gaze sharpens. "Putting a letter like that in our mailbox? Even though she addressed it to me, how the hell was she going to guarantee that Alison wouldn't open it and read it? And then what would happen? Everything would fall apart."

"Everything did fall apart," I whisper. "Ryan, you've been hiding this terrible secret. Are you sure you don't have any idea who might have taken the girls?"

He turns to me, and even though I thought asking him that question might be safe, now I'm wishing I hadn't. It's the way he's standing, one foot slightly forward like he's going to start running, his shoulders hunched a bit like he's going to go for a hit.

Linebacker.

I could run. The idea of making a break for it flits in and out my mind, too fast for me to hang on to it.

Would he follow? Would he let me go?

Sweat breaks out on my palms. My mouth was dry before, but now my tongue sticks to the roof of my mouth. I'm dying to run, to move, for him to say *something*, but he's just watching me with those dark eyes, an unreadable expression on his face.

"Julie," he finally says, and hearing him say my name is even worse than him not speaking. I don't like the way it rolls around in his mouth like he's sucking all the flavor off of it, like when he finishes tasting it there won't be anything left.

"What?" My voice, on the other hand, is a whisper.

Outside, the wind picks up. A branch scratches against the window, and I jump.

"Them being half-sisters doesn't matter."

I don't know if he wants me to agree or not, so I nod. "Right," I say, the tip of my tongue flicking out to lick my lower lip. "Right, of course it doesn't. It was stupid of me to think it might have anything to do with them going missing."

He nods. "Good." He pauses, then clears his throat. "Do you think you need to tell anyone?"

"No."

Yes, yes, yes, yesyesyesyesyesyes—

All the saliva in my mouth dries up. My tongue is thick, like it's going to choke me. I take a step back from him, my panic clearly showing on my face.

"Don't lie to me." He takes a step towards me. "I'm not an idiot. Once the girls are home safe, I'm going to deal with you."

"Deal with me?"

"You're gone. Do you understand? You and your boyfriend."

There's no response to that. I never should have come here, and now I don't know how to get away.

When Ryan speaks again, his voice is dark. "You should leave. Before Alison gets home."

I nod. This was a terrible idea. I don't know what I thought would happen, but this isn't it.

I spin around, the hair on the back of my neck standing up when I realize my back is now turned to him, that he could do anything and I wouldn't know it was coming.

My socks slip on the kitchen tile. Once I'm in the hall, I can barely control myself, and I race to the front door. Shove my feet into my shoes. Grab the doorknob.

Throw the door open.

Without slowing down enough to see what's going on out there, I barrel outside.

Right into the detective.

FORTY-EIGHT
KATE

5:38 p.m.

Julie slams into me, and, without thinking, I wrap my arms around her to keep us both from falling to the porch.

"Julie!" She squirms in my grasp, but I hold her tighter. "Hey! What's going on? Are you okay?"

She twists around, her eyes wide, her mouth falling open when she sees who I am.

"Detective," she says, then exhales hard.

When I realize she's no longer fighting me, I let her go, carefully releasing her, then step back to look at her.

The girl looks terrified. I glance past her, fully expecting someone to be chasing after her, but the hallway inside the house is empty. "Who were you running from just now? Did something happen?"

"No, everything's fine." She wipes her hands on her jeans and glances over her shoulder, but still there's nobody. "I just wanted to get home and was in a hurry."

I think fast. "Who were you talking to, Alison or Ryan?"

She blinks. "Ryan."

Good. Just the man I came to talk to. Again.

"About what?" I eyeball her.

"Just... the girls. And where they might be." She's talking faster now, clearly making it up as she goes along, but I allow it so I can see where she ends up. "He wanted to know if there was anywhere they really like to go, anywhere I'd take them that might be off the beaten path a bit."

"And you didn't think this was a conversation I should be looped in on?"

She has the decency to blush.

"You're hiding something." I pin her in place with a stare. Behind her, I see movement, and my brain registers the fact that Ryan is walking slowly down the hall towards us.

She twists her hands together.

"There's somewhere else you take them. Somewhere you didn't tell me, isn't there, Julie?"

"Yes." Her face is pale, and her hands are shaking. Whatever happened in that house was enough to terrify her. I would normally try to help her through her fear, but she's unsteady right now. She might slip up if I keep pushing.

"I thought so. Where else have you taken the girls?" I'm onto something—I can feel it. Julie can try to hide the truth from me, she can distract me and subvert the truth, but I've been doing this long enough to know when I'm being lied to.

Everyone here is lying, and I'm sick of it.

"There are trails," she says, her voice growing quieter. "I found them one afternoon when out walking with Nealie. She'd been a handful that day, running around, darting here and there, so I challenged her to see if she could run as far as I could."

She falls silent, but I don't speak. These trails she's talking about? They're important—I can tell they are. I need to know more.

"And we found them. There's a privacy fence across the back of the playground separating the neighborhood from the public park it butts up against. Nealie saw a little kitten scoot under the fence and followed it. There's a gap you can squeeze through if you push. It's tight, but she made it, and I followed. We found the trails." She clears her throat and gives her head a little shake. "I know I shouldn't have let her explore, but she was wild that day and needed to burn off some energy. The trails are so nice, and they meander through some woods and then down by the creek, so that's a lot of fun. It's much nicer to be down there when it's hot out than it is to be on the playground in the burning heat." She glances at me like she's hoping I'm going to tell her she didn't do anything wrong.

"Did their parents know where you were taking them?"

She's silent for a moment. "No, I never said anything. And I don't think they know about the trails. You'd have to go to the public park they run through and look for them, and neither the Browns nor the Everetts are outdoorsy people. Besides, you know Ryan. He would have had a fit if he ever thought I was taking Nealie anywhere besides the *approved locations*." She makes air quotes around the words, her mouth twisted.

Yes, I can perfectly imagine how Ryan would have reacted.

From what I know about him, from what he's shown me, no way would he have been okay with Julie taking the girls anywhere outside of where he'd already approved. It wouldn't have mattered to him if there were a dozen puppies for the girls to play with, if they were as safe as can be, Ryan doesn't like it when things happen that he's not expecting.

"I need you to show me these trails," I tell her. "Now. Before it gets completely dark." Overhead, lightning lights up the sky, and thunder makes Julie shake. She wraps her arms around herself and runs her hands up and down her arms.

"It's pouring," she points out.

"I don't care. You could have told us about the trails when it was the middle of the day and not raining, but you didn't. Now I have to try to fix what you did. Do you have a poncho?"

She starts to chew the side of her thumb but catches herself and shoves her hands into her pockets instead. "No."

"Okay. I have a few in my car." I jerk my head towards my car. Behind her, Ryan is standing outside his front door now. I slip my hand into my pocket and press the button on my fob to unlock my car. I'm not facing the driveway, but I see how the lights cast my shadow onto the house when they flash. "Go get one out of the back. I'll be right there."

Julie pauses for a moment, but when I flick my wrist at her, she takes off from the porch like a shot. As soon as she's a few feet away, I turn to Ryan.

"What were you two talking about?"

He doesn't answer.

"Ryan. You're lying. She's lying. All of you are lying, and I can't do my damn job unless you come clean with me!" I punch my right fist into my left hand, but Ryan doesn't blink. He stares into the rain, watching Julie, I'm sure of it, then looks at me.

"Are you and Julie sleeping together?" I ask.

My phone beeps, and I glance at the screen, irritated at the interruption.

Nothing at Julie's apartment. Landlord said she's a dream renter and to come back with a warrant if I want to know more.

I pocket my phone and look at Ryan, the expression on my face spurring him to answer.

"What? No." He scoffs, but the anger I hear in his voice is so real I believe him. "Sleeping with the nanny? I wouldn't do that."

"You've been sleeping around town. Do you think one of the women you were having an affair with is involved with this?" I rattle off the names Julie gave me during her interview.

"I've sent officers to talk to them, of course. But so far, nothing. Still, there's a good possibility one of them knows something. What do you think?"

"They wouldn't."

"You don't think so? Maybe to punish you for sleeping with so many women? Jealousy is ugly, Ryan. There's no telling what a scorned lover might do if they thought you'd screwed them over."

Something flashes across his face. It's not anger. It's different.

Concern.

Worry.

Fear.

"That's it," I say, taking a step closer to him. "You think someone took the girls because of something you did. Maybe not one of the women you're sleeping with but someone else. What did you do, Ryan?"

My mind keeps coming back to the Everetts. It's one thing to take the child of someone who pissed you off, who ruined your life, but another entirely to put your own child in jeopardy. Most people wouldn't do that. Most parents would willingly put themselves in danger rather than allow something to happen to their child.

"Tell me," I say softly, my mind racing as I speak, the words halting. "Who did you hurt? Besides Daniel?"

He turns from me, already reaching out for his front door, but before he can face away from me, I see it written on his face, clear as day, just like he's an open book.

That's what happened. He pissed someone off.

And he knows who it is.

"I don't know what you're talking about," he says, but he doesn't meet my eyes.

"Nealie and Emma going missing is on you." I scoot around to his front and stab my finger into his chest. He winces but doesn't take a step back. "You get that, don't you? You're hiding something because you're weak and scared, but you're not taking into consideration what the girls must be feeling. I'm going out with Julie, but you better be here when I get back. We're not finished."

FORTY-NINE
ALISON

5:43 p.m.

"Don't move." I'm leaning up between the front seats of the Uber, my eyes locked on my front porch.

Ryan's standing there talking to the detective. Or, rather, he's standing there listening to her. Her back is to me, so it's not like I can try to make out her words, especially through the pouring rain, but it's clear from her body language that she's not happy.

She leans forward a bit, one hand resting on the gun on her hip, the other gesturing wildly. Watching her and knowing she's so angry at my husband sends a shiver up my spine.

It's one thing to watch someone in a movie as they read another person to filth. It's another to see it happening on my front porch, to my husband.

"Ma'am, I can't sit here all day." The kid driving is looking at me. He sounds apologetic, but when I turn to face him, he seems to shrink back into his seat. "I have to get home." A pause. "Or I can charge you extra, but I don't think you want me to do that."

"Right. You're totally right." I look back at the house and watch as Julie runs up to the porch. Ryan's just turning into the house, but Julie doesn't follow him. She stops next to the detective, clad in an oversized poncho, then gestures into the rain.

They found something.

My heart kicks into high gear when that thought hits me. Of course that's what's happened. They found something, and Ryan doesn't want to leave the house without me. It makes sense. It explains everything—the dark look on his face, how Julie looks eager to get going but her shoulders slump a little when the detective turns towards her.

I'm out of the car before I realize I'm on the move. Rain hits me in the face, the chill of it making me gasp. I wipe my hand down my cheeks and fling away the water, then run across the yard, ignoring the path.

"Wait! Wait!" Julie and the detective are down the porch steps now and turning to walk around the house. "Wait! Did you find something? Do you know something?"

Is it possible I missed a call? I never felt my phone vibrate or heard it ring, but I guess Ryan or the detective—or even Julie, I imagine—could have called or texted to let me know there was a development, and I totally missed it.

The women stop. Turn. They both have their hoods up, making it hard to see their faces, but I can tell the detective is the taller woman, Julie is shorter, her slight build draped in the poncho.

"Mrs. Brown—" the detective begins, but I grab her arm, cutting her off.

"Please." I can feel my mascara running. Hair sticks to my scalp. My cheeks. I try to ignore the way it feels. "Where are you going? What did you find?"

"Nothing." The detective grabs my arm in response. "We're checking on a possible location they might have gone to, but we don't know anything." She releases my arm and pulls a flashlight out of her pocket. In a moment, it's on, the bright beam cutting through the gloom.

The rain is coming down so hard now it looks like static in the light.

"Where?" I breathe out the word and turn to Julie. "Where? Tell me. Or—wait! I'll come with you! Just let me get my raincoat!"

"Mrs. Brown, go inside." The detective's voice is strong. No-nonsense. "I want you at home, warm, cozy. I don't want you catching cold. Julie and I will go investigate, and if there's anything to know, I'll contact you immediately."

"But my baby." My lower lip trembles, and I fight to keep from crying. "Please."

"Go inside." The look she gives me is pretty clear: listen to me, do what I say, or there will be consequences.

I'm not going to win this one.

"Okay." I turn to Julie. "Thank you for looking for her." My voice breaks, and she looks away. Embarrassed for me? "I need her home, Julie. Find her."

"We're going to try." She reaches out like she's going to take me by the arm, just like the detective did, but her hand falls to her side at the last minute. "We'll look."

"Thank you." It's only as they turn and walk away, the detective's light bobbing ahead of her, that I realize how soaked I am. The rain is torrential, not only chilling me to the bone but washing away any evidence that might have been left behind. That thought makes me shiver, and I turn and race up the stairs.

On the porch, I toe off my shoes and slip out of my jacket. I'll drip all over the floor, but there's no way I'm going to strip completely out here. Not when the neighbors might see.

"Ryan?" I open the door and step inside onto the mat. When I close the door behind me, I consider locking it but leave it open. Julie and the detective will be back.

Or Nealie might come walking through it.

Now tears mingle with the rain on my cheeks.

"Ryan, where are you?" I strip out of my jeans and shirt, leaving them both on the floor. Who cares about water damage to your custom wood floors when your daughter is missing? I couldn't care less about anything but getting Nealie home.

I know Ryan's in the house because I saw him walk in here after talking to the detective, but where is he? I wring my hair out, leaving the puddle behind, and shiver as I hurry upstairs.

I want him even though finding that picture of him with another woman has made me feel sick. It was an older picture, sure, but it had been displayed on the fridge before it fell.

So who was she?

Upstairs, I pause outside Nealie's bedroom door. The room is still trashed thanks to me looking through it for any sign of where she might have gone. I want to go in there, climb into her bed, wrap myself up in her blankets. I want to cocoon myself away from this world and all that's happening until I have her back.

I understand why Carrie did what she did.

That's an overwhelming thought—that I could relate to someone who would willingly drug themselves because that's why she fell, isn't it? A shiver races up my spine and goosebumps break out on my arms, reminding me of how cold I am.

I need clothes. There's the bathroom next, and I walk past it, looking away from Nealie's tub toys, her no-tears shampoo, her purple bath mat.

Then our room. Our door is cracked, the light on inside. I pause in the hall, shivering harder now, desperate for a blanket or a hoodie, or *something*, but there's a little voice in the back of my head telling me to wait.

I listen to it.

"I don't know how to make it clearer that I don't have it right now." It's Ryan's voice, low and cold, a current of danger running through it. A pause, then Ryan sighs. "Believe me, I'm more pissed than you are. You thought you would roll into town. Take what you wanted. But now look what—"

Who in the world is he talking to? It doesn't feel like my hand is attached to my arm as I reach out and lightly push the door open. Just a bit. Just so I can see inside.

Ryan's pacing back and forth on the other side of the room. He steps deftly around a pair of slippers I kicked off this morning and never put in the closet. His phone is pressed to his ear, and even though his eyes flick back and forth across the room, they don't land on anything, and he doesn't see me.

I push the door open a little wider.

"No, you listen to me." His voice goes up a little bit. I'm always glad when that tone of voice isn't directed at me. "We can figure this out. But you have to come clean with me about what you did."

Who is he talking to?

Julie? The detective? No, they're together, and I can't see either of them talking to Ryan in front of the other.

Carrie?

It could be Daniel, calling from the jail. I'm sure he hates my husband right now, but Ryan is the best in the business.

I think hard, trying to work through this problem. Or could it be someone else, some other woman I'm not considering?

"How dare you show your face around here? And then to act like you're innocent, like you're—"

He spins back around, his mouth open like he's going to say something, but this time when his eyes flit around the room, they land on me.

For a moment, his eyes darken. They drink me in, then he hangs up, the motion fluid. I watch as he slips his phone into his pocket, his face already changing, the darkness I saw there a moment ago disappearing, like gray clouds on a breezy summer day.

"Who were you talking to?" I ask. My voice doesn't shake, and I'm proud of that.

"Why are you all wet? And where are the rest of your clothes?"

"Answer my question first."

He shakes his head. "Nothing you need to worry yourself about, Alison. Get cleaned up. Put on some clothes." He pushes past me, his shoulder knocking into me as he goes.

I turn and watch as he stalks down the hall then turns to head down the stairs. He may think this conversation is over, that I'll do what he says, but I know one thing.

I have to get into his phone.

FIFTY
ALISON

5:56 p.m.

As soon as I hear the sound of Ryan pop open a beer, I slink into the kitchen, doing everything possible to look calm, in control.

Yeah, right.

Until Nealie is home, until I know what Ryan is hiding from me, I don't think I'm ever going to be able to relax again.

Thunder booms and rattles the glasses in the cupboard. Keeping my face as neutral as possible, I reach up and take one, then fill it at the sink and take a sip.

Ryan turns towards me and tosses the bottlecap on the counter. It sounds cheery when it lands, and I wince.

"Julie and the detective are outside right now because they think they have a lead." I take another sip of water, trying to soothe how parched my throat is.

"You didn't tell me that."

"You didn't ask." I point at him. "You were on the phone, obviously busy, then upset at me for coming into the house all wet. So, no, I didn't tell you about Julie and the detective. What was her name? Kate?"

I need to watch my tone. If I'm not careful, he'll clam up and I won't get anything out of him. I force a smile.

He doesn't respond. Instead, he drains his beer, then slams the bottle down on the counter. I wait for him to yell, to get upset, to show some emotion, but he's stoic, like this conversation doesn't matter.

"I'm going to shower." He announces it to the room, then grabs another beer from the fridge.

Shower beers. They've always been Ryan's thing, ever since we first met. Hard day in the courtroom? Shower beer.

Great day in the courtroom? Shower beer.

We find out I'm pregnant? Shower beer.

Our daughter goes missing? You guessed it.

He's predictable. Add to the fact that he's pissed off at me, and I'm not surprised when he stalks out of the kitchen and into the laundry room without another word.

I take another sip of water.

A moment later, he walks by on his way to the stairs, the beer clutched in his hand like he's trying to choke it, his boxers on display.

This stripping down he does? It's a terrible habit, one I've hated since we got together. Ryan strips down here before each shower so he doesn't have to carry everything back down to the laundry room.

His boxers he'll leave on the bathroom floor until I get fed up with them existing there and take care of them myself. It's the way it's always been between the two of us.

I've always hated it, but now I can use it to my advantage.

As soon as he reaches the second floor, I leave my glass of water and bolt from the kitchen into the laundry room. There, I have presence of mind to close the door behind me. My hand trembles as I lock it, then I rush to the pile of clothes next to the washing machine.

It's a jumble of fabric, and my hands shake as I dig for his phone. It's in his pocket, just like I thought it would be. I tap the screen, then slide my thumb across it to bring up the lock screen.

His passcode has always been our anniversary, and I type in the month and date—0418.

My heart is in my throat when I press enter, but suddenly the phone brightens.

I'm in.

I don't have a lot of time. As soon as he realizes that he left his phone in his pocket and his pants down here with me, he'll come flying down the stairs for it.

I tap on his recent calls.

I'm in there. Work. Other lawyers, but I don't care about any of those. It's the most recent call I care about. But it isn't saved under a name, of course.

I shove my hand into my pocket to grab my phone. No way will I be able to remember this number without taking a photo of it. I have a terrible memory to begin with, and the area code isn't local, which would make it that much harder.

But my phone isn't in my pocket.

"Are you *kidding* me right now?" I stand, my legs shaky, and press my ear against the door. No noise. No footsteps. No Ryan coming to look for me and his phone.

I still have time.

In a lot of houses, you can hear the plumbing moan and groan when someone runs a lot of water through it, but not ours. That's what happens when you buy really expensive houses—they're well built, silent, made from the highest-quality materials.

And while all that is well and good on any normal day when I don't want to have to hear Ryan showering or hear Nealie singing at the top of her lungs, right now I wish more than anything there would be a clang to let me know the shower was running.

But it's silent.

My hand is sweaty. I wipe it on my jeans and unlock the door. Lean out. The fact that I've now hidden from my husband behind a locked door twice today isn't lost on me. When I step out of the laundry room, I have to decide.

Do I go nice and slow and hope that he won't hear or see me if he's already back downstairs? Or do I run?

Fear prickles the hair on the back of my neck. It's dark out, the night pressing in on the windows. Rain lashes against the glass, and I have a sudden horrible thought of Nealie out there in the rain by herself, of her crying and wet, but I push that thought away because this number means something to Ryan, and I can't let him hide what it is, no matter how much easier it would be to ignore it.

I race to the kitchen, terrified that Ryan will appear on the stairs, that he'll hear me, that he'll give chase and be right on my heels, his breath hot on my neck. A shiver races up my spine. Goosebumps break out on my arms. I might be in dry clothes, but my hair is still wet, and a drop of water races down the side of my face.

And then I'm in the kitchen.

"My phone," I mutter, grabbing it. For a moment, I lean against the counter, then I drop into a squat, hiding behind the island. If Ryan were to come downstairs right now, he wouldn't be able to see me unless he walked around it or looked over it.

I have to hope that if he comes downstairs, he'll head straight for the laundry room and not look for me. If he looks for me, if he finds me snooping in his phone... I'm not sure what he'll do.

My first thought is to dial the number from my phone so I have it saved. But what if they pick up before I can hang up?

And then they might call Ryan, tell him I'm onto them.

So instead I take a picture of the number and click off Ryan's phone. Just in case, I upload the photo to my Google

Drive, then delete it from my camera roll. While I'm at it, I also delete the photos I took of the files in his office. Everything is now safely hidden. I turn my phone off and put it in my pocket.

I need to get the phone back into his pants pocket. It's the best way to ensure he doesn't know I was snooping.

I grip it in my hand. Take a deep breath.

Stand up.

And look right into Ryan's eyes.

FIFTY-ONE
ALISON

6:05 p.m.

"Ryan!" I step away from him, my back pressing into the counter. Yes, there's an island between us, but Ryan looks so angry, so focused, that it feels like he could come up over it, could get to me before I could move. "What are you doing?"

He's dripping wet, a towel wrapped around his waist. Normally, I'd take time to admire his strong muscles, how they wrap around him, twisting as he moves, but all I can do is stare at his face.

His eyes are dark. His lips pressed into a firm line. Ryan exudes danger, which is what I'd imagine the lawyers opposing him on the stand must feel.

It's exactly what I felt when he wouldn't let me call the cops this morning.

It's terrifying.

"I came to get my phone," he says, walking slowly around the island. "But it looks like you already picked it up for me."

I should say something. Should somehow pretend that I didn't mean to take it, that I was going to bring it to him, but that wouldn't explain why I was hiding crouched behind the island.

Instead of lying to him, because I'm sure he'd see right through whatever I said, I hold the phone out to him. He moves faster now that his prize is within reach, snatching it from me before I even realize he's going to take it.

"What were you doing with my phone?" he asks, but now he's not looking at me. He's clicking his phone on, stabbing in his password, and scrolling through the most recently used apps as if that will tell him exactly what I was doing.

"Just... looking." I swallow hard. Is it better to keep lying or to try to come up with some reason that might make sense? The way he's standing, his shoulders hunched forward, his muscles tight, I figure I better come clean sooner rather than later. "I wanted to know who you were talking to."

"And you thought you'd snoop?" He holds his free hand out. "Give me your phone."

I don't move.

"Alison! Phone!"

I'm shaking as I pull it from my pocket and hand it over. He moves quickly, tapping in my password before navigating to my outgoing calls. *Thank goodness I didn't try to call that number.* Next he checks my messages, then finally opens my camera roll.

He's good. I don't think I would have considered looking in someone's camera roll for a photo if they'd been snooping in my phone, but Ryan is a lawyer. He deals with this kind of thing every single day.

That or he's just gotten really good at hiding what he's up to.

"I told you my phone call didn't matter." He finally looks at me as he turns off my screen. There's a faint click, and I reach for the phone, but he pulls it away from me, already shaking his head. "I think I'll hold on to this, Alison."

Just like he did before.

Rage washes over me, and I fight to keep it at bay.

"But what if the police call about Nealie?" Desperation claws at me. I know Ryan can be ruthless, but this is cruel. "Or Carrie? What if she decides she needs me? That she wants to talk?"

"Then I'll handle it. I'll screen your calls, your texts. No way am I giving this back right now." He waves my phone at me, and I feel my heart sink. "Whatever you think you're doing, you need to stop."

"Tell me who you were talking to." I have to fight to keep from screaming at him. Yelling in his face would feel really good for a few seconds, but then he'd only be more angry. "Do they know where your daughter is?"

He's already shaking his head. "Who I'm talking to is none of your business, Alison."

"But Nealie." I reach for him, but I'm not surprised when he takes a step back from me and my hand falls uselessly to my side. "If they know what happened to Nealie, or can help us find her, or—"

"He doesn't know!" He slams his hand down on the island, the loud crack snapping me out of my spiral. "You need to get a hold of yourself. He doesn't know. I don't know, but I'm trying to figure it out. What, exactly, are you doing? How are you helping?"

I know I shouldn't say it. I know that showing him my hand, letting him know that I have any little bit of information on him is a bad idea, but the words leave my mouth before I can stop them.

"I found an old photo of you earlier. With a woman. At Julie's boyfriend's house."

For a moment, he pauses. It's like the pause before a huge thunderbolt breaks the silence, and I realize I really screwed up. "What did you say?" He takes a step closer to me. "What the hell were you doing at Theo's house?"

"I went—"

"With him? Did you go with him? Did he invite you over there?" He waits for a response, and even though I don't answer, my face makes it clear. "No, you didn't go with him, did you? You went by yourself. How did you find out where he lived?"

My mind races as I try to think of a way to get out of this. "I—"

"You were in my office." His voice holds a note of wonder, like he can't quite believe what he's working out on his own. "You were in my office. You're the one who took his file, aren't you?"

"No!" I'll take responsibility for the things I did do, but I'm not going down for all the stuff he's imagining me doing.

"No? Then how did you get Theo's address?"

When did he step closer to me? Ryan's almost right in my face. I can smell the body wash he used, but even stronger than that, I smell something else. Body odor. *Fear*.

"I saw his file, but I didn't take it from your office, I swear I didn't! I recognized your handwriting on the tab, but I'm not the one who took it. You have to believe me."

He blinks, trying to sort through what I'm saying and obviously struggling.

"But you saw it? Where did you see it?"

Where Julie put it. It had to be her. That's the only thing that makes sense. She saw his office was open and got curious. When she went in, she found more than she was looking for. *Or maybe it was Theo.* He could have come in, found the office open, gone snooping... No, that doesn't make sense. I believe it was Julie. She's so comfortable here.

But Ryan was talking to a man. Was he talking to Theo?

I feel like an idiot. We let Julie into our house, and she brought Theo into our lives. I trusted her with my daughter. And she's... what is she doing? I don't know, but I feel like this is a dangerous game. One I didn't want to play. One where Nealie is at the center. In danger.

"Alison. Earth to Alison." His words are playful, but his tone isn't. Ryan snaps his fingers in front of my face. "I asked you a question that should be easy for you to answer, but instead you're standing there gaping like you don't speak English. Where did you see the file?"

"By the gazebo."

His eyebrows crash together. What I said sounds ridiculous, I know it does, but I don't have the mental energy to come up with a lie right now.

"The gazebo? You mean the one in the neighborhood here?" I nod, and he scoffs. "So you want me to believe that someone came into our house, got in my office, stole the file and then took it to the gazebo for some light reading? Then, when it was time for them to go, they decided to leave it there as evidence of their crimes?"

Well, when he puts it that way.

"Do you think I'm stupid? Who the hell would have taken the file from the house in the first place? What person would think—" Abruptly, he falls silent.

I see it as soon as he realizes who took the file. It was just like when I put two and two together. The only difference is I want to know why Julie did what she did. I want to talk to her, try to see her side of things, ask her what was going through her head.

And Ryan looks like he wants to kill her.

FIFTY-TWO
JULIE

6:14 p.m.

The rain is dripping down my back. It's soaking my clothes, wicking into any dry spots left, and I'm freezing.

We've been up and down these paths three times, the detective growing more and more frustrated, me trying to shrink away from her. Just when I think we must be turning back towards the house, towards my car, towards my freedom from Blackwood, she whirls on me, her flashlight in my face.

I wince and hold out my hand to block the light.

"What were you doing bringing the girls down these paths?" She's shouting over the rain so I can hear her, but even though I know she's being as loud as possible, it's still difficult to make out her words.

"We were just on a walk!" I yell the words back, growing more and more desperate to get out of here. "It was just a walk!"

"Bullshit." She drops the flashlight out of my eyes but keeps it trained on me. She's breathing hard. My shoulders hurt from crawling under the fence. I'd seen the scratch on her cheek after she'd made it under. It was bleeding, but she hadn't seemed to notice.

She speaks loudly to be heard over the rain. "You had no reason to bring them back here, not after the first time when Nealie slipped under that fence. Sure, there's a creek, but you and I almost died getting down there. No way would you bring the girls you nanny down that way. And where did the trails end? A parking lot. Where were you taking them? Or did you meet someone there with them?"

I can't answer. The afternoon I lured them to the parking lot with the promise of some ice cream was the day we did their DNA tests. Theo met me there. I can still see him sitting on the curb, a cooler full of melting ice cream next to him, the DNA kits sitting to his other side in the shade.

We had the girls open wide and swabbed their cheeks, telling them we were testing them to find out what their favorite kind of ice cream was. Then we let them dig into six different flavors to test our hypothesis.

I'd been terrified they might tell their parents, but when I promised them we could have another ice cream taste test if they kept quiet, they agreed. Then Theo drove away with the leftovers and mailed the tests, and I brought the girls back home.

And after that? Everything fell apart.

Daniel lost his job. I no longer nannied both of the girls at once. I found out the truth about their father.

And now here I am.

Even though I'm soaking wet, I still feel it when sweat breaks out on my brow. I'm grateful for the rain right now because it means the detective won't be able to see me sweat.

"Why did you take them out of Blackwood?"

I snap back to the present. In my mind, I'm in the parking lot with Theo and the girls. He'd been so happy to help me

DNA test them, so willing to ensure I got the answers I wanted. And you know what? I'd been thrilled with his help. It had meant a lot to me that he was willing to help me out, to handle the tests while I took care of the girls.

And now I wish we'd left well enough alone.

But he'd wanted to double-check Carrie's letter before we used that information as blackmail. Just in case. And I hadn't questioned it.

"It was just a walk. We were bored of being in Blackwood, and I thought a change of scenery would do them good."

"You're lying to me." She steps closer to me, going so far as to bump into my chest. "I hate it when people lie to me. Do you not care what happens to the girls, Julie?"

It feels like a switch flips inside me. To be accused of not caring about them? For someone to dare to say I don't give a crap about them when anyone who knows me knows how much I love them? How I've kept their secret, how I've tried to share bits of information about them with each other so they don't totally miss their best friend?

Their sister?

"Of course I care!" I scream at her.

She grins. It's hard to see her face in this light, but there's a crack of lightning, its bright fingers stretching across the sky, and I see her expression for a moment before it's too dark again.

"Then tell me what you were doing with them. Tell me why you'd take them out of the neighborhood, what business you had doing that. It wasn't an easy thing, getting them out of Blackwood. Whatever secret you're hiding, Julie, you know as well as I do that coming clean about it could be the difference between life and death for them. Literally."

I don't answer. I *can't* answer. My tongue is thick. My throat is dry. I'm coming apart at the seams, and if she keeps pushing, I know I'm going to crack.

"Do you want their blood to be on your hands?" She's no longer yelling, but she doesn't need to. Those words are the most painful ones I've heard since we found out the girls were missing and this horrible day started. "Because that's your future. If something happens to them, I won't rest until you get punished for it. No way will I let anyone walk away unscathed when they could have helped Nealie and Emma."

"Were you sleeping with Ryan?" I know I shouldn't ask, but I can't help myself. Her file? Right there with the others? No way would Ryan have a file on her like that if there wasn't a good reason. Or rather if he didn't think he had a good reason.

She blinks. Her flashlight drops a few inches. "What did you say?"

"He has a file on you." I'm feeling bolder now, like I've turned the tables on her, like I'm finally the one in control. I know it's not true, that she's the one with the real power here, no matter what I might tell myself, but it feels good to not be running scared. To make her question everything.

"I've heard."

That admission makes me blink. "You already know?"

"I know a hell of a lot more than you do."

"I doubt that, since I'm the one who told you about all of his affairs in the first place." My stomach twists. I need to protect myself. If the choice comes down to him or me... well, that's an easy choice. "It had to be hard finding out that you're not the only woman he was screwing."

She takes a step back from me, but then I watch as she rolls her shoulders, fixing her face. Whatever damage I did to her is already over. She's a bulldog with a bone, and she'll be damned before she lets anyone distract her from what she's doing.

"Tell me what you know." The light flicks back up to my face.

I wince but don't step back, don't raise my hand to block it.

"Tell me!"

"He's having so many affairs!" I scream the words into the night, into the storm, into her face. All of the rage I felt when I found out what kind of man Ryan really is bubbles up inside me. It's been kept simmering just below the surface for months now, but I don't have to hide it any longer. "Am I the only one who put two and two together about the girls?"

Never mind that I saw the letter from Carrie. Never mind the fact that I was in the house to look for dirt on him. Never mind that Theo—

Her mind must be going a million miles a minute because she catches on to what I'm saying a lot faster than Theo did when I explained everything to him. He'd been slow on the uptake, shocked, like he couldn't believe it.

"Are you saying that Nealie and Emma are siblings?" Anger laces every single word, and I get why.

I nod. "They are."

"You're sure?"

"I DNA tested them both. That's why I brought them on these trails. To make sure it was true." I'll come clean about that but not *why* I needed to know if they were really siblings.

Her mouth drops open, but she doesn't respond to that. Instead, she gives her head a little shake and rolls her shoulders back. "Does Alison know?"

I consider that for a moment, then shrug. "I don't know."

"Does Ryan know that you know?" When I nod, her mouth tightens. "Go home, Julie. Stay away from him. Let me handle this."

I want nothing more than to do what she's telling me. I nod, but before I can say anything else, she turns and hurries away, her flashlight cutting through the dark.

My stomach drops as I watch her go. The truth is slowly coming out, which will hopefully mean the girls make it home safe.

But that also means someone might find out what Theo and

I have done. He's been lying to me, and I have no reason to assume he'll stand by me as this all falls apart.

I have to figure out a way to make sure he takes all the blame.

FIFTY-THREE
RYAN

6:22 p.m.

This time when I get a text, I tap the green call icon. Whoever's sending them loves to hide behind their messages, loves to harass me from the shadows, but I'm tired of it. They're a coward, and I know how to deal with people like them.

Theo. It has to be him. He's the only person who would text me these things.

He has to have two phones with different numbers. The one I talked to him on before my shower and this one. That would make sense if he really wants to mess with my head.

But I'm done letting him.

The balls on him to come to my office acting like a client, only to blackmail me... He wanted money, said he'd disappear if I gave him a quarter of a million dollars.

Then, when both girls disappeared, the ransom note asked for half a million.

I'd laughed him out of my office. People don't blackmail me. That's some crap you see in the movies, something only jokesters try to do when they're down on their luck. He swaggered in, acting like he owned the place, acting like I *owed* him something.

I should have told Kate right then and there about this blackmailing son of a bitch.

I thought that was all of it. I didn't see him around town, but that didn't stop me from doing a little research on him. Imagine my surprise when I found out he's dating our nanny.

If there's one thing I don't believe in, it's coincidences.

I'd told Alison to get rid of Julie, but she's been unwilling to do so. She loves Julie, Carrie loves Julie, everyone loves Julie.

I didn't move fast enough, and it was all because Alison was right—Nealie adores Julie. Taking her nanny away from her would have been cruel, although necessary. I wasn't about to do it without someone in the wings, someone better.

And now the bastard has taken my daughters and raised the price. He denied it on the phone with me earlier, but maybe this way I can catch him by surprise.

The phone rings and rings and rings before finally clicking over to voicemail. It's the first time I've tried to call this number, the first time I've put two and two together about who's harassing me. It has to be him. But when the voicemail picks up, I don't hear his voice. It's an automated message telling me that the mailbox hasn't been set up.

"Dammit." I hang up, stabbing the screen harder than necessary, then open the text back up.

Price just doubled.

I stare at it, my heart thudding hard in my chest. I'm trying to think of something to say in response, some way to talk him down off the ledge, but my brain isn't working fast enough.

Another text comes through.

I close my eyes, not wanting to read it.

But I have to know. I force myself to look.

Unless, of course, you only want to save one daughter.

Another message pops up.

You choose. Nealie or Emma?

I drop the phone to the kitchen counter and turn to throw up in the sink.

FIFTY-FOUR
KATE

6:31 p.m.

They're sisters.

And Julie, Carrie, and Ryan knew it and hid it from me. Anger washes over me, but I push that emotion to the side as I race down the sidewalk towards the Browns' house. The fact that I used to care for Ryan, the fact that I thought we had a future together, that I would have done anything for him, all of that falls by the wayside.

I'm pissed.

It's still pouring, but I pause under a tree long enough to type out a text to Aletha.

Nealie and Emma are sisters. Ryan's the dad. I'm going there to talk to him now.

Her response is immediate.

Need backup?

Water drips from my hood as I tap out my response.

No.

I've got this under control. Having Aletha here might be nice for backup in case Ryan gets angry, but I don't want to drag my feet on this. Time is ticking.

My phone rings, but I silence it after glancing at the screen. Aletha doesn't want to be left out of the case—I get that. But I don't have time to wait for her to join me right now.

I don't slow down as I race up the porch stairs. It feels like I'm outside of my body looking in as I raise my fist and pound on the door, then immediately turn to the side and start pressing the doorbell.

I'm not leaving here until I get answers.

My phone rings again. Aletha. I pause, considering, then silence it.

"Ryan!" I cup my hands around my mouth and yell at the door before stepping back and kicking it. It feels good to take some of my anger out on his house, and I kick it again. "Ryan, open this door right now!"

"I'm coming!" It's Alison—she's the one who swings the door open, her eyes wide, her cheeks flushed. She stares at me for just a moment before words pour out of her. "Is it Nealie? Did you find her? Did Julie know something? Where did you go?"

"I need to speak to Ryan." It's rude to push past her, but that's exactly what I do. I don't care about dripping on her floor; I don't care about the way my hip knocks into hers to push her out of the way. Ryan is in this house, and he needs to answer for what he did.

Now.

"He's in the kitchen." She closes the front door and gestures down the hall, but before I can make my way in that direction, he appears, wearing only a towel, clutching two phones in his hand.

"What's going on?" He doesn't sound confused. He sounds angry.

Good. Be angry. I want to hear answers.

I could hold back. I could question him without Alison here so she doesn't have to hear how her husband has been lying to her for so many years, but I don't want to take the time. I want to get answers now, so we can find the girls as soon as possible.

"When were you going to tell me the truth about Nealie and Emma?" I don't know why I'm trying to be as vague as possible. It's not like I owe Ryan anything. I don't need to shelter him, to prevent him from getting hurt.

Not when he's the one who keeps running around behind his wife's back.

"I don't know what you mean." He takes a step forward, but it's Alison who speaks again.

"What's going on?" She grabs my arm and squeezes it. It hurts, but I don't have the wherewithal to push her away from me. "What truth? What are you talking about?"

When I don't immediately answer, she turns to Ryan. "What is she talking about? Do you know something? Do you know where the girls are?"

"Your husband has been lying to you," I say. "To all of us, in fact."

"You don't know what you're talking about!" he shouts, stepping closer to the two of us. Beside us, I feel Alison tremble, but she still doesn't let go of my arm.

"I know that Emma is your daughter." The words fall like boulders in the silence of their house. They don't land softly; they ricochet, immediately causing damage I know will never be repaired.

"What?" The word leaves Alison in a breath. "What are you talking about?" She turns to her husband, who's now staring at me like he's never hated another person as much as he despises me. "Ryan! What is she talking about? Why would she say that?"

"Emma and Nealie are half-sisters," I say, wanting to get the truth out in the open before Ryan tries to spin it. That would be just like him, for him to put on his lawyer hat and try to hide the truth of what he's been up to. I point at him. "You had a baby with Carrie, and then the two of you hid it from your spouses. If we had known they're sisters, that might have helped us with the search. Who else knows that? It might be part of why they were taken. We might have already been able to bring them home!"

"What have you done?" Alison finally lets go of my arm. She moves quickly, slapping Ryan across the cheek. The sound rings out in their house, but he still doesn't respond. "Were you ever going to tell me you were having an affair with one of our friends? Is *that* why you wanted to have Daniel fired? Not just to cover up the fact that you screwed up at work but to hide that you screwed his wife?"

He shakes his head. "No, we didn't have an affair. You don't understand."

"You wanted Daniel fired—" I begin, but Alison cuts me off.

"Don't tell me what I do or do not understand!" She's shrieking now. "Is Emma your daughter?" He nods, and she flies off the handle. "Oh, and so you expect me to believe that you didn't have sex with Carrie? I knew the two of you were really good friends, but this is above and beyond the lines of friendship, Ryan."

"We didn't sleep together! She kept having miscarriages and was afraid Daniel would leave her. I donated her sperm, but that's as far as it went."

Alison claps her hands over her ears and turns away from him, moaning as she does. She squats on the floor, keening, the sound painful to listen to.

"You're at the center of this." I whip around and stab my finger into Ryan's chest. He blinks but doesn't step away from me, doesn't argue. "This entire time you knew there was something more to this case than someone taking two little girls. You knew there was a connection, and you didn't do a damn thing about it. You should have told me."

He doesn't respond. Instead, he rakes his fingers through his hair and shakes his head.

"Nothing to say? You didn't come clean then, and you don't think you should come clean now?"

"You don't understand."

"Try me."

"Carrie and I have been friends for years. How in the world was I to know that something like this would happen?" He stares at me, but I'm not going to let him bulldoze me like he has in the past.

"Who did you piss off?"

Alison's still on the floor, her hands still tight to the sides of her head. No way is she listening to us right now, not when she's still whimpering and rocking back and forth.

"Nobody!"

"And the lies keep on coming." I turn to walk away from him. The kind thing would be to help Alison up, to comfort her, to make sure she's okay, but I don't have it in me right now. Not when this information might be what we needed to crack the case wide open.

"Where are you going?" Anger laces each word.

I whip around to face him. "I'm going to try to find your daughters before someone kills them." He pales, and I have to admit, the sight of him looking nervous for the first time since I've met him feels good. "But first I'm going to go tell Daniel the truth about Emma's parentage."

"You can't do that." He lunges for me and grabs my arm

exactly where Alison had been holding me earlier. "Kate, I'm serious. You can't do that. He doesn't know. It'll destroy him."

"You should have thought of that before you did what you did." I yank my arm out of his grasp, and I'm glad when he lets me go. "Someone has to clean up your mess, Ryan."

If I was angry before, I'm pissed now. It's one thing for Ryan to keep making mistakes, to keep making messes and refuse to clean them up, but it's another entirely for him to try to stop me from doing my job.

I'm at the front door when I hear movement behind me. Turning, I watch as Alison stands, her legs unsteady, her eyes wide. "How many more children do you have, Ryan?"

I freeze. Turn all the way around to watch and listen. I'm staring at her back, but I see how tight her muscles are, how she's leaning forward a bit at the waist, like a sprinter about to take off from the blocks.

She continues when he doesn't answer. "How many? You told me about the accident when you were in high school, but how many kids do you really have?"

"What accident in high school?" I hurry back to the two of them and stand directly between them. With the way Alison is standing, like she's ready to fight Ryan, I'm tempted to put my hand out to stop her, just in case. "Tell me everything."

FIFTY-FIVE
JULIE

6:37 p.m.

Theo never gave me a key to his house when we moved to town, but I remember he told me that his bedroom window doesn't lock. His house is the last place I want to be now that I know he's been lying to me, but I'm freezing, and if he's not here, I can pop by, get warm, and leave before he knows I was ever around.

I'll be fast.

"Theo?" I lift the window and poke my head inside. It's cool in there, the AC obviously working overtime to keep the humidity out of the house. The rain finally stopped, but I'm dripping wet, and I got my phone wet while helping the detective look for the girls. So much for using a police-issue poncho.

No phone. Soaking wet. Theo's house is much closer to Blackwood than my apartment, and his car wasn't out front when I drove by. I rang the doorbell, and he didn't answer. I just need some dry clothes. A place to catch my breath. And then I'm going back out there to find the girls.

Everything is falling apart. What was supposed to be a simple job, in and out, get the money and run, has exploded. I told him over and over I didn't think it was safe to work a job in the same town where he'd bought a home, but he was adamant that Ryan was the perfect hit.

Ryan. Not Alison, not Ryan and Alison. *Ryan.* By himself. Because he didn't want to just take his money, did he? He wanted to hurt him.

And now look at what's happened.

I take a deep breath, hoist myself up, and climb through Theo's window. For a moment, I fumble my way across the room, then I flick on the light. The cozy glow makes climbing through the window worth it.

"Theo, you home?" My footsteps are silent as I walk down the hall, circle through the kitchen and living room, then back to his bedroom. I'll take a quick shower to warm up, dry off, change clothes, and get out of here. When I'm no longer dripping wet and freezing, I'll be able to make better decisions. Besides, my apartment is going to be the first place he'll look for me. There's no reason he'd think I'd come here first.

Wherever he is, I'm sure he's looking for me and probably wondering why my phone isn't working. If I thought he had some rice here, I'd pop my phone in there, but he eats so many of his meals at my place that I doubt his kitchen is stocked.

In the shower, I turn the water as hot as it will go, letting the steam envelop me. Today has been exhausting. It blows my mind that this morning Theo and I were eating leftover Chinese in my kitchen. Huge tears run down my cheeks as the full extent of the day catches up with me.

The girls going missing. Theo lying to me. His second phone. My altercation with Ryan, which, in hindsight, was the stupidest thing I could have done.

I dry off, using a fluffy blue towel that I wrap around myself. As I do, my eyes fall on the toothbrushes by the sink. One blue, one pink.

But I haven't left a toothbrush here.

That thought reverberates in my mind as I walk into his bedroom to look for something to wear. Whose toothbrush is it? And has it been there a while? I guess it could be an old toothbrush, one from someone who came to visit Theo a long time ago. I want that to make sense. I *need* that to make sense.

Did he and Tabitha actually get together like she wanted? Or is this toothbrush from someone else? Another girlfriend maybe? A hookup?

I push that concern from my mind. I'm naked and need clothes. The closet behind me is empty and open, which means if he has something for me to borrow, it'll be in his dresser.

My hair's dripping, and I take time to twist it back before opening the first drawer. Theo's underwear. I close it and move on to the next one. Theo's socks. Next: his T-shirts. Then: his belts. All I need is a hoodie and some sweatpants and I'll be good to go.

I grab the next drawer pull and yank it open. Bright colors pop out at me, colors I'm pretty sure Theo would never wear. Relief floods through my body as I pull out a pink T-shirt. This will work. I don't know where it came from, but it should be fine for me to borrow.

But when I hold the shirt up to look at it, it's much too small for me.

Like... so small it could fit a little kid.

I drop the shirt to the floor and pull out the next item of clothing. They're pajamas, soft ones covered with little kitties.

Exactly like the ones Nealie has.

"Oh my God." My fingers tighten on the fabric, and I can't seem to let go. I stare at them in my hand, the kitties playing and prancing, and I feel like I'm going to throw up.

Finally, I manage to drop the pajamas before racing back into the bathroom. Without taking time to lift the seat, I fall to my knees in front of the toilet and throw up. I haven't eaten a lot today, and it's mostly bile. When I'm done, I flush and rinse my mouth, then walk back into the bedroom.

What does it mean?

I can't make it make sense. Why would Theo have clothes for a little kid? Why would he have pajamas just like the ones Nealie wears?

Because they're Nealie's.

It's the only thing that makes sense, but at the same time, it doesn't make any sense. There's no way for Theo to have taken her pajamas, not unless—

"Oh my God." I stumble back from the open drawer. When the backs of my knees hit the bed, I sink down without thinking about what I'm doing. "Theo has her pajamas. He has the clothes for a little girl. He took—"

I can't go there.

Instead of continuing down that path, I force myself to think about the rest of the day. Trudging down the paths with the detective, pushing through the pouring rain to the parking lot, finally coming clean with her about what I knew about Nealie and Emma—*and how willing Theo was to help me with the DNA tests*—only I didn't tell her that part of it, did I? I kept it to myself.

And what about the files in Ryan's office? If I hadn't gone in there, if I hadn't snooped, no way would I have ever known about Theo's file being in there. I still don't know why Ryan has a file on my boyfriend—*yes, you do*—but there has to be some reasonable explanation. I just don't know it yet. I remember him walking with Ryan—*keep thinking, there's something there*—and how they'd both held their left hands out to the side a little bit with each step, how their right ears tip over at the top just a little bit. I think about Theo, how gentle he was when he met Nealie and Emma for the first time, how he got right down on the floor with them and played like he didn't have a care in the world—*like an older brother*—yes, like an older brother, like someone who wanted to take care of them.

Oh my God.

The file.

The siblings.

The affairs.

My head hurts. I stand, pushing myself off the bed so I can get out of here and try to think straight. I'm halfway to the front door—because why go back out the window—when headlights cut across the windows.

Theo's home.

FIFTY-SIX
CARRIE

6:39 p.m.

If Ryan had chosen me, then none of this would have happened.

I grab my phone from the coffee table and thumb it on. The light is bright, and I blink against it before navigating to Facebook. What was the name of the cheerleader Ryan knocked up so many years ago?

We'd been so young. It was an accident. She'd told him she was going to take care of it, but then she left town to live with an aunt and we never spoke of it again. I know Ryan was relieved to have her out of the picture, to have any proof of his mistake out of town, but what if...

No. Not a chance.

Hurrying now, I navigate to our high school's Facebook page. The chances of her commenting on it recently are slim to none, but our high school loved its cheerleaders and football players, so much so that it has Facebook albums with shots from every year's squads and teams.

I need to calm down, but my heart races as I flip back

through the squad photos. Each time I tap the arrow to go back a year, I feel like I'm that much closer to digging up an answer.

Until I'm there. I squint, using my thumb and pointer finger to enlarge the photo, then quickly scan the girls' faces. So many of them look alike—blonde, with dark roots and big boobs and—there she is.

Of course I recognize her. How many football games did I spend watching as Ryan watched her, watching as they made eye contact throughout the game, watching as she jumped into his arms after a big win?

Vanessa Roberts.

And then, for our senior year, she was gone. What would have happened between her and Ryan if she hadn't gotten pregnant? What would have happened if they'd stayed together and gotten married? There wouldn't be an Alison, or Nealie, and I don't know if he would have agreed to help me have Emma.

Without Vanessa getting pregnant and ruining her relationship with him, would he have turned back to me for comfort and support? There's no way to know now, but I'm still curious.

Now that I know her name, though, I can learn more about her. My heart hammers away as I type it into the Facebook search bar.

She pops right up. Since her job is listed as *Stay at Home Mom,* I can tell she doesn't work outside of the house. I also see that she never moved back home. She's about three hours from here, but that's all the information listed. Other than that, her account is locked down. I'd have to add her as a friend in order to see anything else. I hesitate, my finger hovering over the button, then tap it.

Why not? What do I have to lose? And besides, it's not like she's going to be sitting around looking at her phone on a Saturday night. Chances are good she'll be out with friends or her husband. No way do I think she'll—

She accepts.

If I thought my heart was hammering away before, that's nothing compared to how hard it's beating now. I quickly go to her profile, then click on her photos. Without any idea of what I'm looking for, I start flipping my finger, moving from photo to photo, my eyes scanning as I take it all in.

There are so many comments. My eyes flick over the names of people who have written notes on her photos or been tagged in them.

Eric.

Stephanie.

Tabitha.

And then I see it. The man standing next to her is young enough to be her son, and if the similar eye and lip shape didn't give it away, her holding a Mother's Day balloon certainly would have.

She kept her son.

I stare at him for a moment, almost unable to believe what I'm seeing. He's been all over today helping look for Emma and Nealie. But what if he's the reason they're missing in the first place?

I'm so focused on looking at him that I almost don't realize what I just saw. Swearing, I swipe back, going one, two, five photos back before I see her again.

Aletha.

I know her.

FIFTY-SEVEN

ALISON

6:45 p.m.

"Ryan had a child when he was in high school." The words are lead in my mouth, but I force myself to say them. If being honest, if coming clean, if hurting my family is the only way to bring my daughter back, I'll burn this house down myself.

"How do you know that?" Ryan looks like he wants to take a step closer to me, but the detective is in between us, her hand out towards me like I'm the danger she needs to stop.

"I'm not an idiot." I ignore how confused I'd been in the gazebo when I'd found Theo's file. I couldn't reconcile why my husband would have something like that on him, why he'd want that detailed information.

And then it all clicked. The file, the photo of Ryan in Theo's house. How he'd talk briefly about his high school girlfriend but then quickly move on to other subjects, like it was too painful for him to revisit.

I'd been pretty sure I was right, but judging by the way Ryan is acting right now, I hit the nail on the head.

"I saw your file on Theo and then the photo of you with a woman in Theo's house. It took me longer than I'd like to admit to figure out what was going on, but I'm going to chalk that up to the fact that our daughter is missing."

Kate's head turns back and forth between the two of us. "Stop. Back up."

I can't. Not when it feels like I have this secret burning a hole inside of me. I've only known the truth for a short period of time and Ryan has known for... how long? And he's kept it quiet. I can't understand how he could be so calm about this, how he could lie to me over and over without any remorse.

"How many kids do you have?" I fling the words at Ryan, but he doesn't even have the decency to blush. "One from high school," I say, holding up a finger. "Nealie and Emma." Two more fingers. "How many more? Or do you have so many that you've completely lost count?" I'm on a roll now and don't think anything will be able to stop me, not even when I jut my thumb at the detective standing shocked between us. "Did you knock her up too?"

"Okay. Enough." The detective clears her throat and takes me by the arm, pulling me further away from Ryan.

"It's time for you to come clean, Ryan," she says, turning to speak to him.

I bark out a laugh.

"If you can't listen quietly, I'm going to have to ask you to leave the room." She looks at me and waits until I nod. "Thank you. Now, Ryan, tell me everything. I want to bring Nealie home, but I can't do that if you keep lying to me about what's going on around here."

He nods at the detective, studiously avoiding my gaze. I feel the flush in my cheeks; my hands are in tight fists. If the detective weren't here with us... I could hit him.

I know I could.

"Emma is my daughter." He pauses like that's enough, but when the detective doesn't respond, he continues speaking. "Carrie couldn't get pregnant. Well, she couldn't *stay* pregnant. It was really hard on her and on Daniel. I don't know that they were going to make it if they didn't have a child. She and I have been friends for so long that when she reached out to me and asked me for help, I did it."

"You shouldn't have done that." I can barely speak, I'm so angry. It's one thing to know what my husband did, another to hear him talk about it. He's so nonchalant, like making this decision, having another child, wouldn't affect us.

"The two of us have been friends for so long that it just made sense. What was I supposed to do—turn my back on her? Let her suffer over and over again for the rest of her life when I knew I could easily help her?"

I can't keep quiet. "Yes! That's exactly what you should have done if you weren't willing to talk to me about what was going on!"

"Alison." The detective turns to me and takes me by the shoulders. I have to drag my gaze away from Ryan. "I know you're upset, and you have every right to be, but I need you to calm down. You need to take a deep breath, or I'm going to have to ask you to leave the room while I finish talking to Ryan."

"Yeah, right. Like I'd be willing to leave the two of you alone again."

She flushes. Good. She screwed up sleeping with Ryan. I'm angry, and I want her to hurt the way I do.

"Ryan, continue." She gestures for him to keep speaking.

My husband clears his throat. "Daniel doesn't know. He'd go ballistic, and that was the last thing Carrie wanted. We thought about telling you, Alison, but figured the secret would be too much for you to handle. Obviously."

I don't answer.

The detective nods at him. "Tell me about the high school baby."

So he does. If he's to be believed, he has no contact with the mother, no idea where she is, no idea if the child is even around. My head spins as I listen to them talk around me like I'm not here.

"Do you think she told the baby who you are?"

His voice is low when he answers. "I doubt it. We never saw each other again after she moved. Hell, we never even spoke. She was going to get an abortion." He runs his hand through his hair. "As far as she's concerned, I'm probably some deadbeat dad who wasn't there for her when she was pregnant and didn't give a shit that she had my baby."

"How old would the baby be now?"

"Thirty-three," he answers without hesitation.

"Great." She flips open her notebook and scribbles it down. "And how many other children do you have, Ryan?"

"Is this related to the case?"

"I'd say so."

"I don't know."

Is he lying? I have no idea. I don't know anything anymore. One thing makes sense though, and that's why he didn't want to call the police this morning. He'd probably been terrified his mistress was going to show up.

I feel words building in me until I can't keep them inside any longer. "You don't know how many kids you have because you lost count or because of how many women you've banged?"

"Stop." The detective turns to me. "Just take a deep breath. Go get a glass of water. It's been a long day, we're all exhausted, and you two will have a lot to work out in the future, but right now my priority is Nealie."

"Fine." I cross my arms.

"This child from your high school girlfriend," she says to

Ryan, "is there any chance they might have found you? Tracked you down?"

His expression changes for just a second, but it's long enough for me to know that she hit the nail on the head. He's putting up a big front about not having any contact with his high school girlfriend, and that might be true or not, but he knows who his child is.

"They did," I say, stabbing a finger through the air at him. "Your child reached out, didn't they?"

The detective whips around to face me. "Kitchen. Now. You aren't part of this, and if you interrupt me one more time, I swear to you that I'll arrest you, and then you won't have to worry about what your husband is confessing to because you won't be anywhere around to hear it."

"Fine." Anger washes over me, but I know when I've lost. Instead of arguing, I stomp around them, making a big show of heading towards the kitchen.

But instead I stop in the hall. Press up against the wall. And listen.

She sighs and addresses Ryan once more. "Your child contacted you. What did they want?"

There's silence, and I can just imagine him chewing his lip as he thinks. "Money."

"How much?"

"Quarter of a million."

"Small payout for missing every part of their life so far. And, let me guess, you told them no."

"I did."

"So this child kidnapped your other kids. Julie knows about the girls being siblings. Carrie obviously knows. Somehow, this child found out."

He doesn't respond, but I hear him thunk his head against the wall.

"You know who it is." Her voice is high. Tight. "Who is it?

They took your daughters, Ryan, and if you don't give up the name, I can't guarantee a good outcome."

"She knew," he says. "Julie knew, and she told him."

The detective doesn't respond, but I don't need her to figure this one out.

It hits me immediately who he's talking about.

Theo.

FIFTY-EIGHT
JULIE

6:51 p.m.

I'm frozen with fear as Theo's headlights grow closer, seeming to illuminate the living room.

Run.

I need to run away from here, away from the thought that he has something to do with Nealie and Emma going missing. It's a thought that I can't shake, like a virus that's infiltrated all of my cells, but if I stand still and let that fear paralyze me, he's going to find me.

And he'll see it all over my face that I know something.

I should have figured it out earlier.

Move to a new town. Find a mark, but not just any mark. I've never believed in hurting people just because you can. They have to be bad people, people who don't deserve what they have. People who aren't willing to help others. People who have more money than they need and never think of anyone other than themselves.

People like Theo's dad, who abandoned him and his mother when she was pregnant.

And then, once we carefully chose the right mark? Get into the house as a nanny and find some way to blackmail them. Profit.

Rinse and repeat.

Rich people hide behind their money. They cover their sins with Gucci and Dior, but even the nicest clothes and fanciest cars can't hide the fact that so many of them are abusive. That they treat not only their own kids but also treat the poor like crap. That they don't deserve what they have.

And that's why we take it from them. That's why people like Ryan deserve what happens to them. It's Theo's thing, and I've always been more than happy to help him.

Remember how happy he was to help with the DNA tests?

I'd thought Theo was so curious about Ryan because he wanted to get a huge payday this time and he needed solid proof that we could use to blackmail Ryan. I always thought Theo was embarrassed about how he grew up, about not knowing his dad. But Theo's probably been planning this for as long as he and I have worked together.

He used me, and I played right into what he wanted me to do.

Theo, what did you do?

I can't deny the fact that I think he had something to do with Nealie and Emma going missing. The clothes in his dresser are a dead giveaway. What I can't understand is why he would do that, why he would think it was a good idea to—

I had no idea he'd found his dad. No idea he'd plan revenge like this.

Or that he'd make me an accomplice to his plan.

I don't know if I'm more upset that I'm just now figuring everything out or that he's lied to me from the beginning.

And now Nealie and Emma are in danger because of what we've been doing.

There are footsteps on the porch.

Unfortunately, Theo's house is small, and there isn't anywhere to hide. Besides, I just used his shower. He's going to know I was in here. He's going to see my dirty clothes and the dresser and *know* that I know.

I race to his bathroom and gather up my clothes. Best to let him think I just got out of the shower and I haven't started looking for anything to wear quite yet. If he figures out that I know his secret...

My heart is in my throat as I glance around. The drawer where I found the clothes and pajamas is still open. I dump my clothes on the floor and rush to close it right as I hear the front door slam.

"Hello?" He doesn't sound worried, more interested. For a moment, I wonder how he knows I'm here, then I realize he can see the light from the bedroom streaming into the hall. "Who's here?"

"Just me! Hi!" I shove the drawer. It closes halfway and then catches on something. Frantic, I yank it open and feel around inside for what caught.

"Julie? What are you doing here? And how did you get in?" He's coming down the hall, moving faster than I am.

My fingers brush something hard and I try to knock it out of the way. I have to wiggle the drawer with my other hand to create enough room to move it.

It's still stuck.

"What are you doing in there?"

"I was going to look for some clothes I could borrow," I tell him. "I was soaked from the rain and thought I could swing by. I just got out of the shower."

"Let me help you." I hear the edge in his voice as I grab the thin thing in the drawer—a pencil? A chopstick?—and snap it in half.

He walks into the bedroom right as I push against the

drawer with all my weight. It slams shut, and I barely catch myself before falling.

"Hey, you okay?" He grabs my elbow to steady me, and I feel my skin crawl. "Wow, you weren't kidding about looking for clothes. How did you get in?"

"Bedroom window." My voice is strangled, and I force myself to smile at him. "I was drenched after helping the detective look for any sign of the girls and didn't want to drive all the way home. My phone died in the rain, so I couldn't call you and let you know I was coming. I hoped you would be here and helped myself in when you weren't. I hope that's okay."

"Of course it's okay." He smiles at me, but I notice the way his eyes flick over the dresser. "Did you find anything to wear?"

"I haven't looked yet." I try to keep my face as calm and relaxed as possible as I lie to him. On the inside, my heart is pounding, my stomach is tied in knots, and I feel like I'm going to throw up.

But on the outside? I'm hoping I look calm. In control. *Honest.*

"Then I'll get you something. Scoot." He touches my shoulder to move me out of the way. It's involuntary, when I jerk away from him, but I can tell from the expression on his face that he's realizing things aren't normal.

"Julie." He takes a slow breath. "You're acting weird."

"I'm just cold. Tired." I force a smile.

A pause. "Why don't you step back and I'll get you something warm to put on?"

I do what he asks, somehow managing to keep a smile on my face as I give him space. It's clear he doesn't want me looking over his shoulder as he digs through the drawers.

Turning so I'm looking in the other direction, I clear my throat. "So what have you been up to since I saw you?"

"Work stuff." A drawer slams shut. "Here you go."

I turn and take a hoodie and sweatpants from him, my eyes

flicking behind him to the dresser. All of the drawers are closed, but I know which one has the little girls' clothes in it.

"Julie, you okay?" Theo's voice is kind. It makes me want to cry. For years we've told each other everything going on in our lives, and I want to do that right now. I want to break down and come clean with him.

But I can't trust him, so instead, I lie. "Yeah, I'm great. Why?"

It feels like the air shifts.

"I wish you wouldn't lie to me." He sighs, the heavy sigh of a parent who's caught their kid up to their elbow in the cookie jar. When he crosses his arms and levels his stare at me, I know I messed up.

But how does he know?

"You're being ridiculous. I'm changing in the bathroom and going," I scoff and try to hurry past him, but he reaches out and grabs my arm, squeezing it hard enough to make me stop.

He shakes his head like I've disappointed him. "It's pretty obvious the two of us need to have a talk."

FIFTY-NINE
ALISON

6:52 p.m.

"Central, I need an address for Theo Roberts." The detective steps into the hall beside me, her radio held to her mouth, her eyes wide. She looks panicked, like she's seen something terrible, and I think she's going to hurry back out into the rain, but she pauses at the door and turns back to the two of us. "Don't you dare move. Stay in this house—do you understand?"

"I understand," I whisper, but Ryan speaks over me.

"We won't go anywhere."

She nods, suddenly looking uncertain, but turns back to the front door and then is out it in a hurry, the sound of the driving rain filling the house, then it's cut off as she slams the door closed behind her.

The door is barely closed before Ryan spins on me. "What did you do?"

"Me?" I'm terrified and angry and filled with horror, but the one emotion that takes control is my anger. "You did this! You couldn't stop sleeping with people, could you? You just had to keep sleeping around, and that's why—"

"I didn't know my child was alive until just recently when he showed up in my office threatening to tell the world about me, about the girls! She was going to get an abortion, but someone must have talked her out of it. You can't blame me for that, not when I didn't know anything about him even being born."

"He came to your office, and you didn't tell me? We could have avoided this entire thing!"

"I wasn't going to tell you! But then he kept texting me, harassing me, and when we talk, he acts like he's not. He's playing mind games. He's insane."

"And what about Emma?" My heart's beating so hard it hurts, but I'm not going to back down right now. Not until he sees what a jackass he's been, how he's hurt me, how all of the danger we're in can be traced right back to him.

"That's different. It wasn't like Carrie and I were together. It was clinical, like I told you."

"Clinical." I spit the word at him.

"Yes, clinical. She was going to die without a baby, Alison—you saw that. Don't act like you didn't. She needed me."

I scoff. "You've always chosen her."

He shakes his head but otherwise doesn't deny it.

"If you had just told me about Theo and Emma we could have worked this out already. We could have the girls home." I think about the young man who sat next to me on the front porch when I was so stressed out. It's almost impossible for me to imagine him as a kidnapper. He'd been so comforting, so kind to me.

Is it true he's the one who helped Nealie sneak out of her window?

My throat closes up.

But he's... her brother. Oh God, Theo is Nealie's much older half-brother, and while that thought makes me sick, the one thing I can try to lean on to keep from falling completely apart is that he wouldn't hurt his sister.

No big brother would hurt his little sister. *Sisters*. That's just not how big brothers operate. They're protective and caring. Unless... unless he was jealous of Nealie. Wanted to hurt her to hurt Ryan.

"Do you think he'd hurt her? Hurt them?"

"How the hell am I supposed to know?"

"He's your son, for starters," I snap at him. "Have you two not talked after he tried to blackmail you?"

Ryan grows silent, and my stomach sinks.

"You bastard. Did you know this entire time that he was the one who took the girls? Were you hiding it because you were afraid of what people would think about you for having another child out there?"

"I didn't know it was him." He glares at me. "The person texting me—"

"Oh, good God, you've been *texting* with him too? What, do you two catch up during the day? Call each other before bed?"

I... I can't believe this. Not only has Ryan been lying to me from who knows when, but his lies are the very things that put Nealie in danger. Not to mention her half-sister, which is another can of worms I'm going to have to sort through later, when I can handle the fact that my husband and my best friend have a child together.

"I don't know. I talked to him on the phone, but that number is different from the one that keeps texting me. Why would he have two phones? I thought it was him—it makes sense it would be, but two phones? Come on. If you would take a breath and let me talk for a moment, you'd finally understand what's going on."

Fine. Instead of responding, I motion for him to continue.

"Theo came to me a month ago and told me he wanted me to pay him, or he'd tell everyone that he was my son."

It feels like my blood chills. I know where this is going, but I don't like it.

"He wanted a quarter of a million dollars and he'd disappear, but that was it. No threats."

"No threats?" I clear my throat. "He was going to embarrass you in front of everyone, and you don't consider that a threat?"

"Compared to our girls going missing? No, I don't." He glares at me. "He wanted the money. I told him to get lost."

Now my heart is in my throat. There was that much money in the business accounts, but that was before I—

"But we don't have the money." Ryan grits his teeth together. "It's... gone."

"Gone?" I swallow hard.

This is how Ryan finds out that I was going to run.

I'm terrified of what's about to happen.

He nods. "Someone wiped out the business accounts. They took a little off the top of each of them, month after month, until they swiped everything that I'd need to pay Theo. To get him off my back." He stares at me.

Does he know?

Sweat breaks out across my forehead, but I don't move to wipe it away. "Do you think he'd accept the quarter million to bring the girls back? I know the note asked for more, but..."

The fact that I might have kept Nealie from being returned —even inadvertently—makes me feel sick. My legs feel like they're going to give out, but I don't allow myself the luxury of sinking to the floor. Ryan is already angry at me. If he knew that I was the one who had taken the money, he'd go apoplectic.

It had been so easy too. I took little amounts at first, just testing the waters. For a respected law firm, it didn't make any sense that Ryan wouldn't be more on top of his finances, but the truth was that he didn't keep an eye on it. If he had, he would have seen how I started taking more and more. First I moved it to a separate account that was still connected to the business. From there, it was easy to sweep it out for myself.

All I wanted was to be able to afford a new life without him. One with just Nealie and me. She deserves to be part of a family where the parents love each other, where they're not running around on each other, where they trust each other. And I was going to give it to her. I'm basically a single mom now, and I figured that taking her from Ryan before she got any more attached was the best move.

But now I've shot myself in the foot. I had Nealie and no money. Now I have money and no Nealie.

"Does it matter? We don't have it either way." Ryan runs his hand through his hair. His face is flushed, and he looks like he's been sick. "I think Kate—Detective Martin—is on top of it. I think we have to trust her. Even if I had the money right now, I don't know if Theo would take it. He's dug his grave."

This Ryan isn't the man I married. I don't know why he's not out there right now trying to bring Nealie home. He should be taking control right now. Fixing this. But he's not, and I can't wrap my mind around why that is. "Is that who you were talking to before your shower?" It's not something that matters, not really, but I'm desperate to piece together what's going on.

Ryan sighs. "Yes, Alison. Obviously. Although he swears he didn't take the girls. That he just wanted money to keep quiet about my children."

"And you believe him?"

"Of course not. Can't you keep up? Now, we need to get back on track. Figure out what to do about Nealie. How we can help her."

"And Emma. You know, your other daughter."

He ignores my sneer. "What I can't understand is where the money went." He yanks his phone from his pocket and starts tapping on the screen. "It was being siphoned out regularly, and

I'm sure I can track it—I just haven't had the time. But it suddenly stops—" He lifts his head. Stares at me.

"What?" I ask, even though I already know.

"It just stops, Alison."

I swallow hard. Take a step back. See, this is one part of my plan I never really thought through—what would happen if Ryan caught on to me taking the money. I always assumed I'd be out of here well before he figured out something was going on. Then things fell apart after forging Daniel's signature, and I felt so guilty about what we did to Carrie. I didn't want to leave her behind without knowing she'd be okay.

Especially since she could turn me in at any time.

"Weird." I take another step back. What I wouldn't give to have that nosy detective show up at the house right now.

"It stopped right around the time you left the company." His thumb twitches, clicking off the screen. Ryan slips his phone into his pocket and takes a deep breath. "What do you have to say about that?"

Nothing.

I have nothing to say.

That's why I run.

SIXTY
CARRIE

7:14 p.m.

With Daniel locked up for pushing me down the stairs, I don't have to worry about the loud click the front door makes when I close it behind me. This worked out perfectly, even though I'm sore and I know I'll hurt for days. Having Daniel out of the way means I don't need to sneak around, don't have to slip him sleeping pills to get out of the house.

I would feel bad for him, locked in a cell for something he didn't do, but he's not the one who fell down the stairs. Even though I did it to myself, it hurt more than I imagined.

I'd love to call Ryan and let him know I'm on the way, but instead I step out into the growing dark, my purse held close to my body. Knowing Ryan, he'll want to play this safe. I can easily imagine him telling me to turn around and go home. That we'll take care of everything tomorrow, that he'll handle it.

That Emma will be fine.

But it's not just Emma I want. It never has been.

And now I have nothing left to lose.

I walk faster. The Browns' house is only two houses down,

but today the trek feels like it takes forever. For a moment, I pause, then glance over my shoulder at our house.

It looks like every normal house in Blackwood.

Rich. Safe.

I scoff and turn back, ducking my head as I walk. While the streets had been crawling with officers earlier, the rain scattered them. The storm has passed, but it's humid, the damp sticking to my bare skin and making me feel like I'm breathing water.

At the large magnolia at the corner of Ryan's property, I pause. It feels silly to hide, to pretend I'm not here, especially when anyone would be hard pressed to see me through the dark, but I stand there a moment, looking at the house.

There's no movement. Adjusting my purse, I step around the plant, but the garage door rumbling and raising makes me freeze. I'm torn between running up to the car—it's Ryan's, isn't it?—and staying where I am.

In the end, I stay still.

I watch as Ryan hurries out of the garage. He pauses by a large bush at the corner of the house, then bends down. When he stands back up, he wipes his hands on his pants and runs back into the garage. A moment later, his car backs down the driveway. Instinctively, I crouch. He reverses out into the road, then speeds away, his headlights sweeping the bush above my head. I duck, but there's a soft revving sound as Ryan presses down on the gas.

I'm sure he's gone, but I give him a moment to get out onto the main road, then I stand and hurry across the yard to the front porch. Normally, I'd stay on the sidewalk, but I don't care about wet shoes or tracking mud or beating down the grass.

There's something about the way he sped off, about the fact that he was alone, about the fact that he didn't call me with an update that makes me nervous.

I want to follow him, but something pushes me to go to the house first.

I knock on the front door, then take a step back. There are a few lights on inside, making the house glow, but Alison doesn't immediately answer. Moving quickly, I step to a window and cup my hands to peer inside.

The entryway table is knocked over. Keys and a potted plant lie on the floor, the dirt from the plant scattered across the hardwood. There's a huge family photo hung right above the table, and it's been knocked. It hangs cattywampus, like something hit it and then nobody stopped to fix it.

A smear of red on the wall catches my eye.

Blood. It has to be blood.

My breath catches in my throat, and I reach for my phone without realizing what I'm doing.

What I should do is call 911. Or the detective. I'm pretty sure I have her card in my purse somewhere. If someone is hurt, they're going to need help. I could get that help.

I click my phone on. If I hadn't framed Daniel... only, no. He doesn't need to get involved in this. Daniel wouldn't know what to do. He wouldn't understand what's going on. It's best that he's out of the way right now.

I flick my finger across my screen, but I don't call the police. Or Alison. Or even Ryan. He's obviously okay. I saw him driving away from their house, which means...

"Alison." Whatever happened in there to make him drive away like that while the entryway is a mess had to involve Alison.

I chew my lower lip, then back off the porch, away from the front door. My feet lead the way, and I don't realize where I'm going as I run over to the bush where I saw Ryan stop. With a tap on my phone, I turn on the flashlight, then shine it on the ground.

There. Right there. It's what Ryan brought out here and dumped.

My breath catches in my throat, and I tug off my sweater,

carefully using it to pick up the knife. I don't want to get blood on me. Don't want my fingerprints on the knife.

It sounds like screaming in my head. I do my best to ignore it, but the sound grows louder and louder. Being gentle, I wrap the knife in my sweater and tuck it under my arm.

I'm taking it with me.

The knowledge that I should call the cops, that doing anything else is stupid, washes over me, and I tap my phone back on. Turn off the flashlight. Take a deep breath to prepare for what I have to do next.

My finger hovers over the green call button, but instead I tap another app.

Where's My Friend?

There's no delay after I tap it. It opens and refreshes, a moment later showing me the little icon for Ryan. I can only imagine how Daniel and Alison would feel if they knew that Ryan and I kept tabs on each other like this.

Well... I wouldn't call it *keeping tabs*. He promised me forever ago that he would always be there for me, and this is the best way for him to keep that promise. When I get worked up over something, or I'm worried, knowing that I can find him, can go to him if I need to, makes me feel better.

Not that I ever have, of course. I'm not crazy. No way would I show up at his office or the courthouse, but just being able to check and see where he is calms me down when my brain won't shut up.

I spin away from the front door and hurry back down the steps, across the lawn, and down the sidewalk. My car's in the garage, and I let myself in, then crank it. Mash the button to raise the door.

"Hurry up," I mutter as I fit my phone into its holder. On the screen, the little blue car representing Ryan takes a right. The map automatically zooms out so I can keep him in view.

The pink icon representing my car starts to move as I back down the driveway and speed out of the neighborhood.

I have no idea where he's going, but I press down on the gas, eating up the distance between us. Twice I run a red light, wincing and blinking as I do, hoping nobody will hit me. I slide through a stop sign, then another, then finally slow down and turn into a little neighborhood.

On my phone, the little blue car has come to a stop. A few minutes later, I tap the brake and slow down before parking down the street from him. I don't know where I am or what he's doing here, but I want to make sure he's okay. He's that important to me.

For a moment, I sit, hoping that he's still in his car, but the dome light doesn't click on, which means he's already on the move, and I missed him. I take a deep breath and slip out of the driver's seat, carefully closing the door behind me...

And where am I?

I've never been much of a runner, but I run now, racing up to his car. It only takes a moment to tell that he's not in it, so I turn to the house he's parked in front of. It's small. Unassuming.

My palms are sweaty, and I wipe them on my pants as I think. Instead of approaching the front of the house, I'll loop around. Maybe there will be a side door that's left open. That thought makes me think of Daniel leaving the back door open at our house. He's the reason Emma went missing.

But I'll bring her home. With Ryan.

Resolve flows through me. I hold my purse tighter against my body and hurry towards the side of the house. Before I reach it, though, I hear raised voices.

I freeze. Turn. As quickly and quietly as possible, I hurry to the front of the house, to the main windows. I duck low and press up against them, watching everything.

SIXTY-ONE
RYAN

7:29 p.m.

I knew from the moment Theo walked into my office that he was my son. Even though I haven't seen his mother in decades, looking at him was like looking at her. He has her eyes, her mouth, her attitude. And from me? His height, his broad shoulders, his nose. The way he's staring at me right now, like he'd love nothing more than to punch me in the face? Yeah, that's from me too.

He looks confused as I push past him into the house but recovers quickly, closing and locking the front door behind us.

"Where are Nealie and Emma?" I'm trying to keep all emotion out of my voice, but it's almost impossible. Never in my life have I hated anyone as much as I hate this man. To waltz into my life like I owed him something, to act like I should hand over so much money just to pretend like he doesn't exist?

He's maddening.

I want to kill him. And you know what? I might.

The detective headed straight to Theo's house.

Leaving me with my wife? That was a mistake. Alison was

so angry and mouthy and kept blaming me, even though she was the one stealing money from my business.

And I snapped. While I was taking care of Alison, I got another text from that unknown number with this address. It's time to end this.

"They're somewhere safe," he tells me, but there's something about how he pauses before he speaks that has me worried. He won't make eye contact.

He's scared.

"You were so willing to text me photos of them before," I say. "Bring them out. Prove that they're fine."

He frowns. "I haven't been texting you. I don't have the girls." Every word is slow, deliberate, but it takes me longer than I'd like to admit to understand what he's saying.

"You don't have the girls? But you texted me this address. Told me to come here."

"You don't listen! I haven't texted you. Not once."

My mind races as I try to make this all make sense. Theo's adamant about not being the person who's texting me, threatening me and the girls. But if it's not him, then who? "Who else is involved?"

Theo shakes his head. Spreads his hands out in between the two of us like that's going to be enough to convince me that he's telling the truth. "I swear to you, Julie and I wouldn't hurt your daughters. Taking them was never the plan—you have to understand that. They're not here." His voice is tight.

"And what was the plan? Show up in town and screw me over? Is that what you thought would be a good idea? Tell me who has my daughters!" Yelling isn't going to solve anything, but I want to get through to this asshole. It's impossible for me to believe he's my son, that I could ever father someone who acts like this, who is so willing to screw someone over. Anger washes over me, the same anger I felt when Alison finally confessed that she'd been planning on taking Nealie and leaving me.

The same anger I felt when I stabbed her, over and over, her eyes wide, her blood so bright red.

"We just wanted money! That's all we wanted! We don't hurt kids!" He's yelling back now, and it feels good. I don't get to yell at work—I have to think things through and be careful, be on top of it, but now I get to scream just like I did with Alison. I could throw things too. I could hit him, I could—

His eyes flick down to the front of my shirt before he looks back up at me. I don't need him to speak to know what he's thinking.

The red stands out against my white shirt, blooming there, bright and accusatory, but I didn't want to take time to change my shirt before hurrying over here. Dropping the knife outside the house was stupid. I should have left it in my house, or dumped it in the river, or *something*, but I wasn't thinking straight. All I knew was that I couldn't bring it with me, that I had to have it somewhere I could find it, but not in my car.

I'm thinking straight now though.

"We?" I don't pause, the words spilling out of me. "Tell me what Julie did." She's been sneaking around, a little rat in the house, getting information about me and my family and feeding it to Theo. I wonder what she thinks about all of this, what lies he tells her to make her follow along with his plan.

"Julie." He scoffs, glances over his shoulder. I look too, but it's dark down the hall. If she's here, she's quiet. Hiding. "She told me everything there was to know about you. She finds the information about the families she nannies for. I simply get the money from them. But she never would have agreed to hurting the girls. She loves them. She's better than that. Than this. I know you don't trust me, but Nealie and Emma weren't ever a part of it. We just wanted to blackmail you for money. Normally I call our marks, but I wanted to see you in person. I wanted to meet you. I needed to."

I hear what he's saying, but my mind is caught up on one thing he said.

The families she nannies for.

"You've done this before?" I was in control a few minutes ago, but now I feel that slipping away. I can't wrap my mind around what he's saying, what he's implying, that they've done this before, this is what they do, they find people and screw them over—

He barks out a laugh. "Over and over. It was my idea, of course, but Julie was pretty easy to get on board when I made it clear we were only going to be taking money from people who didn't deserve what they had. I never told Mom about this, of course. She moved on from you." He leans forward, his eyes glinting. "I didn't."

Moving away from him is a sign of weakness, but I can't help but step back from him. He looks evil. Truly evil. I feel off balance and reach out for support, but there's nothing for me to grab.

"How did you find me?"

"Mom knew your name. It wasn't tricky to find you when I looked you up online. Julie and I had been making money for a while now off of rich people with questionable morals, and I brought her here without telling her who our mark was going to be. Alison loved her." He grins. "So did Carrie. And let me tell you, *that* was a surprise. Two more biological kids. You've been busy, Dad. Julie was so excited to find out that Emma is your daughter because it was the perfect blackmail. But I already had a plan. *I* was the blackmail. My existence should have been enough to make you pay."

I'm sweating, but I'm too afraid to move and wipe my brow. The way Theo's watching me, it makes me worried he might attack me. The adrenaline I felt when taking care of Alison is subsiding, but it's still there.

"All you had to do was give me the money." Theo sounds

disappointed, like the roles are reversed and I'm a kid who didn't do what his father asked. "And then we would have left. None of this would have happened."

My mouth is dry. I force myself to swallow, then lick my lips. "Theo, I just want the girls back. You can have money—I'll get it for you! I'll get you whatever you want. Just, please. Give me back the girls."

He sighs, and the sound is heavy. "Dad—can I call you Dad? I'm so used to Julie calling you Mr. Brown or Ryan, but *Dad* just sounds right, doesn't it?"

I don't respond.

"Anyway, Dad, if you'd played the game and gotten us the money like I asked you to, this would all be over. But you didn't, did you? You thought you'd be cute and ignore me. Well, that's fine. But then someone else got involved, and that's when things went south. That's when your girls went missing. But I didn't take them. I just wanted money. Remember that."

There's movement in the hall behind Theo. A figure. I have to fight to drag my eyes away from his face and look past him.

It's not Julie. They're taller, with broader shoulders. For a moment, I think it's another man, but they step into the light of the living room and it's a woman. One I recognize immediately. One who's been around the house all morning helping look for the girls. Her uniform let her come and go, but now the sight of her in it makes my stomach lurch.

"Tabitha," she says, pointing at herself. "Welcome to my home! Theo and I connected online when we were looking for our father, and when he told me about his little scheme with Julie, I wanted in. He said no at first, that it was just him and Julie, so I thought I'd up the ante a bit."

I can't speak.

"We've been texting for a while now, but it's so good to chat with you in person."

"You're my—" I can't say it. I can't even *think* it. Coming face-to-face with one adult child is bad enough, but another?

Aletha. Her name was Aletha Bradshaw. Not Tabitha. I don't know where that came from. Why is she calling herself that when she's Aletha, a cop, someone to help, not my—

"Yes, I'm your daughter!" She throws her hands into the air like we're celebrating. "What a fucked-up family reunion, huh? Yeah, it was great luck when Theo and I found each other. I was looking for whatever deadbeat knocked my mom up when she was in college; he was looking for whatever deadbeat knocked his mom up in high school."

My mind whites out.

She grins at me. "Now, what do you say we talk about our little sisters?"

SIXTY-TWO

KATE

7:32 p.m.

I have my gun drawn as I press myself up against the front of Theo's house. There's a light on inside, but it's silent, and I can hear my heart hammering away as I inch closer to a window to peek inside.

There are multiple cars parked on the street, but the constant rain keeps the neighbors inside. Thick clouds cover the sky, making it darker than it normally would be. I shiver and inch forward, ignoring the drop of rain that runs from my temple down my cheek.

This is the address dispatch gave me. He has to be here. And, with him, the girls. That's my only thought right now, that the girls are going to be inside this house, safe and sound, that the fact that it's so quiet doesn't mean anything bad.

They have to be okay.

Another step, and I slowly turn, peeking in the front window. Sheer curtains hang on both sides, but there's enough of a gap between them for me to look into the living room. My eyes flick over it quickly as I drink it in, then I take my time, looking slower this time, for any sign of the girls.

There's nothing. It's sterile, uninspired. I see what I would expect in any house—a couch, a coffee table, a stack of magazines. There are no toys, no snack plates, nothing primary colored or plastic, or that requires an insane amount of AA batteries.

"Where are you?"

My hand falls to my radio. I don't like to second-guess dispatch, but I call it in anyway.

"This is Detective Martin. Verify that address."

The response comes back immediately. I'm at the right place, but then where the hell is everyone? Two seconds later, I hear Aletha's voice.

"Just checking in. Still no sign of Julie."

I respond quickly. "Ten-four. Keep me updated if you find her." Without thinking about what I'm doing, I glance over my shoulder, but nobody's here. No nosy neighbors are watching, nobody's walking their dog.

I'm not leaving without getting inside.

The thought has taken over, and I move quickly to the front door and twist the handle from right to left. It doesn't budge and, for a moment, I consider going back to my car.

But then I think about Nealie and Emma.

I raise my gun before I've fully formed the thought of what I'm about to do, and I use the butt to knock out the pane on the front door. There's a crash, then tinkling glass, and I freeze.

Nothing moves.

I holster my gun and reach inside, careful not to nick myself on the sharp edges. In just a moment, I turn the handle and let myself in. Moving faster now, I close the door behind me. Lock it.

I'm in, and sweating, and breaking tons of laws, but there's no time for a search warrant, not now, not when I'm so close and the girls could be in danger. I hurry through the living room, already pulling my gun, and loop through the entire house.

The bathroom. The bedroom. The kitchen.

It's a small house, so it doesn't take me very long to look through it. Disappointment weighs heavy on my shoulders, along with fear.

I'm walking back through the living room while my mind races. The magazines on the coffee table are tapped into a neat, perfect stack. The kitchen is tidy, the bathroom is neat. On the wall hangs a huge woven tapestry, looking a little out of place. Honestly, it seems like something you'd find in a college dorm, not in an adult man's house.

I walk over to it. When I reach out and finger the edge, it pulls easily away from the wall. I tug it to the side, my heart racing when I see what's behind it.

A door.

When I radio Aletha, my voice is a whisper. "I found a door that looks like it leads to a basement. I'm going to see what's down there."

Her response is immediate. "Give me ten minutes and I'll meet you there. Don't go alone."

"There's no time," I whisper, then press the button on my radio. "Negative. I'm going down. Stand by."

There's a click like she's going to respond, but I turn the knob to off before she can. It's dangerous, but I need it quiet, on the off chance that whoever's in the basement doesn't know I'm coming.

Slowly, I turn the deadbolt, then open the door enough for me to look inside, and I'm half-relieved, half-horrified that I'm right: there are basement stairs here. There's a soft glow from down below, but it's not bright enough for me to see much of anything. I feel like I'm walking blind as I descend, and I pull my gun as I do.

Three stairs down.

Four.

Five.

There's a stench, and I wrinkle my nose. Feces.

Six.

Seven.

I hear movement, and I freeze.

There's whispering, and I wait, then slowly descend, hurrying the last few steps and turning, my gun already out in front of me, my finger on the trigger. Hair on the back of my neck sticks up, and I take tiny breaths of air, fighting against the fear already eating at me.

Are the girls down here? Are they okay? Still alive? Hurt... or dying?

A scuffling draws my attention, and I grab my flashlight with my free hand, clicking it on and shining it into a dark corner. Two girls, hugging each other, blink into my light. I barely take in the rest of the space, but I see a cot, a bucket for a toilet, a dirty puzzle spread out on the floor.

"Girls," I say, but before I can say anything else, there's movement to my side. I turn, my flashlight and gun swinging out ahead of me, the person running at me making my finger tighten, tighten, tighten—

Julie rushes me, her hands over her head, something held between them. She's screaming, her mouth wide open, the sound filling the basement. I barely have time to notice the cut on her forehead, the blood running down her cheek, how her face is puffy and red like she's been sobbing.

I drop the gun to my side and bend my knees, driving my shoulder up into her stomach. She exhales hard and drops to the ground, the hatchet she held crashing to the floor next to her.

I kick it out of the way and train my gun on her as I hurry backwards to the girls. They're clinging to each other, both crying loudly. I debate squatting to check on them but need to keep my eye on Julie.

She doesn't move, but I'm not going to risk looking away from her.

She had the hatchet over her head, ready to bring it down on whoever came into the basement.

To defend the girls? To defend herself?

I'm breathing hard as my mind races and force myself to look away from Julie. The girls are clinging to each other, their faces wet with tears. "You girls okay?"

Emma buries her face in Nealie's shoulder, but she nods.

"Stay right here, okay? Just stay by me." I look away from them, back over at Julie, who doesn't move. My eyes are locked on her as I reach down. Turn on my radio. Pressing the button on the side, I prepare myself for what I'm about to say but then stop.

Julie was down here with the girls. She obviously was involved—somehow. Does that mean she'd been lying to me all day about knowing what happened to them? It could. She could have been stringing me along while knowing full well that the girls were safe.

Then it hits me what I had to do before I came down here.

I unlocked the door, which means only one thing: Julie was locked in here with the girls.

Whoever locked them down here did the same to her.

And they're still out there.

SIXTY-THREE
RYAN

7:44 p.m.

Tabitha—Aletha—*my daughter*, whatever I want to call her, holds up one finger to tell both Theo and myself to be quiet. I stare at her, clad in her officer's uniform, a gun on her hip, her earpiece barely visible.

She frowns, touching it and tilting her head to the side like that's going to help her hear better. After a moment, she smiles, the grin spreading across her face.

My gut twists when I look at her. All of my research into my children, all of the times I hired someone and begged them, bribed them, did everything in my power to get information about any of them that may exist, and she was a ghost. There was nothing to find. No information on her.

But this entire time she's been living in my town.

She changed her name and got a job in a career where nobody would expect her to be the bad guy. When someone commits a crime, nobody looks twice at the police. Everyone assumes they're the good guys, that they wouldn't do anything wrong.

"Ten-four, Detective. I can be there for backup in a few minutes." She releases the button on her mic and grins at me. "You'll never believe what that call was."

My mouth is dry. Even if I had a guess, I don't think I'd be able to speak. It's all I can do to keep my legs under me, especially when I feel like I could collapse at any moment.

"Do tell, sister." Theo takes a step forward, almost like he's afraid of being left out. My eyes flick to him but then go right back to Tabitha. Aletha.

My daughter.

"That was the great Detective Kate Martin," she says, her eyes locked on me. "You know, Dad, the one you've been screwing? Anyway, she made it into Theo's basement. Want to know what she found there?"

"Nealie." I gasp out my daughter's name.

"And Emma. Don't forget your other daughter," she admonishes. Her lips curl up, and she squints at me for a moment.

She's enjoying this. It hits me out of nowhere—this is the most stressful moment of my life, and she's enjoying the fact that she's in control and I have no power.

"And Emma," I parrot. "Are they okay?"

"Well, they are *now*. Detective Martin found them in the basement with Julie. And get this—Julie tried to attack her. With a hatchet."

"Julie?" Theo's voice is strangled, and he takes a step closer to her. Rage washes over his face, and I see the way his hands clench into fists. "Is she okay? Did she hurt Julie?"

"Kate laid her out, but she's alive." Aletha cocks an eyebrow at her brother. Her hand shifts a little, resting now on the grip of her gun. "I had the girls locked up in the basement. Tell me how Julie ended up locked in there with them, brother. I thought you wanted to keep your hands clean of all of this. That's what you kept saying—that you wouldn't get involved if I took the girls."

"And I did keep my hands clean! Until you locked them in my basement." Rage pours off Theo.

"Oh, please. You were blackmailing him. I just took it up a notch."

He closes his eyes. Takes a deep breath. "You dragged me into this. Julie came over and found their pajamas in my dresser. *You* put them there. I had to do something with her. She thought I kidnapped them! Imagine my surprise when I panicked, went to lock her in my basement, and found the girls."

My mind races as I try to understand what's happening. From the way Theo and Aletha are staring at each other, this wasn't how the plan was supposed to go.

I want to move, but I can't seem to make my legs respond.

I'm stuck here. Watching. Listening.

"I had to put the clothes somewhere, and why not get a little insurance at the same time? When people have skin in the game, they're more likely to play ball. You're a part of this too, Theo." He doesn't respond, and she continues, her voice growing louder. "What, you think I was stupid enough to keep the girls in my apartment? Your house was the better choice, and since you and Julie were connected at the hip, I figured you wouldn't find them there."

"I told you not to get the girls involved," Theo begins, but she laughs and cuts him off.

"Oh, please. Obviously Daddy here wasn't interested in forking over any amount of money, no matter what you were going to tell people about him. We had to make it worth his while to hand over the cash, isn't that right?"

She turns to me, and I force myself to nod, then to speak. "And I would have, but Alison stole it! She embezzled it from my firm." The irony of my wife embezzling from me while at the same time forging Daniel's signature to place the blame of screwing up an embezzlement case on him isn't lost on me. "If she hadn't taken it, I—"

"Wouldn't have done a damn thing, and you know it. I saw how you acted about the ransom note I wrote. It was easy to pretend to find it behind your house." Aletha shakes her head with a chuckle. "Alison was all about paying the money, but you weren't."

"I would have," I argue. "I was looking for the money, but Alison took it." She doesn't respond, and I swallow hard. "What are you going to do now?" It's a stupid question to ask—I can tell by the way she chuckles. "Nealie and Emma are okay, but Julie is hurt, and she's important to you—"

"She's not important to me! She's important to him!" Aletha points at Theo, her cheeks bright red. "I don't care about her." She pulls her gun and hefts it, glancing between Theo and myself.

"You murdered Alison," she says, using it to point at the blood on my shirt. "Didn't you? Or is she still alive?"

"She's gone." When I blink, I see the way my hands stretched out towards her, how easily I'd grabbed her around the neck, what it had felt like to shake her back and forth before throwing her against the counter and finishing her with a knife. She'd run, tried to get away. Hell, she'd almost made it to the front door before I got her and dragged her back into the kitchen. I shudder when I think about all the blood on the walls.

"God, you just keep screwing up." She wipes her free hand across her brow. "You," she says to Theo, "shouldn't have locked Julie up with the girls."

"You weren't supposed to take them—" he begins.

"I wasn't finished. You promised me you could handle her, that she would do whatever it took to get the money, but you were wrong, weren't you? You two made a huge mess, and I have to be the one to clean it up. Typical man." Her gun wavers between the two of us.

"Julie never would have agreed to put the girls at risk. She loves them."

Aletha rolls her eyes. "Oh, I know. I've heard you say how great she is, that she's the best thing to ever happen to you, that she's only going along with your plan to punish people who deserve it. But what about us? We deserve a good life. He doesn't." She juts the gun in my direction.

My stomach flips.

"Julie won't turn on us," Theo says, but Aletha isn't listening to him.

When she speaks, it's her muttering to herself. "One way or another, I'm going to have to spin this."

"Spin it? No, you don't have to spin anything." I hold up my hands to show her I'm not a threat and take a step forward. She turns to me, both hands on the gun now, her arms fully extended in front of her, and I freeze.

"Theo's not going to turn on you. Neither will I," I begin lying at the same time my son speaks.

"Tabitha," Theo begins, but he stops talking when the gun swings in his direction.

"Eenie," she says, looking at me. "Meenie." Back at Theo. "Minie, moe. One of you has got to go." She cocks an eyebrow at me. "Didn't know I was a poet, did you, Dad? There's so much you never cared to learn."

I wince, bracing myself for impact.

"Oh, one more thing, Dad."

When I look at her, she's grinning.

"Strip. Swap shirts with your son."

I want to argue, to refuse, but my fingers are already on the buttons. When Theo tosses me his shirt, I return mine, then pull his on.

And then she pulls the trigger.

SIXTY-FOUR

Later

Emma and Nealie shriek as they run around the playground. It's been just over a year since everything happened, and while nothing is completely back to normal, things are on the way.

No, you know what? They're better than *back to normal*. We had to go through hell to get to this point, but now that I'm here... I can honestly say I wouldn't change a thing.

The girls started first grade this fall, and of course they were in the same class, just like they were in the same kindergarten class. I made sure of it.

No way was I about to back down. These two girls are a special case. They're closer than ever before, like the time they spent apart and the time when they were kidnapped only helped bring them closer. They've even come up with their own little language, like they're twins, which I love.

And they are sisters, so it makes sense if you think about it. They share half of the same DNA, and there's no reason to keep them apart from each other.

Losing them was terrifying, but I like to look on the bright side, and that's this: they're happy and healthy, and they have a family who loves them.

In the end, isn't that the only thing that matters?

"Mrs. Brown." Detective Martin sits down next to me. She clocks the girls on the swings and nods at me. "How's the afternoon?"

"Great." I stretch, noting the way my diamond catches the sun. It's been months since I first put it on, but it's always going to be special. After what I had to go through to get it, I don't ever want to take it for granted.

Daniel had been heartbroken when I filed for divorce, but after I showed him the paperwork proving that Emma wasn't his, he packed his bags. Besides, he didn't want to stay with me after I swore to the cops he'd pushed me down the stairs. Luckily for him, he's had practice defending domestic abusers and got off relatively light. I offered to let him keep the house, but in the end we sold it, and I moved in with Ryan.

Having both of the girls under one roof? It's been heaven, but being Ryan's wife has been even better. It's all I've wanted since we were in high school, and I'm so glad I'm alive to enjoy it. When I told him that I knew the truth—that I know he killed Alison and Theo was innocent, no matter what he and that crooked cop daughter of his said, no matter Alison's blood all over the shirt Theo had on—he saw how right I was about something: that we belong together.

It didn't hurt that I kept the knife he used to murder his wife. Ryan doesn't know where I have it, but what matters is that I do.

And holding it over his head is enough to keep him by my side.

He's facing charges for the forgery, even though Alison was the one to actually sign Daniel's name to the document, but I'll be here for him, no matter what happens. And since she's not here to defend herself, I'll do whatever—say whatever—to ensure he gets as light a sentence as possible. We're going to paint it as her idea and spin it to make people believe he's innocent, that he was clueless as to what she was doing, even though that couldn't be further from the truth.

He knows he needs me. Everything I'm doing for him was more than enough to convince him that he needs me.

And to convince him to be more than friends.

I saw everything through the window that night. I saw how his daughter killed Theo, but how she'd debated between him and Ryan. After that, I'd run to my car and hurried home. I'd barely gotten in the door when my phone rang with news of Emma.

The official story? Aletha kidnapped the girls, but Theo got angry at Alison and killed her before going to Aletha/Tabitha's house to kill her. Too bad Theo knocked out Blackwood's security cameras after he started threatening Ryan for money and never got them up and running again. If he had, everyone would have known he wasn't the one who killed Alison. Instead, it sounds like Tabitha killed him in self-defense. As it was, he wasn't able to defend himself. Detective Martin was a town hero, lauded for saving Emma and Nealie, even though a few of us know the truth of what really happened that night.

The girls were so brave telling the truth about Aletha. They'd been scared to leave their houses that night, but they trusted her because she was in uniform. My blood boils when I think about the danger she put them in, but she's in jail now and not getting out anytime soon. Of course, the gunshot residue on her hand pointed the finger right at her as Theo's killer. She'll never see the outside of a cell again.

And as for Julie? She's locked up, which is what she deserves. The past nannying clients she'd screwed over were more than happy to come forward when they found out it meant she'd go to jail.

Emma runs up to me. She's fallen and skinned her palms, but before I can pull her onto my lap, the detective grabs her.

"Allow me," she says, wrapping Emma in a hug. "Hey, kiddo, you're so tough! You're not going to let those little scratches get you down, are you?" She chucks my daughter under the chin, making her laugh.

I'm seething watching their interaction, even though I keep a smile on my face. I told Ryan I wanted her gone. I don't want Emma or Nealie to ever know that she was sleeping with Ryan, but there's no way to get away from her.

She's a hero.

She saved the girls.

And I can't stand her.

But I can grin and bear it because at the end of the day, I go home to Ryan, Emma, and Nealie. She goes home by herself.

Besides, she has a dangerous job.

It would be terrible if something happened to her.

A LETTER FROM EMILY

Dear reader,

Thank you so much for reading *The Nanny Share*! If you did enjoy it, and want to keep up to date with all my latest releases, just sign up at the following link. Your email address will never be shared, and you can unsubscribe at any time.

www.bookouture.com/emily-shiner

Writing a book isn't always easy, and when the subject matter revolves around children, it can be even more difficult. There are cases every day of children being abducted, and while some have happy endings, there are many that don't. Thankfully, there are many groups throughout the world dedicated to finding these children and bringing them home safe.

Two of these organizations are the National Center for Missing and Exploited Children and the International Centre for Missing and Exploited Children. They do great work. Check them out.

Even with the difficult subject matter, I hope you loved *The Nanny Share*! I would be very grateful if you could write a review. I'd love to hear what you think, and it makes such a difference helping new readers to discover one of my books for the first time.

I love hearing from my readers—you can get in touch on my social media or my website.

Thanks,

Emily

- facebook.com/authoremilyshiner
- x.com/authoreshiner
- instagram.com/authoremilyshiner

ACKNOWLEDGMENTS

Finishing a book is like running a marathon (I would assume—you'll never catch me actually running that far), and it really takes a team (so maybe this is more like NASCAR?). I'm lucky enough to work with the most incredible pit crew ever. Move over, A Team. Step aside, Avengers. I have Kelsie Marsden, Donna Hillyer, and Laura Kincaid keeping me on track and making sure the plot is tight, the twists are twisty, and no egregious commas slip through to the final book. And that's not to mention the rest of the Bookouture team! From the first seed of an idea to final production, so many people touched this book to help bring it to life. Thanks to everyone involved!

A huge thank you to my family for picking up the slack as I resolutely didn't vacuum the entire time I was writing and editing this book. I guess it's my turn now.

Massive thanks to my tea girls. I'd be lost without y'all.

My readers, thank you. Thank you for the support, the love, and the regular DMs asking when I have another book coming out. Here you go.

PUBLISHING TEAM

Turning a manuscript into a book requires the efforts of many people. The publishing team at Bookouture would like to acknowledge everyone who contributed to this publication.

Audio
Alba Proko
Sinead O'Connor
Melissa Tran

Commercial
Lauren Morrissette
Hannah Richmond
Imogen Allport

Cover design
Debbie Holmes

Data and analysis
Mark Alder
Mohamed Bussuri

Editorial
Kelsie Marsden
Nadia Michael

Copyeditor
Donna Hillyer

Proofreader
Laura Kincaid

Marketing
Alex Crow
Melanie Price
Occy Carr
Cíara Rosney
Martyna Młynarska

Operations and distribution
Marina Valles
Stephanie Straub
Joe Morris

Production
Hannah Snetsinger
Mandy Kullar
Jen Shannon
Ria Clare

Publicity
Kim Nash
Noelle Holten
Jess Readett
Sarah Hardy

Rights and contracts
Peta Nightingale
Richard King
Saidah Graham

Printed in Great Britain
by Amazon